THREE GOTHIC DOCTORS AND THEIR SONS

BY THE SAME AUTHOR

*Minor Confessions of an Angel Falling Upward

*The Cannon and the Quill, Book One: We All be Jacobites Here

*The Cannon and the Quill, Book Two: Princes of the World

Jester-Night (Book 1 of the Ambir Dragon Tales)

Watch Out For the Hallway: Our Two-Year Investigation of the Most Haunted Library in North Carolina (with Tonya Madia)

Roommates from Beyond: How to Live in a Haunted Home (with Tonya Madia)

*Part of the Stanton Chronicles

THREE GOTHIC DOCTORS AND THEIR SONS

PART OF THE STANTON CHRONICLES

JOEY MADIA

New Mystics Enterprises
Leavittsburg, Ohio

ACKNOWLEDGMENTS

This novel is adapted from *Three Gothic Doctors and Their Sons*, a musical with book and lyrics by Joey Madia and music by Knight Berman, Jr.; and *Frankenstein* by Mary Shelley, *Island of Dr. Moreau* by H.G. Wells, and *The Strange Case of Dr. Jekyll and Mr. Hyde* by Robert Louis Stevenson.

The musical was performed in 2014 and 2015 at Trans-Allegheny Lunatic Asylum in Weston, West Virginia. Produced by Seven Stories Theatre Company. Direction by Max Gould. Performed by Robby Justiss and Joey Madia.

In 2021, the musical will be filmed and streamed while being performed live in Los Angeles. It will then be edited and released as a film.

AN INTRODUCTION TO YOUR NARRATOR

Good Reader: As is customary in narratives such as these, I begin with a brief introduction, which I have titled clearly and concisely, as might appear above the lead of an article in the *Evening Standard*, where I was, until recently, employed.

It is my hope that, in these few pages, you will come to understand how my background, interests, and experiences led me to the peculiar and oftentimes painful position of being the author of the supernatural story you now hold in your hands.

Before we begin, I must ask up front for your indulgence, patience, and perhaps forgiveness, for I fear my fifty-plus years as a newspaperman have provided me with little opportunity to practice the skills required of a narrative such as this. What meagre craft I have mustered I must credit to the considerable number of Gothic and other novels of similar ilk I enjoyed in my youth, in my precious moments of leisure, and in my twilight years. Credit must go as well to the instruction I have received—sometimes gentle, sometimes brutal—from the many gifted and even famous authors that I have come to know and admire in the course of my life in London.

That said... At the risk of grandiosity, it is my humble hope that this narrative—and others I am outlining based on stories of interest involving murder and various grades of mayhem I pursued under the employ of WT Stead and others—might gather me enough of an income to make up for that which I have lost in my retirement.

As I looked my seventy-fifth year on Earth in its cold, judgmental face, I found that I did not have the heart to continue.

Besides my advanced age, I would not wish the life of a city beat reporter on any who seek my counsel. The politics and personalities take you piece by piece over time. As recently as a handful of years ago, I was extending this self-same warning to the youngest generation of Stantons, although the point has become moot—my brother's son, Uriah, has committed to his uncle's occupation in America, despite my best attempts at warning him off the path.

I say this because the things I describe as taking place on the crowded streets and in the back alleys of the abject poor and drawing rooms of the wealthy in our bustling city of London and elsewhere in the world would not be believed by me—nor would I ask you, Good Reader, to believe them—had I not soberly and with full God-given faculties witnessed and at times engaged in them myself.

On the Obtainment of Materials for the Tale I Endeavor to Tell

Most of the journals on which I have based this narrative I acquired some years ago, having been retrieved with a bloodstained, weather-beaten haversack in a ruined, ransacked laboratory, part of a complex of dwellings on the Isle of Rousay in Orkney. Within the haversack were two journals of a would-be doctor of ultimately of no historical consequence, a Colt Cloverleaf revolver, schematics of several complex scientific instruments, a well-worn map marked in blue pencil of a journey from the South Pacific to Rousay (with several stops along the way), and the journals of three infamous doctors—Jekyll, Moreau, and Frankenstein—of whom the reader is without a doubt aware. To say the oft-told tales of these flawed and broken men have fascinated as much as they have repelled does not begin to capture the truth. By the turn of the century, there were no less than four stage adaptations of the story of Jekyll and Hyde in major cities such as London, Boston, and Philadelphia, and there have been over a dozen films to date. Although *Frankenstein*'s list of adaptations is far shorter, at two stage productions and a film, it is no less of an obsession with your average workaday citizen. The scandals surrounding each of these doctors were considerable, both shocking and (dare I say) thrilling in their own unique ways. The horrific experiments these tragic geniuses performed on humans and animals in the second half of the nineteenth century caution us all to not mistake science for religion, nor ourselves for God.

The man who retrieved these journals, papers, and objects—whose request to remain anonymous I do not intend to honor—had them sent to me, knowing my interest in their gruesome subject matter and experience with some of the more supernatural and occult—and hitherto untold—aspects of each particular tale. Indeed, in the case of Henry Jekyll, I had more than a passing connection, for it was within a mere handful of months of my joining the staff of the *Pall Mall Gazette* in 1885 that I was assigned to report on the brutal murder of a respected Member of the House of Lords named

Sir Danvers Carew. I am sure the reader recalls the name of the man—nay, the *monster*—who brutally beat and stomped this bastion of good will and benevolent leadership on a city sidewalk in front of numerous witnesses—the degenerate madman Edward Hyde. A creature of evil so bereft of the slightest morality that he had left half the hickory cane he used to enact the repugnant deed at the scene of that horrible crime. It was Jekyll's lawyer, Gabriel Utterson—to whom Carew was carrying an urgent letter—and a certain Inspector Newcomen of the fabled Scotland Yard who found the other half of the malevolent instrument of death in Hyde's soiled, repulsive den.

The contents of that letter—which I was able to read, though the details contained within must remain at present private—made a clear indication that Carew and others were close to making the worst kind of connections between Hyde and his misguided benefactor.

As to the cane, the skilled investigative work of the men of Scotland Yard quickly indicated that the imprint of a blunt object left in the skull of Sir Danvers Carew matched exactly the silver knob on the end of the monster's makeshift weapon.

The bloodlust of this brutal instrument was far from ending there. A full decade later, in 1894, Inspector Newcomen's nephew, Jonathan, who had followed in his uncle's footsteps at the venerable stronghold of advanced police detection, confided to me that the cane had been stolen from the Black (or Crime) Museum housed at Scotland Yard. The perpetrator was none other than a blind mechanic named Von Herder—the very man who had created the ingenious silent air rifle used by the hunter-turned-assassin Colonel Sebastian Moran to kill Ronald Adair and to attempt to kill none other than Mr. Sherlock Holmes.

One can only guess at the macabre motivations that led Moran to order Von Herder to obtain and repair Hyde's hideous instrument of death, but the damnable thing was almost Holmes's undoing in the empty house across from 221B Baker Street when he sprang upon Moran after the successful ploy with the plaster bust. Were it not for Dr. John Watson's reflexive actions with the butt of his revolver, Moran, who had gained the upper hand, would have added the self-styled consulting detective to the cane's list of victims, for he had it high in hand with the intent to bring it down upon his opponent's skull.

You will not find this detail, Reader, in the pages of Watson's narrative. The doctor left it out to save the staff of the Black Museum any and all embarrassment.

By this time, I had known Dr. John Watson for nearly fourteen years. The circumstances of our meeting were thus: While I was serving in India in the Sixty-Sixth Berkshire Regiment of Foot, convalescing in Peshawar (the circumstances of my wounding will await a later tale... I am already dragging on and they are so fantastical that I must first build your trust with the narrative herein contained), Watson, an assistant surgeon attached at first to the Fifth Northumberland Fusiliers before reassignment to the Berkshires, was brought into the medical tent, having suffered serious wounds to his shoulder and leg at the Battle of Maiwand. During the weeks of our recovery, John and I developed what I most humbly call a deep, abiding friendship. Whatever meager skills I display with narrative I have primarily learned from him.

Throughout my in many ways remarkable journey, I have had the pleasure to know not only Dr. Watson, but also his best friend and colleague, Sherlock Holmes. Further, although Holmes would disagree, I will defend the position that I contributed in measurable ways to the investigation of a case in 1894 whose disappointing outcome bears directly on the narrative at hand, although, because of that very outcome, a close conspiracy has kept it out of the celebrated catalogue of their cases. As Dr. Watson's faithful readers know, Holmes rarely allowed public disclosure of his failures.

I have also had the honor of calling the inestimable playwright and creator of *Peter Pan*, JM Barrie, my friend. I was groomsman at his wedding to the actress Mary Ansell. My acquaintances further include WB Yeats, Bram Stoker, Henry Irving, HP Lovecraft, and another excellent purveyor of tales of ghosts as well as episodes of historical occurrence such as the *White Company* named Arthur Conan Doyle—a brave, curious Scotsman (is there any other kind?). I am proud to call Doyle a fellow traveler in the pioneering studies of the so-called supernatural by the Society for Psychical Research, of which I also am a member.

How I Entered the Shadows of the Occult
Perhaps it is as simple as my being born on All Hallows Eve, the Celtic festival day of Samhain, more popularly called Halloween—31 October.

Although, of course, there has to be much more.

At first, I studied the occult as a means of coping with my darkest experiences as a journalist employed by the *Pall Mall Gazette* by better understanding the underlying mechanisms behind them. Once that door had opened, however, I found myself increasingly drawn in. And—much like the three doctors I have mentioned, by means of forsaking sleep and the company of friends and the occasional lover—thrusting myself nightly into the midst of the coarse, hand-scrawled pages of the treatises penned by men braver and more learned than myself on subjects as far-flung as alchemy, witchcraft, physiognomy, vampires, werewolves, addiction, demonology, natural philosophy, vivisection, and madness.

Of all of these, perhaps madness is of primary interest in the tales I endeavor to tell. For what else can account for the Faustian pursuits undertaken by this trio of doctors and the other villains and murderers you shall meet should this narrative sell enough copies for a publisher to agree to pay me to tell you more.

Like a weak candle in a too-dark room, my studies of these manuscripts, from the ancient to the modern, did not shed sufficient light to illuminate the corners where I knew the answers lay. As a consequence, I found myself turning to mentalism, mesmerism, and the unholy specifics of ever darker and more dangerous occult rituals from ancient Egypt to the gold coast of Africa, from the Caribbean islands and American colonies to the Harz Mountains in the witch-kissed German Brocken.

But, as Nietzsche wrote in *Beyond Good and Evil*, "He who fights with monsters might take care lest he thereby become a monster. And if you gaze for long into an abyss, the abyss gazes also into you."

I had already nearly crossed paths with one such monster, Edward Hyde.

I was soon to gaze into the abyss brought into being by another.

Not wishing to spoil future installments, I must mention only in passing that, in 1888, I was assigned, at the still tender age of 26, to the serial murder case that has cast a pall over the CID, Scotland Yard, the Crown, and the *Gazette* ever since—

That of Jack the Ripper.

I do confess, although that case drove me deeper into the occult knowledge-seeking laid out in detail above, it was five years earlier, in 1883, that I became a contributor to the spiritual quarterly *Borderland* (launched by WT Stead) and the following year, an apprentice to the Society for Psychical Research.

Before moving on, I must share one last fact about our saucy man Jack: No one has ever come close to sharing the truth of the Ripper murders—a conspiracy of the powerful that I plan to expose at some future date. Both my theories at the time and I were made to seem so outlandish and insane as to be suppressed by all those I have listed above as suffering from their failure to solve the case.

My relentless questing for the truth in matters that would chill the blood of most men—and chilled my own aplenty, although I have always mustered the iron will required to carry ever on—may very well be a longtime family trait. Those who fancy the tales of the Golden Age of Piracy may be acquainted with my ancestor, Joseph Stanton, who sailed with the cutthroat Charles Vane and was associated at times with the infamous captain called Blackbeard. According to family lore and the scant documents from his time that I have been able to acquire from various record houses in the Caribbean and America, Joseph was involved in dark and sinister dealings after his father was murdered in cold blood in plain sight of his sister Julia, who, forced to feed the family by engaging in the world's oldest, saddest profession, carved Joseph out of her life by means of a letter received by him on Christmas day in the hard year 1715.

His father Artemus's murderer? A madman assassin doing the bidding of a demonic cult that very nearly toppled the world's greatest empires... and still might, if we do not remain always vigilant and willing to stand our ground. Although the parents of this dark angel of death named him Devon Ross, he came to be known as *Faccia del Diavolo*. I shall revisit this sordid tale at an opportune moment later in our narrative.

To Him Whom I Owe the Most
If I have whet rather than quelled your appetite to read on with this narrative and to look forward to those I am planning (be so kind, if I have earned it, to contact the publisher to ask them for more), I owe it to my years of tutelage under WT Stead. It was he who pioneered the multipart series, which had carefully crafted, heart-racing endings for each segment so the reader would have no choice but to run to the newsstand to purchase the next edition carrying the latest revelations of whatever lurid story that genius of investigative journalism was pursuing. I was fortunate enough to assist—ever so slightly—in his series on child prostitution that arguably changed the face of journalism forever, while doing a hell of a lot of good.

(Please indulge my off-color language in the service of historical accuracy.)

And so it is to my dear friend and mentor—who was tragically lost with more than fifteen hundred other souls on 15 April 1912, when the brashly pronounced as unsinkable HMS *Titanic* struck an iceberg and sunk to the bottom of the Atlantic—that I dedicate this narrative. A champion of the little man to the end, Stead was on his way to America to take part in a peace congress at the request of President Taft. Witnesses also reported that he selflessly helped women and children into the inadequate number of lifeboats—a situation he had cautioned against in a short story he published in 1886 titled, "How the Mail Steamer Went Down in Mid Atlantic by a Survivor." He also gave up his life jacket, a gesture that very well could have cost him his life hours later when he and John Jacob Astor IV, both of their feet frozen, let go of a raft and sunk to their deaths.

I must also mention that Stead often proclaimed that he would die by lynching or drowning. Knowing the man perhaps better than anyone else, lynching was a response to those who railed against his pioneering style of journalism, accusing him of sensationalism at the expense of the truth. History shall judge him on the morality of his actions, as it does with all men and all things of weight.

I attribute premonition and intuition to his prophesying his death by drowning because he published another story, in 1892, this one titled, "From the Old World to the New," which told the tale of one vessel rescuing passengers from another that had disastrously *struck an iceberg*.

One last remembrance: It was related by witnesses whom I personally interviewed that WT regaled the dinner guests the night of the tragedy with our adventure with a mummy one night at the British Museum—another tale that I might be coerced to tell if the present endeavor goes well.

I miss you, my friend. *Veritatem sectantes*. I shall continue in pursuit of the truth.

A BRIEF NOTE ON THE NARRATIVE

Having before me the journals of Drs. Frankenstein, Jekyll, and Moreau—and those of a fourth and, for many reasons, more central character, as you shall see—I saw before me three distinct paths on which to proceed.

For the first, I could simply transcribe the pages of their narratives word for word, linking them together with my natural journalistic ability by way of brief passages of commentary and analysis. Seeing as other authors have already endeavored to handle these journals in almost this same manner—although passing them off as fiction rather than journalism—I quickly abandoned this route.

The second would be to simply read the journals and then abandon them completely, constructing a narrative loosely based upon them taken solely from memory. I would allow myself an author's considerable license, introducing purely fictional characters, locations, and events.

Keeping in mind that this is not (yet) my strength with the pen, I abandoned this possible path as well, after a few aborted and admittedly dreadful attempts—at least according to my good friends Barrie and HP Lovecraft (who was taken to his eternal rest seven months ago), whose feedback, while brutal, was altogether accurate.

I often think of what my talented Irish brother in the pen, Bram Stoker, whom we lost in 1912, would have thought of it, having written his own fictionalized accounts of monsters and the occult using an epistolary form.

And so it is the third path that led to the volume I now, at long last, present. A mixture of journal excerpts (not marked out as such except on the rare occasion when I felt it the cleanest way to proceed), my own experiences as an eventual participant, and the filling of gaps with speculative text (based on my knowledge of the occult and experience with similar cases), employing some limited license to hold the reader's interest. I should also mention that I undertook to interview those who might shed further light on these matters. The first was Edward Prendick, who originally brought the frightful matter of Dr. Moreau to the world's attention through a series of newspaper interviews with our fierce competitor and eventual buyer of fourteen years ago, the *Evening Standard*, the editors of which had deeper pockets than WT Stead with which to help the destitute and cruelly ridiculed Prendick.

In a later manuscript, given to some falsities and hyperboles in order to hook and frighten its audience, Prendick referred to me in passing as a strangely able man, a mental specialist who had known Moreau in London before his departure for the unnamed island—a tale for another time, Dear Reader—and who seemed to credit his story.

Understand me when I say, there was no seems. For I took it all to be true.

This world has a voracious appetite for fiction but little stomach for the possibility that much of what they wish to dismiss as shadows beneath the bed and the well-drawn emanations from the madman minds of writers like the Brothers Grimm and Edgar Allan Poe are actually based in fact.

I also interviewed colleagues, police staff, household staff, and others who had firsthand knowledge of the narrative's major players.

It is this last mode of information gathering that provided me with the material for the opening scene of this narrative, to which I invite you to proceed without any further delay.

CHAPTER 1

Robert Peary Walton—fresh from withdrawing from the course in medicine at University College Hospital, where he had less than a year to go before securing his degree— fidgeted with the hem of his coat from the back row of the venerable old auction house. He was doing so in an attempt to refrain from checking his pocket watch, which he had been doing every five or so minutes, much to the chagrin of the two men of means who flanked him.

Glancing instead at the brochure an attendant had handed him as he had entered six hours earlier, Walton managed a smile. The pair of Ming dynasty vases just sold to a diminutive Irish woman whose wealth made her an Amazon amongst her peers were just above the item that Walton had spent the day waiting to secure.

The wait had been almost painful. The remainder of the Utterson family had decided to move to the country, and the list of what they were selling was as long as it was impressive.

Banging his gavel on the oak podium behind which he executed the duties of his office, the auctioneer croaked out in a thin voice that betrayed his considerable years, "Lot 141. The final auction of the day. The journal of deceased doctor Henry Jekyll. According to the affidavit submitted by the Uttersons, Gabriel John Utterson, Esquire, was given this record of Doctor Jekyll's work by the man himself mere hours before his tragic, and dare I say infamous, suicide."

Patting the envelope full of pound notes in his left breast pocket, where he had laid it over his heart, Walton sat up straighter as the moment of bidding began. He would not enter early on, but rather dash in like a hawk to snatch its prey after it has circled safely above, taking full and careful measure of its hungry competition.

Unlike many in attendance, his funds were limited and he must not tip his hand as to how anxious he was to get what he had come for.

The bidding proceeded, facilitated by the able actions of the auctioneer: "The bidding starts at fifty pounds. Do I——yessir. Seventy-five pounds. Do I hear seventy-five? Very good. One-hundred pounds. One-hundred pounds is the current bid. Do I hear—yes ma'am, one-hundred and twenty-five pounds… excellent, *excellent*! Who will pay to learn the secrets this journal of Jekyll's holds?"

Enough of that, old man, Walton thought, ready to descend. *You shall drive the blessed price too high!*

When the brisk bidding of the opening slowed as the auctioneer coaxed it to two-hundred pounds, indicating that the bulk of the bidders were now considering the cost and not *just* their curiosity, Walton tucked his wings and dove down for the prize.

"Two-hundred and twenty-five pounds from the back," the auctioneer announced, acknowledging Walton's thrust-high, waving paddle. The accompanying murmur from the rows in the front was excellent news to his ears. The auctioneer craned his neck to look about the room. "Going once, going twice. Sold to bidder 23. On behalf of the Utterson estate, I thank you for attending today's very successful auction."

As the audience began to disperse, either to retrieve their new possessions or out into the street, Walton removed the envelope from his pocket, smiling at not only securing the object for which he had come, but in doing so, still reserving nearly a hundred pounds toward his next-stage expenses, which would no doubt be considerable.

Walking briskly toward the side room where he would complete the final transaction, Walton found his way blocked by a parasol and floppy, moss-hued hat accented with a large pair of ostrich feathers. Behind and beneath them was a delicately boned, pale girl in her twenties with small lips and large, brilliant blue eyes.

Her voice was as delicate as her features. "Excuse me. Doctor Walton, is it? I am Daphne Utterson. Gabriel Utterson was my grandfather."

His annoyance at the delay for now outweighed by his interest in the peculiar girl in front of him, Walton answered, "It is *Mister*, actually. Pressing issues have necessitated a leave of absence from my schooling—although I might not return at all once all is said and done… Uh… n-no matter. Thinking aloud, as is my all too embarrassing habit. Pleased to meet you, Miss Utterson. I am in a bit of hurry, sad to say, so if you will excuse me…"

She made no move to let him pass. "I have a question, if you don't mind."

Trying his best to hide his impatience, and failing, Walton answered, "Be quick about it. I have a ship to catch."

"What is your interest in Henry Jekyll's journal?"

Taken somewhat by surprise by her question, Walton paused a moment to formulate his answer, though he had no time to waste. "I am a man of science, Miss Utterson, pursuing a certain line of inquiry that could prove the salvation of humankind. And there are certain crucial elements in Jekyll's work applicable to my own. Ah... There is my apprentice, waiting by the door for me to complete my transaction. I really must depart. Pleasure to meet you, Miss Utterson. I do sincerely mean that."

The anxiety in Daphne Utterson's clear blue eyes as she looked into his own was something Robert Peary Walton would replay in his mind and reflect upon almost daily for the remainder of his life.

"Be careful with it, doctor. It caused my grandfather and especially my mother countless nights of despair. The answers that you find may not be the ones you seek. Read its words with caution, Mister Walton... will you?"

Watching her walk away, Walton did his damnedest to shake her image from his mind. Five minutes later, Jekyll's journal in hand, he joined his apprentice, Tom Paris, who was holding his cheap workman's timepiece face out, as if Walton needed reminding of the relentless press of their schedule.

With the jovial tone he almost always employed, Tom put away his watch, remarking, "I see ya 'ave secured the object of yer 'eart's desire, suh! An', may I ask, wit' no small, passin' interest, who was that lov'ly bird whom you was chattin' up?"

Tom's Cheapside accent and simpleminded enthusiasm for life would normally make him a man Walton would cross the street to avoid, but his particular set of skills were invaluable to Walton's enterprise, so he was willing to overlook Tom's annoying, abundant shortcomings.

Flipping through the journal, Walton said, "Another busybody committed to educating me to the dangers of my path..."

Abandoning his grin, Tom replied, "May'ap 'er warnin' is worth a listen, suh."

Slamming the journal closed, Walton said, heading through the exit and onto Leadenhall Street, "Not now, Tom. Not when I finally possess the journals of Jekyll and Frankenstein and a map to Moreau's island. Speaking of, the ship will not remain at anchor for us. Not even for a moment. Are you all in, Tom, or should I leave you at the threshold?"

Lighting up his face with another brilliant smile, Tom hooked his thumbs in the pockets of his vest. "I am wit' ya, suh. Now as always."

Flagging down an Austin London taxicab, Walton looked at Tom with a smile of his own. "That's the man I hired! Schooling is behind us, Tom. We shall succeed where these others have failed. Warnings be damned. It's an undiscovered country, Tom, and we shall plant our flag squarely in its heart."

CHAPTER 2

A few essential details on the journey to Moreau's secret island, gleaned from the captain and a few of the crew of the Portuguese tramp steamer called the Boa Sorte

Gonçalo Costa, captain of the steamer *Boa Sorte*, though no stranger to the fierce storms that often sprung up in the South Pacific, testing the mettle of crews and their vessels alike, knew there was something about the way the clouds darkened and the winds blew so inexplicably cold that day that it had nothing to do with weather patterns and everything to do with where it was they were headed.

Cursed islands bring hazardous events, even to a tried and tested crew on a ship whose translated name in English means Good Luck.

Crossing himself and kissing the crucifix he had worn around his neck since he was an altar boy in Lisbon, which he still called home in his fortieth year, Costa wished to God that he had heeded his intuition and refused the medical student and his pleasant companion when they had first enquired about passage to a certain forbidden island.

Not that Walton's money had tempted Costa right away. Far from. He had first gone to church and consulted with the local priest, Father António, who had assured him that there was nothing but superstition and a desire to sell newspapers behind the horrific stories of animal–human abominations created on the island in question by a doctor named Moreau.

"*Deus* would not allow such things, *meu filho*," his parish priest had said.

Even then, although he was a man of great faith who gladly paid his tithes to the Holy Church at the appointed times of the year, Costa had sought further insight and advice. Leaving his first mate in charge of the *Boa Sorte*, he made the trek to the edge of the forest a handful of miles from Lisbon, to a small thatch-roofed cottage, home of the local *curandeira*, Senhora Martinez. Inviting him into her cramped, dim-lit cottage full of foul odors and fouler oddities, she accepted his payment in silence, motioning him to sit on a hand-hewn stool by the fire. Throwing her runes and gazing into the leaves left in a cracked earthenware mug after Costa consumed a strong, pungent brew ladled from a cauldron she continually added to and fussed over as they waited for the potion to take effect and the expected visions to come, the *curandeira* frowned.

"The spirits show me nothing of note in the leaves," she whispered, tossing the cup into the fire and meticulously placing her runes into a box that, according to its faded, peeling label, once held fine cigars. "But the brew shall do its work."

Nearly an hour later, much of which Costa could not recall, there had been nothing but impossible to decipher whispers and vast fields of soundless black—broken at times by howls, moans, the whine of complex apparatus, and the glow of red and yellow eyes.

It had told Costa nothing he did not already know. Of course such things would be heard and seen from the depths of a South Pacific island in the middle of the night. He had experienced many such occurrences himself, making unscheduled landings to obtain fresh water or make emergency repairs. As to the whine of the machinery—an echo of the evil doctor's work.

The wet weather and torturous humidity on the island would almost certainly have made it all by now inoperable.

Laying a few more coins on the table for her troubles, Gonçalo headed home, where he received the news that his eldest daughter, Renata, sick with fever, was returning to her family from her position as schoolmistress in the home of the powerful estate owner, Baron Riviera, half a day's journey away. This bad bit of luck, coupled with a poor price negotiated for his cargo on his most recent trip, forced the determination that Gonçalo should accept Walton's offer, which he did.

Now, weeks later, as the storm raged, stressing the hull and rocking the masts and booms to their limit before the crewmen could scurry up to secure them, Costa made a decision.

Throwing wide the double hatch to the lower decks, he rung the water from his cap and opened the door to Walton's room. There he was, as always, pouring over the two leather-bound journals of disparate sizes and colors that he was never seen without.

To a simple man like Gonçalo Costa, too much reading was, as his grandmother cautioned, *queimar as pestanas*—to burn one's eyelashes.

"We have to turn around, Senhor Walton," Costa said, remaining in the doorway. "This storm is nothing to be trifled with and we cannot risk getting any closer to the island. Not with the rocks that I know with utmost certainty lie in wait just beneath the water on the approach to the shoreline, anxious to smash our hull. I apologize. But my men I shall not risk. *Ir com os porcos.* That shall not be our fate."

Removing his spectacles, which he carefully folded and placed on the desk as his lips pursued and tired eyes narrowed, Walton hissed, "You have been paid, captain, and I *must* make landfall today. It is my destiny. If yours is to die with the swine, so be it. Continue on your course!"

Shaking his head, Costa replied, "To hell with you and your destiny, *senhor!* You have *ter muita lata*—some damned gall! I heard rumors aplenty about that cursed island. The things there that have happened. It is a most unholy place. This storm is an omen. A God-sent portent to warn us away. Go back to London. Go back to school and your medicine practice. Perhaps I interpreted incorrectly the visions brought on by the *curandeira*'s brew..."

"Damn your superstitions, Captain Costa! They are the Dark Age lies and limitations that my contributions to science will finally and forever destroy! You, sir, make a stronger case for my need to reach that island than any I have hitherto expressed! I demand you take me there. Tonight! You have no idea the importance of the timing, Costa! Storm be damned!"

By way of a reply, Costa returned to the helm. Hearing the hatch thrust open behind him a moment later, he knew that Walton had followed him. Good. He was not afraid of this obviously insane Englishman. He had known them aplenty. They swarmed the world with their colonialism, false manners, and odd ideas. Like locusts, they were a plague.

Above the increasing din of the storm, Costa shouted to his crew, "Turn this boat about and batten the hatches, *rapazes!* Check the booms and cranes. We shall ride her out as best we can and make steam for safer ports and then for home as soon as we are able." Feeling Walton's hot breath upon his cheek, Costa turned to face him. "You will just have to find another way to reach the island. I shall refund a fair portion of your—"

"Keep the goddamned money!" Walton yelled, pulling his wallet from beneath his already soaked-through coat. He had refused a slicker on more than one occasion and Costa had one day ceased to make the offer. "As a matter of fact, I have plenty more, and I shall not need it on the island. Let me purchase one of your lifeboats!"

As if in answer from his god, for he doubted Walton had one of his own, Costa heard a deafening crash of thunder overhead. "*Estás a meter água!* You are mad, *senhor*! These waves will bash you to pieces before you are six feet from our side. Besides, it would be most irresponsible of me to release one of our lifeboats to you. This storm only worsens!"

Thrusting the entire wad of notes, all he had in the world, into Costa's chest, Walton said, "Better to take my chances out there than remain amongst cowards like you! You will still have ample boats should you need them, but really Costa, no doubt, according to your witch doctor, casting me from your ship, as a sacrifice to the sea gods, will make the storm magically disappear. You have nothing to lose by taking my offer."

Feeling his face tighten in rage, Costa pushed the money away. "You do not think I know who you are, Robert Peary Walton—but I do! No man takes passage on the *Boa Sorte* without my learning about him all I can! There is talk of you in London... yes! You left your school before they could remove you. And these journals—Satan's scribbled words! I must have been insane to have them on my ship."

Walton laughed. "Are you through, Captain?"

"Not yet. I know who was your ancestor. Why do you not show common sense, as he did! Know when nature has control. When you cannot win!"

If he were at that moment turned into a viper, Walton would have, with pleasure, sunk his poisonous fangs into Costa's pulsing throat. "Common sense? Cowardice! Abandoning Victor Frankenstein when the ice began to press upon his ship... What wondrous things he could have learned had they captured the doctor's creation!" Raising the wad of money toward Costa's rain-lashed face, he said, "I have no more time for talk. Take these notes... They are more than generous to cover the loss of the lifeboat." As Costa took them, anxious to be rid of this lunatic and remove from danger his crew and his ship, Walton yelled, "Now stand aside!" Leaning over the railing, he shouted into the open hatch below, "Tom! Throw our bags into one of the lifeboats. Make sure anything delicate is safely cushioned and packed. Especially the radio transmitter. And do not forget the rifle!"

A few seconds later, Tom's head appeared in the hatchway. "Whatya mean, suh? We best be hunkerin' down!"

"I will not have it, Tom! Not from you! The captain refuses to complete our contract, so we are going ahead on our own. I have purchased one of the lifeboats."

Tom felt the blood draining from his face. "But, suh... the storm... we won't suhvive it."

Leaving the helm, Walton jumped down rather than using the steps, grabbing Tom by the collar and pushing him into the hull. "Check your gut, Tom. Now's the time to decide if you truly want in on this. *Fully* in. It was wrong of me not demanding it before. So make your choice. Get our things as I ask and meet me on deck within minutes or stay here with these superstitious Portuguese rabble. You might even be a stevedore one day. Marry some island girl and have a brood of half-breed children. But *I* am going to that island."

Tom never knew what the reason was that led to his next decision. The prospect of Walton's vision of him coming true, or fear of being alone with the Portuguese after Walton had so thoroughly insulted them, or the look on his employer's face, which was enviable in its determination.

What matters is his reply. "I am wit' ya, suh. Ya know it ta be true."

Minutes later, as the storm continued to rage, as Tom did his best to secure their belongings and a few small barrels of water and some food that the crew had insisted they take into the lifeboat, Captain Costa grabbed him by the arm. "You are not as crazy as he is, boy! I beg of you—do not match him in his madness. We will drop you somewhere nice. Someplace where you might secure work, meet a lovely woman..."

Pulling himself away, Tom prepared to lower the boat as Walton—his haversack of precious journals and carefully packed bottles of tinctures, salts, and chemicals slung on one shoulder while his Enfield bolt-action rifle hung from his other—stepped into the lifeboat.

As Tom worked the winch and pulley system to lower the lifeboat into the sea, Costa called down, his crucifix in hand, "God then bless you both. And if he is a good and wise God, as I know him to be, may he protect you from whatever horrors you will surely find on that island!"

As they rowed away, Tom gazed into the storm as a jagged bolt of lightning lit and split the clouds, followed quickly by two monstrous crashes of thunder and a raging, pelting rain.

"We're takin' on water!" he exclaimed.

Handing Tom a bucket, secured to an oarlock by a length of braided rope, Walton said, "You will have to bail. But first protect the transmitter. We have to keep it dry! I will get us to shore." As he took Tom's oar and adjusted his position to better push against the waves, he yelled, "Damn the gods for trying to keep me from my destiny! I WILL NOT LET THEM WIN!"

*****

I am sure you can imagine, Dear Reader, how the scene progressed. Walton straining against the oars, Tom struggling with the bailing bucket, as the storm sent its fury against them. For hours it continued, as the lights of the retreating *Boa Sorte* blinked and dwindled before disappearing beyond the horizon.

And then, as Tom turned to empty the bucket for perhaps the two hundredth time, a wave knocked him off balance, his head striking the gunwale and all the world going black.

He awoke some hours later, to find himself lying on several layers of palm fronds, coarse sand and jagged rock all he could see around him. The storm had finally passed. Sitting up, he first smelled and then felt the subtle warmth of a fire. Above him was a glowing silver moon and a sky resplendent with stars.

Then, in silhouette, there was Walton, standing over him seemingly nine feet tall like the intrepid conqueror of obstacles he was wholly proving to be.

"Ah… there you are, Tom. You gave me quite the fright. But it seems you have survived." Crouching down to check an egg-sized bump on Tom's left temple, Walton put a calming hand on his hired man's shoulder as he shrank back from the pressure, light as it was. "Easy now. You rest yourself, Tom. I have the promising start of a fire going. I shall make us a light breakfast when the dawn at last arrives and then we shall hike to the lab."

Feeling himself drifting slowly into sleep, Tom smiled as Walton rummaged through their provisions, humming lightly to himself as though he were preparing tea and muffins for the queen in a posh English drawing room rather than stale water and hardtack on a tiny Pacific island that could very well be the means of a most painful and ugly death.

CHAPTER 3

A page from Walton's journal, written that very evening, illuminating his plans.

—5 April 1929

As I sit here comfortably on a twisted length of driftwood, digesting a dinner of *bacalhau* and *enchidos*—salted cod and sausage—courtesy of Captain Costa's crew beside a dwindling fire on the shore of Moreau's Island, I cannot help but smile at the divine providence shining down on me from the above-inscribed date. For it was twenty years ago tomorrow that my hero and namesake, Admiral Robert Peary, first broke through the icy obstacles of the Arctic Circle and set foot with a few brave pioneers upon the Northern Pole. Men whose mettle I wholly understand. For it has been the unending application of my own fierce Will and the divinely transmitted guidance of a nameless Angel who speaks to me in dreams that, at long last, through boundless effort and countless miles, I have come to sit within a few hours' walk of the laboratory of the ill-remembered, much-abused genius, Dr. Abraham Moreau. Three long years have I secured and studied the most detailed maps I could find of the islands of this vast, unyielding ocean, guided by nothing but the cruelly vague clues left in dusty library archives and self-serving newspaper articles by the coward Edward Prendick. Who can hope to understand the deft, Divine work we endeavor to accomplish, my nameless Angel and I? Inspired by the great Admiral Peary, I have arrived at an Arctic Circle of the mind—a vast expanse of new knowledge that shall save the beastly and imperfect Human Race from its multitudinous and vile stupidities. My environment shall not thwart me, nor shall I be swayed by the faulty logic of dull morality like my ancestor, Robert Walton, for whom some claim I am also named. He who looked into the eyes of genius in the person of Victor Frankenstein a century and a half ago, who held his letters and retrieved his detailed journal, which, found by me in my grandmother's attic on a long-ago day, began me on my quest. My ancestor—who professed to be an equal of the inestimable Dr. Frankenstein—lost heart and turned back from his own anointed fate as the ice began to thicken and his men began to shake. I shall not shrink from my own sacred fate, as did my father and his fathers before him. I will not settle for safety in an airless, crowded office making loans to men of greater stature and grander plans and claim from that a worthy legacy. I have studied mathematics, biology, chemistry, natural philosophy, medicine, and the works of the Alchemists. I have gone for days with neither food nor sleep, as I chased the infinite in the infinitesimal. Then, as a recent reward for my endless, expensive efforts, there shone upon my path a mystic blessing as profoundly brilliant as the force of seven suns—an item in *The Evening Standard* announcing an auctioning of the estate of the venerable Uttersons. The very same family from which had come the lawyer and confidant of the brilliant Henry Jekyll. An auction to take place mere miles from where I was until recently enrolled at University College Hospital. It was on that day that I at last possessed, coded though they were, the formulas and procedures Dr. Jekyll had used to bring forth Edward Hyde. Long have I studied the precious pages of Frankenstein and Jekyll... Tomorrow... *tomorrow!* I shall hold in my hands the third and final key to unlocking the doors of my own angelic vision. No matter the trials, no matter so many think me mad... I shall raise a modern man. A new Adam, as beautiful as the Morning Star, genius Lucifer himself—devoid of all Evil, a child of a new breed of God-man, impervious to disease, unencumbered by the inevitabilities of death and decay, and he shall call me Father, and I shall call him Son.

Now to get some sleep, for tomorrow shall soon arrive.

CHAPTER 4

Walton and Paris approach Moreau's compound after hiking through the jungle.

While Tom—as fit and vigorous a specimen as Walton had hoped he would be when he hired him—hacked the thick foliage in their path with a black-bladed machete, his employer kept consulting a crude map he had fashioned by pouring over Prendick's various narratives. He had been mumbling, "Should be soon, should be soon…" or some similar variant for the past half hour.

Hacking through a tangled cluster of monstera and vines of green jade, Tom stopped where he stood, feeling the map Walton held before him crumple against his back as he undid the bright red bandana around his neck, using it to mop up some of the sweat pouring steadily into his eyes. "Look there, suh. That must be the lab awright."

Stepping around Tom and peering through the foliage just ahead, Walton nodded. "It is indeed. Five long years I have waited. Hurry along now."

As curious to see for himself what lay inside the laboratory as was Walton, Tom hacked away at the vines between them and the building with renewed vigor.

A few minutes later, they stood before the door, both men winded from their efforts.

Waving his hand as he tested the strength of the planks of rough-hewn wood that barred them from entry, Walton said, "Hand me the hatchet and the pry bar in the duffel bag, Tom. I would like to do the honors."

After doing as Walton requested, Tom stepped aside to let him at his work.

Examining the two by six that ran from the upper left corner of the doorframe to the lower right, each end of it affixed with a trio of broad-headed nails, Walton set the pry bar at its midpoint, against a seam between two vertical planks, using the flat end of the hatchet to drive it in.

"If you would be so kind as to pull with me, Tom," Walton asked.

Grabbing the pry bar at the top while Walton planted his feet and kept a grasp further down, the two men strained as the nails began to pull free with a high-pitched groan and the tip of the pry bar further separated the seam.

Throwing the two by six into the bushes near the building, Walton aimed the hatchet at the opening they had widened, striking the wood with a surprising ferocity half a dozen times, until it began to splinter and separate from the doorframe. Taking in a few great gulps of air, Walton, whose shirt and vest were soaked through with sweat, whispered, "Give me a hand pulling this wood away. We are almost in."

Employing the crowbar and hatchet as needed, the two eager adventurers soon found themselves facing the door, which had a thick iron locking mechanism that was not only engaged, but also rusted from the humidity. Luckily, there was a small glass window reinforced with thin wire mesh in the center of the door.

"Now we know for sure why the door was boarded up, and so thoroughly," Walton said, as if he had found it all exactly as he had expected.

Handing the hatchet to Tom, he said, "If you would be so kind as to make quick work of that window, we should be able to reach inside and undo the lock with ease."

Which is exactly what Tom Paris did.

"Afta you, suh," he said, stepping aside as the door slowly opened, reticent as it was due to its three rusted hinges.

Lighting a lantern, which he extended through the doorway like a talisman, Walton chuckled with glee. Before him was a large open room. Two operating tables stood at its center, several feet apart. Around the perimeter were shelves and benches full of books and medical equipment. Every few feet, lanterns hung from the ceiling.

"Get these lit, Tom," Walton ordered, waving his assistant inside. "So we can have a proper look around."

Once all of the lanterns were lit, Tom exclaimed, "It's like ya lab at UCH. But... macabre. All these bones, an' skulls, an' appendages, 'uman but not quite... Cor blimey, suh... Itsa 'ouse a' death, it is!"

"Nonsense, Tom. It is only the trail of Moreau's work. Meaningless detritus. The price of progress. Help me find his journal."

An hour passed without a sign of the prize. Tom could hear Walton's frustration mounting as he pulled books, instruments, and Moreau's "meaningless detritus" off the shelves with increasing force and speed. "It has *got* to be here..."

Several more minutes passed before Walton, in his frustration, pulled down a five-foot bookshelf, its contents hitting the packed dirt floor of the laboratory with a cacophony of crash and crunch, books and bones, and glass.

"My God, Tom! The Angel blesses me yet again! Hand me the pry bar and hatchet!"

Tucked into a custom-built recess in the wall was a metal case a few feet square, a padlock securing its lid. As Tom handed him the requested tools, Walton said, "Bring the lantern close. This has to be where he hid it!"

Laying the point of the bar on the lock, Walton brought the hatchet down on the top end, laughing with delight as the mechanism fell away. Lifting the lid and peering inside, he yelled, "Yes! Here it is. How apt that I should be the one to first set hands upon it after such a relentless search."

Grasping a faded green leather-bound book, Walton stood while extending his arms to their full length above his head.

"Ya 'old it like it were a piece a' the True Cross or the skull of a saint..."

Bringing the journal slowly down so he could hold it against his heart, Walton whispered, "They, my good son, are naught but superstitions. This journal and its contents are scientific fact. Mark the date, Tom. April 6. You know full well its importance to my quest. Can you feel that? Fate is bathing us in its light."

As Walton unwound the twine that held the journal closed, Tom took the opportunity to look around the room. Taking in the bloodstains on the operating tables and the hooked points and serrated blades on the instruments strewn about the workbenches, Tom said, "I ain't so sure 'bout this, suh. By the looks a' the equipment, this was less an operatin' room an' labo't'ry than a torcha chambah."

Not bothering to turn around or lift his attention from the journal pages he slowly scanned, Walton said, "Your mind has been warped by the lies of the coward Edward Prendick. Those scribbled notes and interviews of his constitute nothing more than a biased, cowardly account of Doctor Moreau's work. They were, without question, motivated by the basest combination of ignorance, fear, and exaggeration. You must be wiser than the rabble who were swayed by his narrative, Tom."

Before Tom could offer an answer, a half-human scream split the quiet of the day from deep within the jungle.

"What in Christ was that?" Tom asked, retrieving the Enfield and raising it to his shoulder from just inside the door. "Please, suh. 'Tis not safe 'ere. Take the journal an' let's find a safa dwellin', eh?"

Showing no sign of fear, Walton said, "Nonsense. How naïve of you to think there would be nothing left alive upon the island. We are staying. Moreau's residence is no doubt near. Find it and get us unpacked. It is your turn to make us dinner. First thing tomorrow, you must find the materials you need to build a radio tower, yes?"

Still gripping the rifle as he peered into the jungle in the rapidly dimming light, Tom said, "I may start on that tonight. In the meantime, where will you be?"

"Right here, of course. I need isolation. I was for too long thwarted by prying eyes and moralizers. Give me a hand with this table. I want it directly under that lantern."

As they worked to situate the table and straighten its collection of beakers, burners, and instruments, Tom said, "I remember your arrival in London when ya travelled from Portsmouth ta start at uni. All us hired workers envied ya, rich an' smart an' all as ya were. But look what you've become. Ya rarely sleep, 'ardly eat... So many who respected ya at the start were laughin' behind ya back. I've come 'ere ta protect ya as much as ta help ya. An' it's not just the promise I made ta Kath'rine..."

Pulling a turned-over stool from beneath the toppled bookshelf and placing it behind the now work-ready table, Walton answered, "I don't require your protection, Tom. As to Katherine, she knew what I was when she agreed to our engagement. Her breaking it off was an illumination of her faults—of her unworthiness to be my wife. She was not for the long haul and full commitment a quest like this requires. Your promises to her are no concern of mine. You had no right to make them. She should find someone else. Let him be her protector. I ask you not to mention your promises—or her—again."

Leaving his station by the door, Tom approached the table, knowing he would not get another chance to prevent an almost certainly tragic outcome for them both once he left the lab. "Yer chasin' ghosts, Robert. Think a' yer father. Yer family reputation."

Placing Moreau's journal before him like it was the Holy Grail, Walton said with a sneer, "So it is Robert now, is it? Do not forget yourself, Tom. Our relationship has not changed just because it is only you and I—and whatever else remains—upon this island. As to my family... Cowards! Every last one of them... My father worst of all, providing funds to men with larger hearts and innovative ideas while he sat in his cage at the lending house. Yet, when I, his *son*, needed it the most, he refused to help me. His *only son*. Leave me now, Thomas. I have important work to do."

Hearing in Walton's voice the clear indication that the conversation would go no further, Tom gathered up their things and exited the lab.

Opening the cover of the journal and moving his lantern closer, Walton closed his eyes and said, "I do now command of you, oh mighty Moreau, to rise up from the dank grave of your defeat and reveal the heart of your sacred secrets to me..."

CHAPTER 5

Moreau's island laboratory, many years earlier.

Over the course of the more than a decade since he had been banished to this tiny Pacific island—by his own will and choice, as he so often told himself—Abraham Moreau, former resident of London, had taken great pains to bring as much civilization—as much order, routine, and decorum—as he could to his daily life.

Tonight was the exception. Tonight he would not be at table for a four-course meal served promptly by his household staff at seven p.m. sharp.

Not tonight. Not when he was so tantalizingly close to a breakthrough.

After which, when he had returned triumphant to London, how clearly they all would see what the spark of revelation in a genius' mind could do.

Once a physiologist of great renown, he had suffered his first of many insults when, due to complaints by a few jealous colleagues regarding the nature of his pursuits, he had been driven out of his rooms at University College. Desperate to continue his work, he met a man in charge of a highly organized criminal gang in the East End underground who was willing to fund his research in return for certain services. Forced to apply his growing skills in vivisection and grafting between species to the most horrid of enterprises, he found himself thwarted and pursued by a man he had hoped to make an ally through an appeal to his considerable intellect. When that last ditch effort failed, he had escaped to Costa Rica—along with a troubled young doctor, his eventual assistant, Alex Montgomery—to gather necessary supplies before arranging for transport to this island.

Glancing up from the latest hybrid specimen strapped to his operating table, Moreau surveyed his laboratory with pleasure. Both this building and the four others he had designed and overseen the construction and appointment of to his exacting specifications were marvels by any standards, and none were as high as his.

Oh yes, of course, as he readily admitted, there had been the occasional mistake. The infuriating setback. Though never had he strayed—even as Montgomery had slowly sunk into a cesspool of alcohol and pangs of regretful conscience. He, though, had never considered walking away as his creations—his children—had reverted time and again to their despicable animal ways.

Why would he? Not when each failure yielded new discoveries, new advances toward success.

Returning to his work—the careful separation and elongation of the paws of a she-panther (how crucial for their survival and education was the dexterity that came with manipulation of objects with the hands!)—he heard, from just beyond the threshold of where his cultivated compound ended and the ungovernable jungle began, the high-pitched yell of his most rebellious child, hyena-man, followed by a chorus of guttural growls and the rustle of the foliage as he was chased away.

Moreau would soon have a visitor, and the timing could not be worse.

Placing his scalpel, as well as a needle and length of catgut, into a surgical pan, Moreau tugged a blanket from a neatly folded pile on a shelf to his left, partially covering the she-panther, who gave as her response a low and lowly moan. Kissing her gently on the forehead, he began to wash the blood from his delicate surgeon's hands as the door to the laboratory opened, revealing a tall, shaggy, gray-furred figure in a makeshift, burlap-patched parody of cleric's robes. As the man-creature entered, Moreau could hear its long, curved toenails clicking on the hard-packed floor and the breathy snuffling that the creature was trying so hard to hide.

Banging his ceremonial staff, which was seven feet in height, on the floor three times so the shells, tiny skulls, ribs and other bones, brightly colored and pure white feathers, rabbits' and hens' feet, and other adornments clicked and rattled against it and each other, the man-creature said, as though in a trance, "Not to go on all fours. Not to eat flesh nor fish—that is the law. Not to suck up drink. Not to claw the bark of trees—that is the law. Not to chase other men. Not to shed blood—that is the law. Are we not men? To go tearing with the teeth and hands into the roots of things, snuffing in the earth... it is bad. Evil is he who breaks the law."

As if in response, the she-panther howled in pain, attempting to break free of her restraints, just as a great roll of thunder exploded overhead and torrents of steaming rain began to fall beyond the door.

"For pity's sake, my friend," Moreau said to the man-creature, who had been dubbed the Sayer of the Law for his crucial role amongst the doctor's children, "you know better than to come here while I am working! Say the words again and be gone, or I will be forced to make an example of you."

Suppressing a growl as it rose in his throat, Sayer did as he was told, increasing the rhythm and the banging of the staff as the words were intermixed with snorts and snuffs and huffing, hissing breaths. "Not to go on all fours. Not to eat flesh nor fish—that is the law. Not to suck up drink. Not to claw the bark of trees—that is the law. Not to chase other men. Not to shed blood—that is the law. Are we not men? To go tearing with the teeth and hands into the roots of things, snuffing in the earth... it is bad. Evil is he who breaks the law."

As Sayer recited the laws, Moreau took the opportunity to fetch his whip from a table, although he held it behind him in the shadows so his visitor could not see it.

His recitation done, Sayer fell to his knees, laying his staff beside him and clawing at the dirt and straw between his muscular legs.

Snapping the whip at the creature's shoulder, producing a pitiful yelp that sent the she-panther into hysterics, Moreau yelled, snapping the whip again for emphasis, this time in the air, "There must be Law, even for one's children. Say the words I've taught you!"

"Evil is he who breaks the law. Yours is the hand that makes, yours is the hand that heals, yours is the House of Pain. Yours is the lightning flash, yours is the deep salt sea, yours are the stars in the sky. Our Father, He is great. Our Father, He is good."

With each word forced from his thickly muscled throat, Sayer calmed, until, by the end of this latest recitation, he was curled in the fetal position at Moreau's booted feet.

Crouching down so he could stroke the mewling creature's head, Moreau whispered, "Do you understand what I have sacrificed to bring you and your siblings into this world? Once upon a time, I was Doctor Abraham Moreau, celebrated in the greatest of cities and known throughout the world. Now I labor in secret, an outcast, misunderstood and cursed. I dwell in the shadows with the ghosts of grand discovery, awaiting the day that I will get my due—the day the gods shall genuflect and pronounce that Moreau has surpassed them."

Grasping his father's hand, stroking each of Moreau's well-formed fingers with his gnarled and clumsy own, Sayer struggled to say, "Father, am I not five-man like you? Why then must you give the others and me the Pain?

Smiling with a mix of love and disappointment, Moreau answered, "How is it that you do not know? It is my goal—as it has been from the start—to cure deformities and control genetics for the good of Humankind. A perfect race of beings, devoid of all evil. And you, my most capable of sons, shall be its Adam."

"These are 'big thinks,' Father. They hurt me in my heart."

Jumping to his feet and snapping the whip in Sayer's face, Moreau, gone from gentle father to vicious tyrant in the quickest of instants, exclaimed, "The heart? Do not speak to me of the heart! A mere mechanism to circulate the blood, and nothing more... It knows no emotion. Such a notion is baseless and ignorant and I shall not abide it!" Resisting the urge to strike his creation again—the she-panther had finally quieted down and he did not wish to rouse her—Moreau took a calming breath and continued. "It is abysmally worthless notions such as these that have kept me on my quest despite its countless setbacks. Where do anger, hate, fear, cravings, desires *truly* live in the body of a man? This is what I wish to know, so I can starve them out!"

Pulling himself tighter into his position on the floor, Sayer began to weep. "The Pain you make on us, Father, is a kind of Hell."

Slamming his fist into a nearby table, Moreau felt his face turning red. Damn these unintelligible beasts! "Pleasure and pain have nothing to do with Heaven or Hell! Suppressed sexuality... this is our Age's answer to these matters... Industry plots and plans its brutal wars, all the while accusing *me* of being the monster!" Realizing he was at this moment living up to that role through his booming voice and dark demeanor, Moreau forced himself to quell his flaming temper, taking a seat and running his hand through his short white hair. "I have never troubled about the ethics of the matter. The study of Nature makes a man at last as remorseless as Nature. And if this road is paved in Pain and bathed in Blood, it is, in the end, no matter."

From the floor, he heard only snuffing.

"Somehow you damnable creatures always regress." Pushing back his chair and approaching the weeping mass, dropping the whip as he did so, Moreau asked it, sternly but without malice, "What is the law?"

Grasping its staff and forcing itself to stand, the creature managed to growl out, "Not to go on all fours."

Then, together, they whispered, "Are we not men?"

Taking his creation by the elbow and leading him to the door, Moreau said, "Go now, my son. The hour is late but I am far from finished. This House of Pain awaits me and I must answer its call."

CHAPTER 6

Something comes forth from the jungle.

T he lanterns had all but burned the last of their oil when Walton, having been sitting in the same hunched position for hours, taking in page after page of the details of Moreau's work, read aloud, "'The study of Nature makes a man at last as remorseless as Nature.'"

Glancing at the most recent page of the dozens he had filled in his own journal over the course of the session, he gingerly straightened his back, the vertebrae and muscles groaning and popping as he did so.

"Remorseless is what we must be, Abraham," he said, turning his head to the left and right to loosen his neck muscles. "Your downfall was in trusting your creations. They were far too primitive; you had too far missed the mark. Not that the fault was your own. You did not understand the things that I have learned. For you did not have access to the cumulative work of you and your fellow travelers."

Stretching his legs before sliding off the chair and approaching one of the operating tables, Walton ran his hand along the edge from the bottom to the top. "This is where you worked on the she-panther. Oh yes... I can feel it clearly enough. Already I begin to feel closer to you, to the presence of your ghost. How close had you come before chaos descended upon you? Before hyena-man led his brethren against you? That damned Montgomery... Never trust a drunkard. Or another doctor. Tom, for instance, is simple. Tom craves just enough adventure to be useful but has not enough ambition to overstep his bounds. His moral barometer, however... Well... should the time come, if he presents half the threat Montgomery did, I shall not hesitate. The stakes are far too high."

Closing both his and Moreau's journals, Walton slid them back into his haversack with those of Jekyll and Frankenstein. As much as he wished to proceed, it would have to wait until morning. He needed some food and a sound evening's sleep.

Locking the journals in a cabinet, the key of which he slipped into the pocket of his vest, Walton began turning down the near-exhausted lanterns when a shrill cry came from the jungle, not far from his door.

"Ah," he said, reaching for Moreau's whip from its place on one of the nearby shelves. "One of Abraham's creations is seeking to find its father. I can play the role as well as anyone. Much can be learned if I can trap, sedate, and examine it."

Situating himself in the shadows just inside the laboratory door, Walton uncoiled the whip. He had practiced for many months with whip, knife, pistol, and rifle—any means necessary should he have to meet violence with violence of his own. Letting the whip dangle, carefully adjusting his grip, Walton readied himself as the sounds of the beast came closer to the door, the scream replaced by a series of vicious growls.

"Come inside now," he whispered. "Come and see your father." Looking to the ceiling he silently added, "Guide me now, my nameless Angel, that I may succeed where Jekyll, Moreau, and Frankenstein and so many others have failed."

Half expecting an answer now that he was actually on the island, what Walton heard next was the sound of the bolt of the Enfield rifle being pulled back and then forcefully engaged.

Tom.

Putting his face into the broken window of the door, Walton hissed, "Dammit, Tom! Get in here and get behind me. I tell you, it must not be harmed!"

Keeping the rifle out in front of him, trained on the jungle, Tom backed through the door, which Walton left half way open. Pulling Tom to the side and back into the shadows, he hissed, "Get behind me, you damned fool! And do not shoot, no matter what the creature does, unless I should command it."

Doing as he was told, Tom tensed as the creature came closer, the quality of its blood-chilling growl somewhere between a lion and a gorilla.

Then, in an instant, it was through the door, dropping its center of gravity to move on all fours with a speed that was hard to track. Beakers, burners, and books all toppled over as it charged around the room. Thankfully, the lanterns upon the tables were all empty of oil or burning so low they extinguished themselves as they fell to the floor.

Still Walton stood his ground, cocking back his arm to release the whip and punish his would-be prey with a sharp dose of pain.

But the creature—which looked to Tom as though a jaguar had been crossed with a long-tusked boar—must have sensed Walton behind it, for it abruptly turned, charging at him hard with a terrible roar.

Tom shot it dead, directly between its piercing yellow eyes, the bullet from the Enfield hitting with enough force to not only stop the creature's charge but throw it backwards, where it lay, breathing its last, no more than three feet from where Moreau was standing.

Pulling the bolt back to eject the spent .303 cartridge and throwing it home to engage another one, Tom stood over the beast, ready to finish the job at the slightest sign of movement.

"Cor blimey, what a stench! Look at it, suh. 'Alf jaguar, half... 'tis a demon, suh. We done it a service ta put it outta its mis'ry, I tell ya!"

Instead of an answer, perhaps a sign of gratitude, which Tom was expecting, he felt the barrel wrenched to the side by two powerful hands.

"Did I tell you to shoot it, you git?"

Walton crouched beside the beast.

Did he stroke its forehead?

"I had the situation handled," he said. "Now put that damned rifle down and help me get it up and onto the table. I might yet save its life and learn its secrets... A journal can only offer so much!"

As Tom complied, while trying not to gag as he lifted and held his end of the infernal, bleeding beast, he again began to question his agreeing to accompany Walton to the island. Whatever he had been expecting, whatever he thought he could do, this was well beyond even the tiniest show of sanity or reason.

Once the beast was on the table, Walton began strapping it in, but not before pushing Tom away.

"Bring me a plate and mug. And my pipes. Leave them just inside the door, Tom. Until further notice you are no longer welcome in this room." Standing in shock at Walton's words, Tom soon moved, as Walton yelled, "Now, man! Or you shall quickly wish your place was exchanged with this poor creature here."

Turning back one last time before exiting, Tom saw that he had not been mistaken moments before.

Walton was stroking the creature's horrific head.

And he was calling it son.

CHAPTER 7

What other lessons Walton learned from Moreau.

Despite the application of his considerable skill in surgery, Robert Peary Walton was unable to save the hybrid creature Tom had shot. The damage was simply too great. But his efforts were not without rewards, for, by examining the scars from Moreau's original vivisecting, grafting, and modifying, and extracting and studying various organs, including what was left of its brain (*damn Tom's irrational actions!*), Walton learned methods and modalities he never could from a textbook or journal.

The applications of the contents of the jars upon the shelves—carbolic acid, Royal Jelly, opium derivatives, ammonia, and many others—began to whisper their meanings as Walton moved back and forth between the theories and formulae in Moreau's journal and the evidence of practical application in the creature on which he worked.

Although much of what he had done was crude or even foolish, Moreau had been close! Walton, in his excitement, could see more clearly than ever before his path to immortality.

When he had sliced into, dissected, and examined all that seemed of value in the creature, Walton inserted various parts and pieces into jars of formaldehyde and set about the work of removing the unneeded remains of the carcass to an area beyond a thick growth of bush just outside the door.

Exhausted from the effort—even with so much removed and stored, or simply discarded into the brush, the beast was exceedingly dense with muscle!—Walton leaned against the building to catch his breath.

Tom then appeared from around the farthest corner, Enfield in hand and machete and hatchet tucked into his belt.

"Really, Tom," Walton said dismissively, "you look foolish with all that weaponry. You do. How quickly you have retreated into the basest of emotions. How thoroughly you have surrendered control to fear. I will help you, Tom. And soon. Another week or so with the doctors' journals and I shall be ready to undertake experimentations of my own."

Stepping back as Walton spoke, Tom shook his head. "Not likely, suh. I will not be subjected ta the aberrations that produced an unholy creature such as that one! Look at its remains... an' yerself! Covered in blood an' gore ya are!"

Glancing down in complete surprise at his encrusted surgical apron, Walton flicked his hand toward the pieces of the carcass. "Bury that in the jungle somewhere. Bury it deep, Tom. And in exchange I shall have a bath. A change of clothes. But then I must return to work."

As Tom fetched a wheelbarrow to complete his unhappy task, Walton undid his apron, throwing it in a barrel so Tom could burn it with the rest of the evening's trash. Gathering the journals into his haversack, he walked to Moreau's main house, where he found a plate of bread, fruit, *enchidos*, and cheese awaiting him in the kitchen.

After devouring its contents, he stripped off his gore-draped clothes and cleaned himself in the bathtub.

Intending to read as he lay on his bed—*Moreau's* bed—he arranged the mosquito netting and made himself comfortable.

He soon descended into a deep and dream-filled sleep.

CHAPTER 8

Walton conjures memories of Frankenstein and his Creature.

Walton had remained asleep for the remainder of the day and into the early evening. Had he remembered the grisly contents of his dreams he might have considered abandoning his path, but that was not to be. His nameless Angel would allow no such contrary messages to reach him.

Joining Tom in the dining room, Walton contemplated the half dozen unoccupied chairs arrayed around the table. For whom had they been placed? Walton knew one was for M'Ling, whom Edward Prendick had derisively described as a "bear, tainted with dog and ox." *Tainted?* Prendick, again through his narrative, had *also* described M'Ling as fiercely loyal to the drunkard Montgomery. Willing to give his life...

Had there been others? If so, why had Moreau not mentioned them? Why had Prendick left them out of the tale?

Chewing on the mystery as he did his vegetables and meat, Walton sat in silence throughout the meal, knowing full well Tom was in agony over it and its unsettling possibilities. As soon as he was finished, he slipped his haversack from the chair where he had hung it and excused himself, warning Tom in no uncertain terms not to approach the lab.

Reaching the front door, he eyed the Enfield rifle leaning in a corner. After a moment's contemplation, he left it where it stood.

Ten minutes later, the lab door locked and lanterns lit, he pulled the journal of Victor Frankenstein from the haversack, running his fingers over its cracked cover and rotting leather clasp.

How many times he had read the tiny cursive through he could not even hazard a guess. There were passages he could recite from heart and yet he continued to read it, over and over again, marking the deterioration of the handwriting as Victor suffered loss after loss. It was a narrative of deep despair, cataloguing betrayals, bargains, murders, and myriad pursuits both on land and in the mind.

How different things might have been had Robert's seafaring ancestor and his uncourageous crew not gone back on their agreement to remain. The final page of the journal, written only hours before Frankenstein finally expired, unable to cope with this final, ultimate grief, had the capability of haunting the present Robert Walton if he let it.

He did not intend to let it do so.

Opening the increasingly fragile journal to the November night that Victor had brought the Creature to life, Walton whispered his summons: "Come forth now, Doctor Frankenstein. The time has come to reveal to me the secrets you have hidden in plain sight. Have I not proven myself worthy? Made an arduous journey as you did, but also succeeded where you failed—for I did not let the captain of the ship on which *I* booked passage dictate terms to me! Speak to me, dear Victor… I promise I shall listen…"

*****

Locking the door of his laboratory in Ingolstadt and opening his journal to a fresh, eager-to-be-filled, white and pristine page, Victor Frankenstein smiled at the storm gathering just outside his curtained windows.

For many months, he had purchased and cobbled together both the mundane and harder to obtain array of laboratory equipment carefully arranged around him. As he dipped his quill into a fresh pot of ink, he felt his shoulders relax as he let the bubbling, dripping, and sparking from the equipment soothe his weary mind. He had not slept for days. The feeling of electricity in the air had made the hairs on his arms stand on end for hours, so carefully had he trained himself to sense it.

Knowing he did not have long to wait—even the lifeless, sutured-together body beneath the blanket on the table behind him seemed to throw off the subtle energies of eager anticipation— Victor began to write:

"I feel as though I am driven on by Destiny. In my ambition to cure mankind of all disease, to crack open and penetrate the hidden laws of Nature, I have walked for years a path which no others have dared to even test. I have made my enemies, yes—it is no matter, for they were not worthy men. I have weathered the slings and arrows of mockery and scorn. My dearest friend, Henry, in his romantic poet's zeal, has warned me that my experiments, because they go against Nature, can only lead to Evil. That I am endangering with my pursuits my family's Honor, Reputation, and Integrity. I shall say this for Henry, as wrong as I know he is—at least he dared to speak it to my face! How many more have accused me behind my back of being Mad! Has any scientist ever been saner? Never has my path been clearer, my purpose more sacred and pure. I pursue Power over Death. No more needless disease, such as the one that took my mother. No longer shall the state of the soul be a mystery held to their breasts by corrupted priests and mystics, for I have cracked the codes of the Alchemists. I hold in my head the means to the elixir of life!"

As a streak of lightning illuminated the street outside his rooms, he added, "A new species will bless me as its creator. No father could claim the gratitude of his children so completely as I shall deserve theirs!"

Placing the quill in the seam between the newly filled pages, Victor crossed the room to his primary apparatus—a bank of two dozen spotless Leyden jars. Checking the wires inside and out and filling each of the jars to the top with room-temperature water, Victor inspected the lengths of thin copper he had connected to an electrostatic machine near the table on which the lifeless body lay.

Pulling back the blanket and gazing with pride at his eight-foot labor of love, Victor checked that he had embedded the lengths of copper from the contacts on the back of the electrostatic machine securely at the proper points along the length of the body. How he had rejoiced when he had found the ancient Asian scrolls full of diagrams of the energy centers used in their priests' healings in a half-buried box in a dusty bookstore two months before.

The nameless Angel of his dreams *had guided him there*. There could be no other explanation, tucked as they were between and beneath broadsides and tattered volumes of the prideful histories of war making and conquests of the Romans, Greeks, and Persians. The shopkeeper, whose name was Vellum-Verlag, had not recalled from whence the scrolls had come, nor could he find them listed in his inventories.

He had therefore asked a pittance, which Victor gladly paid.

Readying the machine to collect, through a rod upon the roof, the unmeasurable energy of a strike of lightning, Victor braced himself for the shock that would light up the room for a few precious seconds.

How exhilarating it was as it struck! Victor laughed with unbridled glee as the water in the Leyden jars heated and began to bubble and steam. Several of them burst—it was no matter. They had done their work. Brushing glass from his arm, he lay his head upon the chest of the mass upon the table as the wires warmed and crackled around him.

"At last the heart begins to beat!" he cried. "Life from death, and I am its master!" Grasping the bandaged chin of his creation, he whispered into the carefully cut slit that lay in line with its ear, "Live, I tell you! Breathe, I *command* you! Live and show the world what wonders Science can do! What I, Doctor Frankenstein, can do!"

So faintly beat the heart and so swiftly had the full fury of the storm come and gone that Victor began to fear his efforts were for naught.

Then a shoulder twitched thrice and a pale, gigantic hand began to move, grasping the air with its fingers like a newborn babe's searching urgently for its mother's milk-filled breast.

"That is good, my child," Victor urged, his heart set to burst with a father's unfathomable love. "Move the limbs that I have given you. Think with the brain that your Creator has bestowed upon you. Sit up now. I command it of you!"

How exquisite the effort his reanimated creation made! With the veins in its neck bulging to the point of near bursting with its desire to please its father, its body at last flexed at the waist.

What a sight it was as it struggled and sweat and, finally, sat itself up.

"Look at you, my child. How you move! Stand now, my beautiful specimen of a New and Perfect Man!"

Assisting the great muscled bulk off the table, Victor watched with mounting joy as his creation made ever more easy use of its limbs, widening its stance and spreading its arms outward to keep its balance.

"How regally you stand there for all the world to worship! Let me see your face, my son, that I may know what I should call thee."

Stepping into the growing light by the window as the storm clouds moved away, Victor's child found the frayed ends of the bandages that covered its face, letting them fall to the floor one after another as it fulfilled its father's request.

When at last the final strip had fallen away, so too did the veil that had clouded the eyes of Victor Frankenstein the many months that he had worked on the suddenly hideous visage before him. "My God...," he hissed, backing away, "What have I done? In all my months of toil, how could I not have seen the wretched, unendurable visage of this... this most unholy *monster!* This vile, filthy demon. Such a thing as even Dante himself could not have conceived."

"*Faaa—ther?*"

The whispered word fell upon his ears like a warlock's darkest curse.

Then the Creature, with a groan, dared to speak the word again.

"*Faa-ther!*"

Turning away from his creation, Victor pleaded, "Do not say that word! I cannot bear to hear it! You are no son of mine!"

Grasping the poker from a stand near the fireplace as he heard the Creature's awkward, ungainly footsteps approach, Victor swung around, holding the length of pointed iron before him like a sword.

"Get away from me! Do you dare to want to touch me? Take your wretched, ugly form to the farthest corners of the world, and leave me to my misery!"

The Creature halted its approach, the pain in its voice filling Victor's eyes with hot and heavy tears.

"I do not understand..."

Digging the heel of his hand into his eyes to grind the tears away, Victor yelled, "Be gone from me, I say! Get thee back to Hell, accursed fiend! Let me never look upon your wretched face again! Do you hear me, accursed demon? *GO!*"

Though Victor could not see it, so great was his fear and disappointment, a mask of deep confusion contorted the Creature's face. "Are you not my father?"

Shoving his tormentor backward, Victor screamed, "Damn you, filthy thing. I claim no such cursed role. I... said... *GO!*"

With a horrid crashing of glass and splintered wood, the terrified Creature complied.

CHAPTER 9

Through Divine intervention, Walton learns the Creature's secrets.

It never failed to make Walton's temperature rise as he read of the swift about-face Victor Frankenstein had made that triumphant November night. Certainly Prendick's description of M'Ling and the corrupted visage of the hybrid beast Tom had shot were proof enough that Moreau—and apparently even Montgomery—were not moved to revulsion by such a small detail as the beauty or ugliness of the face.

"Frankenstein, you coward!" Walton exclaimed on this particular night. "Worthless fool that you were! I am once again embarrassed to read your account!" So great was his anger, so pressing his need to physically express his frustration, Walton threw the journal against the wall, its dried binding causing it to separate into two halves, with the back cover also coming loose and sliding across the floor.

Immediately feeling remorse at his action, Walton crossed the room, retrieving the two almost evenly distributed parts of the book. Bending to collect the back cover, he was astonished to find the inner paper glued to it peeled back, revealing a trio of folded pages on a much rougher paper in a different hand than Frankenstein's.

Taking the materials back to his table, Walton unfolded the three pages that had been until that moment hidden from him.

"My nameless Angel comes to my aid again," he whispered, realizing that the pages he held were in the hand of the Creature itself.

*****

A Monster's Tale, in Prose and in Poem

Oh, how through these many, many months have I longed and readied for this day. To return to the progenitor of my evil Awakening and cause of my terrible Banishment. Through cracks in shutters and around the corners of streets have I watched this man, my Father, waiting for the appropriate moment to execute my long-deliberated plans.

It was not without preparation, without pause and deliberation, for the stakes for us both are incalculably high.

For long have I studied. For long have I prepared. Summoning memories of a life; some life… perhaps many, many lives… previous to this most insufferable incarnation, which I have wished at times to end. To pull from a muddy stream of my all too limited mind the power to understand.

My confusion, so profound, so prevailing, at long last superseded by my anger. As I wandered in the woods, pure instinct driving me to eat what I could gather, pick, kill, or steal. Or to drink from streams and unguarded wells or the odd and precious bottle of something sweet or sleep-inducing left upon a sill. For what had I done? Had I asked to be Awakened? Had I requested to be worked upon and distorted into a demon such as I?

No.

Given no choice in the matter, yet punished still—and oh, so severely—for my appearance, my clumsy, intrusive actions.

I ought to be like Adam, but I am rather the fallen angel. From the first night of my life, when my father so brutally disowned me with his sharp, remorseless cruelty, I have taken to wandering the world. I have been met in all directions with hatred and disdain. I have been chased by dogs and whipped by priests and scum. I have taken my refuge in caves and desolate places no man would dare to enter. But I have also learned. I have puzzled out the familiar yet distant symbols in these wonders men call books. Over time, my memories of the written word—how to read it, to write it, to soak in the salty brine of stories, tales, confessions, recorded nightmares—at last, through the most immense of effort, returned. With such a valuable gift, such a precious birthright, restored to me, I sought out the familiar. Descriptions of demons, both Ancient and Modern, so I might better know the differences and similarities between us.

From shadowy libraries, back alley bookstores, and unlocked drawing rooms did I gather what I needed—Bibles and fairy tales, novels and myths, scientific journals and illustrated travelogues… And, of them all, it was poetry—Milton, Byron, Shelley, and Blake— that I learned to love the best.

Poetry sings to the soul like a dove must to its lover.

Uck… What truly blasphemous talk from a loveless monster such as I, birthed from the depths of Hell!

How can such unholy inconsistencies be allowed to be?

Through simple acts of kindness, dispensed without wanting return.

Simple acts of kindness, experienced by a heart both tattered and abused, offered in earnest through the ministrations of a man whose eyes knew no sight, whose voice held no judgment, whose hands knew no hate.

It was from him, in his humble, dilapidated home that I learned of kindness and of love. What a strange nature is Knowledge! It clings to the mind when it has once seized on it like a lichen on the rock. And the more that I have learned, the more that I despair, for all I ask is love, and all I am given is hate.

And so I offer this, my poem to the world.

In the vast, unending darkness of the void.
A light shone in the mist. It beckoned, follow bliss.
I moved to make a coupling with the sound
A soul to be reborn, met instead with scorn.
Expecting love, a promise not to rend—
Cast into the furnace, hatred made of me a friend.
No father's love, on which I could depend,
Thrown into the gutter, hatred made of me a friend.
In the cruel, despising gazes of the world,
A fist was quick to fly, forced into disguise.
Seeking solace in the books I found
Their comfort was not mine, their truth to me all lies.
Expecting love, a promise not to rend—
Cast into the fire, hatred made of me a friend.
No father's smile, on which all sons depend—
Forced into the maelstrom, hatred made of me its friend.
How I hope to find a place to live—
Where my soul knows more than hate.
How I wish to know another way—
Than the deaths I've made my own…
My curse, to be alone.
In the vast, unending darkness of my life.
No light shows within the mist
No one beckons follow bliss.
Still I dare to hope to hear the sound—
A voice that says, "Reborn." A respite from your scorn.
Shall I know love, a promise not to rend?
No more fire, no more furnace. Hatred is no friend.
Another's love, on which I can depend.

I must have a companion. Hatred is no friend.
Another's love, to help my soul ascend.
He will make my companion.
Or I'll make misery, his last and only friend.

CHAPTER 10

The narrative of Frankenstein and his Creature continues.

It must have been mere moments after the Creature had scrawled his thoughts and completed his poem somewhere within the forested shadows near to where Victor had been hiking by a river near the Alpine village of Chamounix that he had made the decision to at last reveal to his poor excuse of a father what he had become in the hard months since his birth.

Pulling up the wide, deep hood of the crude coat he had fashioned from scraps of burlap and canvas he had pilfered from a factory on his way to Chamounix, the Creature charged through the trees toward his target, the rips and tears caused by thorns, brambles, and low-lying branches not registering in his hyper-focused brain, although they gashed his cheeks and hands as well.

Exiting from the tree line and stopping at the start of a gentle slope above where Victor stood, the Creature called out, "Frankenstein? Is that you, my ever-fallible Father? How very gaunt you seem! How so unlike the proud man who thought that he was God. Your prodigal son has returned. Yes… it is true—the horrid beast you so severely scorned has learned to read! As my proof, I offer you a verse from *Paradise Lost*, by the mystic poet Milton: 'Did I request thee, Maker, from my clay to mould me Man? Did I solicit thee from Darkness to promote me?' Do you hear me, father? Your devil has returned! Educated and determined—and wanting something of you! Come and see me, Father, so I might prove to you how thoroughly I have changed."

As the Creature headed down the slope, he saw Victor attempt to move, to flee from the source of all his nightmares, but his feet seemed frozen in place.

"Are you so frightened of me, Father? It is all right to have me so close. You must not be frightened of me. I bear you no ill will. I have read in Plutarch's *Lives* of the origin of Republics and the gentle men who must govern them. I will not cling to malice."

Staying where he was, Victor raised his walking stick, holding it diagonally in front of his body for protection. "How dare you disturb me here!"

"Father..." the Creature answered, holding his position at the bottom of the slope. "I am disappointed. Are not my new abilities those of a worthy child? Are not the words I chose from this book that I hold, which I have read again and again, proof enough that I am not as you say that I am?"

Turning his head in disgust, Victor answered, "Your words make you all the more an abomination. An affront to God! You are no poetic Angel, but the offspring of Satan himself!"

Throwing the book to the ground, the Creature hissed, "If Satan is my father, than you, Frankenstein, are the very Satan of which you speak! To have made of my visage *this*!" Pulling the hood from his head, the Creature ran his fingers along the rivulets of scars on his face, highlighting their grotesque ridges with the freshly drawn blood. "Only a blind man ever showed me love, so hideous am I to see! But you, as my father... Can you not love me despite my flaws?"

"Flaws?" Victor shouted, "I know the things you have done, the murder you have committed. My poor, defenseless brother... You are a monster, nothing more!"

The Creature let loose a cry that would have moved a statue to weep.

Yet Victor remained unmoved.

"I am shunned and hated by all mankind!" the Creature cried, moving a few steps closer to the target of his frustration. "Shall I not hate them that abhor me? I tell you this, Victor Frankenstein—if I cannot inspire love, I will inspire *fear*!"

Wishing to retreat but remembering the river at his back, Victor answered, holding his walking stick weapon a little higher and tighter, "Come no closer! I warn you! Your soul is as hellish as your detested, devilish form. Your words only worsen my rage. Be gone! I have a life here, as a respected man of science. I have put the mistakes of my past behind me. I have put *you* and your memory behind me! In truth, I am soon to be married."

Putting out his arms for balance to keep from falling, so weak had this news made his legs, the Creature crouched slowly to the grass, his disfigured, bleeding face hidden in his also bleeding hands. "Shall each man find a wife for his bosom and each beast have his mate, and I be all alone? Are you to be happy while I grovel in the intensity of my wretchedness?"

Lowering his voice to a dismissive hiss, Victor answered, "Your condition is not my concern. If you have any pity within you, you will not linger here."

Taking his hands from his face and holding them out, wet as they were with his tears, tinged red from the blood of his wounds, the Creature said, softly but now with the malice he had so wished to contain, "Why should I pity man more than he pities me? I am fearless and therefore powerful. I warn you, Victor Frankenstein—I will not be denied. You will fulfill the request that I have come here tonight to make of you."

An endless well of curiosity ever his weakness, Victor stepped forward half a dozen steps. "What would you have me do?"

"You must create another... A female, made like me, with deformities such as mine. We will live out our days together far away from man. Deep in some jungle or cave. I will never bother you again. I will love her, and she will learn to love me."

Backing away until he felt his heels sink into the muddy bank of the river, Victor shook his head with a violent vigor, such as to remove the words he had heard from his ears before they could anchor in his brain.

"What you request is madness! Never will I create another beast like you, equal in deformity and wickedness. How dare you ask of me to do this monstrous thing!"

Rising up to his full height, the Creature said, "You once did it on your own, with no request—or permission—from me. All that has happened since that moment I opened my eyes, breaking your ignorant trance, is your responsibility, not mine! Do not deny me my request, I beg of you. Call upon the writhing thing inside of you that drove you to make me and use it to give me a mate!"

Watching the Creature fall to its knees, hands clasped in supplication, Victor found himself momentarily pulled toward granting the fiend its request, so fine had some of its sensations become that he felt doing so would be a form of justice. Then, just as quickly, he felt himself yanked hard in the opposite direction until a wave of revulsion for the project unprecedented in its depth and strength overcame him. "I shall never do this thing you ask of me. Never!"

Rushing forward, the Creature shouted, "You are my creator, but I am your master—*Obey*!"

Falling to the muddy ground, Victor dropped his useless improvised weapon and, arms covering his face as the Creature raised its huge-knuckled fists above his head, ready to strike, managed to choke out the following: "I said... *Never*!"

Curling himself into as small a figure as possible, half hoping the mud would swallow him up and offer him protection, Victor closed his eyes against what he knew would be a skull-splitting series of blows. Instead, he heard splashing and the flight of startled birds as the Creature brushed past him and entered the shallows of the river.

Feeling the Creature yanking him by the collar of his coat into the freezing water, Victor refused to open his eyes as its foul, fetid breath filled his nose. "Do this for me, Frankenstein. Do this for me, *Father*, and I shall torment the world no more."

Then the beast was gone, leaving Victor alone with his troubled, conflicted thoughts.

CHAPTER 11

Tom disobeys, but with reason.

R unning his hands over the pages the Creature had penned, and taking in the final lines of the poem—*I must have a companion/Hatred is no friend/Another's love, to help my soul ascend/He will make my companion/Or I'll make misery, his last and only friend—*

for the half-dozenth time, Walton tucked them back into the book. No doubt the Creature had dropped them during their struggle by the river near Chamounix and Victor had tucked them away, perhaps initially as a spur to what he must do and later as a reminder of the carnage his cowardice had caused.

"You were a fool, Victor Frankenstein," Walton proclaimed, placing the two halves and the back cover of the journal aside. "And worse—you were a coward. I would have honored the Creature's request from the very moment he asked. I would have prayed that he and his mate would bring forth a progeny. To which I would be a Grandfather-God. If only the Heavens had blessed you with an Angel such as mine, to spur you on when you faltered and not just to lead you to scrolls."

Getting up and stretching his legs, ready to return to the main house for the night, Walton was startled by a sudden banging on the laboratory door, through which he heard Tom in a state of agitation.

"I know I ain't supposta, suh, but I beg ya, let me in! There's somethin' about, suh. We ain't safe!"

Going to the door but not unlocking it, Walton lifted the end of the scrap of hospital blanket he had used to cover the broken window after forbidding Tom to enter, not putting it past him to spy upon his work. "What are you on about, Tom! Your disregard for my instructions displeases me. To resort to this behavior..."

"I ain't makin' nuthin' up! There is someone on the island. 'E came inta the 'ouse. I was upstairs when I 'eard a rustle a' the silverware from the pantry. I caught a glimpse of 'im goin' out a dinin' room windah."

Considering for a moment, Walton answered, "Perhaps one of the beasts yet remains alive. We must capture it, Tom. It would be of great use to me. You must not kill it—do you understand?"

Needing to see the answer in his assistant's eyes and not just hear the words through the wood, Walton undid the lock and the latch, opening the door only wide enough to fit his face in the gap. "Eh, Tom? I see you have that damnable Enfield. Do not let your fear get in my way, Tom, I warn you yet again."

"Tweren't no beast, Robert. It looked ta be a man. But a monstrous one at that. Short an' 'unched. Wild, wavin' 'air. Long, curved 'ands. And it laughed, suh, as it went. Laughed like the devil 'isself, I swear."

Thinking of the unaccounted-for chairs in the dining room, where Tom had seen the supposed beast, Walton said, "Perhaps Moreau got further than we thought! All the more reason to capture it. Let us go to the house, Tom. Have a meal and make a plan. Traps must be devised. We have work to do. Your salary must now be fully earned, by following my instructions and doing my will. So I ask you again, Tom Paris—do you understand?"

Knowing he had, for the moment, no other reasonable choice, Tom nodded his assent.

CHAPTER 12

The Creature confronts his father on the Orkney Islands.

A Brief Note from Your Narrator

Unable to ask Walton himself, one can only surmise—and here my years as a journalist, interviewer, and investigator make me as qualified as any to answer—that his central disappointment with Victor Frankenstein was the doctor's at times unfathomable vacillation. I was an overly impressionable boy when I first read Mary Shelley's semi-accurate account of the true course of events, which of course she packaged, on advice of her publishers, as fiction. I have it on good authority that the summer on Lake Geneva that Mary (all of eighteen and still Goodwin at the time) and PB Shelley spent with Lord Byron, Doctor Polidori, and Claire Clairmont engaging in their Gothic literary exercises provided the perfect alternate narrative for what actually transpired. I have no doubt Victor Frankenstein was himself a guest at Byron's estate during that time, recently returned from the confrontation recently presented herein. Frankenstein was not alone... he had secured a benefactor who paid for his subsequent travels to England, via Strasbourg (where he met with his friend, the poet Henry Clerval), Mannheim, Cologne, and Rotterdam, amongst other cities and towns. From there, it was on to St Andrews and Perth in Scotland, which ultimately led to his decision to have his laboratory well hidden in the north of Orkney, on the isle of Rousay, on the Eynhallow Sound.

A laboratory paid for and outfitted by this benefactor, Abishua Ravenskald, whose family's means were considerable and whose tentacles had stretched far, wide, and deep throughout the history of the world. In each of the cities mentioned by Mary Shelley—and those purposely left unspecified—Frankenstein met with an array of specialists in the scientific and esoteric arts whose tutelage and access to certain texts, while provided to Victor, furthered the aims of the Ravenskalds. I have spoken with some of these teachers during my own previously mentioned studies in these subjects. The unnamed natural philosopher mentioned by Shelley in passing was merely one of many.

This would not be the last time a Ravenskald would finance the work of a scientist attempting to usurp God, as you shall soon enough be shown, both in the current volume and in my future narratives.

Forgive me. I have digressed, although much of what I have digressed with is crucial to the forthcoming installment of our story. I was speaking of Frankenstein's curious vacillations. Even as an impressionable boy, sitting in my bed in an upstairs room, a cheap candle throwing poor light on the page, I wondered at Frankenstein's sudden turn as the bandages were unwrapped and the Creature's face revealed.

Was it the light of life in the deformed face that triggered his theretofore-absent revulsion?

Was it the realization that the Creature had no soul?

Were it not that Frankenstein exhibited the same about-face when it came to fulfilling the Creature's wish and furnishing him with a mate, one would think that Shelley—no doubt directed by Frankenstein himself—had employed a weak narrative device in order to keep her version suitably tense and full of conflict.

Alas, as you will read in what now follows, Frankenstein's predisposition to vacillation was ultimately responsible for all that befell him, his family, and others whom he loved.

*****

Arriving in Orkney after his multi-country tour to find his laboratory fully outfitted according to his specifications and awaiting both he and his work, Victor donned his lab coat and examined the four bodies his benefactor's local men had secured for him, each of which met the criteria of his extensive, exacting demands. He then made an equally detailed catalogue of the utensils, chemicals, and energy-harnessing machinery he had requested his benefactor's men ship from the lab where he had brought the Creature to life.

Satisfied that all was in order, Victor turned his attention to examining the other hastily but solidly constructed dwellings, three in number, Ravenskald had provided for his comfort in the weeks the work would take. After a hearty meal of lamb, clapshot (potatoes and turnips in butter and salt), and black pudding, he took a walk by the sea, resolving to begin his work at the coming of the dawn.

And so the work proceeded, cut by cut, stitch by stitch, as the days and nights passed, until the morning when Victor experienced his next inevitable crisis. Backing into a beaker full of water, the doctor watched in helpless dread as the contents spread across a table before falling upon a tangle of uninsulated wires, causing the machines to which they were attached to come alive with a multi-second series of pops, sparks, and whirs.

Waving away a cloud of dark, acrid smoke as the machinery shorted out, Frankenstein resolved himself to clean up his mess without delay, part of him grateful his work on the female would be postponed for several hours.

As he finished wiping the remainder of the water from the table with a rag, he heard a voice behind him.

"Frankenstein, you fiend!"

Female—although not wholly feminine—he knew from whence the voice had come.

"Turn and face me, my damnable creator! Do you think I shall supplicate myself to you like the one who came before? The one who now awaits me, for his own selfish, though understandable, aims?"

Clenching the rag with such force as to make the contents that it contained gush upon his shoes, Frankenstein wished himself elsewhere as he realized what the shorted-out machine had accomplished.

"Allow me to explain," he whispered, refusing to turn around.

"There is no explanation," the female creature hissed, struggling against her straps. "No defense. No reason to your actions. You are not God, Frankenstein. Nor are you woman, tasked with the often-overwhelming responsibility of bringing forth a fragile, vulnerable life. To nurture and care for it, even when it disappoints you."

Turning to face his tormentor, Frankenstein asked, "What know *you* of disappointment? Of nurture and of toil? You have been birthed by *me*, do you understand? As a balm to a wound that makes my whole world bleed! You will do what I require. You shall live where I command, with whom and how I command it!"

For the rest of his days, Victor Frankenstein would contemplate the actions he next took.

Anything the female would have said would have greatly bettered the outcome. Any set of words would have seen the project done. Seen the Creature pleased.

But what she did was laugh. Laugh at his hubris, his desires, his self-delusions, and his shame.

Great peals of derisive, dismissive laughter came forth from her sutured throat and meticulously manipulated mouth, until the sound of it so hurt him...

He snapped her delicate neck.

Red with rage, his vision blurred and mind no longer his own, he tore his cursed creation limb from tormenting limb, all the while unaware that the Creature was hidden away nearby, anxious to see his desperate request fulfilled.

Falling to the floor, soaked with all manner of fluid, tissue, and flesh, Victor felt his heart clench as the door to the lab swung violently open, revealing the Creature backlit by the sun like some unholy spectre come to claim its due.

"Hear me well, my tyrant and tormentor!" the Creature screamed, picking up the long-haired head of his would-be mate from the floor and holding it before him so its dim, unfocused eyes stared out at Victor with pointed accusation. "You shall come to curse the sun that gazes on your misery. I shall be with you on your wedding night. And you shall wash yourself in the blood of your broken bride, as you have washed yourself in the innocent blood of mine!"

Placing the head on the ground, the Creature charged at his creator, pulling him up by the lapels of his vest so his feet dangled inches above the cold stone floor. "Hear me well, Victor Frankenstein, for I promise you—I shall be with you on your wedding night."

Pulling himself up and falling against the bloody operating table as the Creature exited the lab, the female's head in his arms, Victor began to weep.

"Merciful, Heavenly God," he whispered, looking toward the sky, "forgive me for what I have done. For I swear I'll make it right."

If, by some misdirected insight, Victor supposed that gathering the parts and pieces of his aborted project into a basket weighted with stone, which he then threw over the side of a boat four miles out in the sea without so much as a prayer, would serve as sufficient appeasement to God or anyone else, he was soon to know his folly.

First it would be Henry Clerval, his closest friend, who would feel the Creature's oversized, calloused, and powerful hands take the breath from his body and light from his eyes.

And, then, Gentle Reader, you know all too well what it was that happened next.

CHAPTER 13

A promised unfulfilled is met with one fulfilled.

Nothing could be further from Victor's mind than the broken promise to the Creature as he gazed at the shining eyes and radiant smile of his new and beautiful wife Elizabeth as they were ferried across a lake to the town of Evian, the spire of its church rising in the moonlight like an old friend standing in welcome.

At the encouragement of his father, the weeks that had passed since Victor's return to Geneva he had filled with the preparations for the wedding. Strictly forbidden were all brooding, study, and malaise—the library had been locked, the key always remaining in his father's frock coat pocket—and Victor had found himself missing the drudgery of study by candlelight not an ounce. Although the image of Henry's crumpled throat and the purplish-red reminders in the shape of the Creature's fingers that had done the deed were never far from his mind, he was eager for diversion. The sight of Elizabeth choosing arrangements of edelweiss, roses, and lilies for the altar and selections of music from Mozart, Bach, and Handel to be played by the hired musicians during the ceremony and at the reception after never failed to banish them from his mind.

On the day of the wedding, all went off without a hitch. There was a moment when, catching him alone in the hallway as the guests danced and drank on the sprawling lawn outside his father's estate, Abishua Ravenskald had pressed him for answers on what had transpired on the Orkney islands. Victor, however, still quick of mind although he had enjoyed already several glasses of celebratory sherry, had blamed it solely on the Creature.

"He had seen the ugliness of what he asked," Victor lied, "and, in an unholy fury, he tore the unanimated corpse, evidence of his hubris, into dozens of parts and pieces."

Satisfied with the answer, Victor's benefactor had presented him with a sizeable wedding gift in gold and wished him well on his honeymoon.

Safely arrived at the inn where they would consummate their marriage and from which they would venture forth for the next two weeks to enjoy the local scenery, shops, and entertainment, Victor, his mind abuzz with the events of the day, left Elizabeth to settle in with a bath and a book while he explored their immediate surroundings.

He had just climbed the stairs to the level where their suite was when he heard a scream from down the hall. Pulling the pistol he had carried since his return to Geneva from his jacket pocket, he ran toward the sound, knowing all too well from whence it came, whose it was, and what dreadful truth it held.

Putting the key in the lock with shaking, stubborn fingers, he flung wide the door to find Elizabeth's broken body draped in a grotesque, unnatural position on the bed and the foul, hellish Creature crouching near the open window.

Why had he not thought to fasten its latch!

Would it have mattered?

Cocking the pistol, he took aim at the great hulking bulk and fired, the ball sending up a shower of splinters and shattered glass as it exploded an inch from the scarred, demonic face of his incessant, terrible tormentor.

"Damn you back to hell, you fiend!" he cried, reloading and re-cocking the pistol and adjusting his aim.

Pointing his finger at Elizabeth's bloody, broken form, still within her dress of lace and silk and ribbon, the Creature dropped from the window as Victor squeezed the trigger.

From the street, Victor heard the Creature cry, "I am satisfied, you miserable wretch! I am satisfied and sated!"

Rushing to the window, while once more loading the pistol, Victor saw the street was empty.

The Creature had again escaped his grasp.

Dropping the pistol to the floor, Victor flung himself upon the bed, cradling Elizabeth's head, which moved unnaturally beneath his hand. Once again, the Creature had taken an innocent life by crushing his victim's neck.

Within days of his beloved's funeral, Victor's father, who had held Elizabeth in his heart as his own natural daughter as much as his daughter by law, had expired of grief and Victor, filled with the scalding bile of revenge, had booked passage on Walton's ship in pursuit of his demon seed.

CHAPTER 14

Walton, in a delirium, is aided by his nameless Angel.

So damned thirsty… Why am I so thirsty?

Reaching across his body toward the three water glasses by the bed, Robert focused his eyes on the one in the center.

The only one that was real.

Acting with authority as his employer was struck down by a sudden, crippling fever—from the food, the island, the fetid atmosphere of the lab, it did not matter—Tom had confined Robert to his bed, with little argument, for the past several weeks.

Although he had been unable to work, his time had been well spent.

Each night, his nameless Angel visited him with ideas. Instructions. Insights. All the spackle and patch he needed to seal the cracks in the wall of information he had been cobbling together from the crumpled brick and stonework of the journals of Moreau and Frankenstein.

Frankenstein… the vacillating coward! Yet unquestionably a genius. Not a father at all, while Moreau played too fully to the role.

Both blind, through no fault of their own. They did not have each other. Nor the nameless Angel.

Not to the extent that Robert believed he did.

In point of fact, it was the nameless Angel that had first whispered in the ear of the brilliant London surgeon that the chemical rhythms of a beast and ultimately of man could be altered by transfusion, vaccination, and inoculation. That the skills of the vivisectionist could be applied to artificially modify the basest animal instincts. To extract from the brain and heart the cravings and desires, the hate and fear, that so harmed and hurt humanity.

It was he, the nameless Angel, his now nightly visitor and teacher, that had taught the Creature to read and had helped it to escape to the frozen north as Frankenstein relentlessly pursued it.

It was he, the nameless Angel, that had led Victor to the ship captained by Walton's ancestor. A true piece of manipulative genius. The first paver on the path to where Robert had been led.

And, of course, he had helped the Creature's creator in prior days as well. No one mind could have designed the machinery needed to bring the dead to life.

Now he spoke to Robert, in whispers and laughs, in distorted images through the blurred natural vision and open third eye of the paranormal and supernatural energies and ethers made possible by the fever.

The fever... a gift!

The fever... a must!

The fever... a rite of passage!

The fever... his way home.

The only obstacle was Tom—so determined to medicate and *cure* him. To give him quinine and extractions of dogwood and poplar. To ply his forehead with cold cloths and help him in and out of freezing baths.

Then, worst of all, constantly requesting to use the radio transmitter to call for help. To summon a ship, of all impertinent things!

Interference! He would not have it.

Not when there was still so much meaning he could glean from the ministrations of this holy, nameless Angel.

His nameless Angel.

Robert would set to work as soon as he was well, but the time had not yet come.

As his blurred, untrustworthy vision failed him and he fruitlessly tried to grasp a phantom glass—the back of his hand knocking the real one to the floor, triggering the hurried footsteps of Tom, his relentless, troublesome tormentor—Robert screamed in his frustration.

For, just before the glass had fallen, his nameless Angel had entered through the window, a roll of documents in his hand.

"Away, Tom! Away from this room and from me, do you hear me! I have need to be alone. Alone with my... my..."

Robert was unable to finish, so quickly had the injection taken effect that Tom had so deftly administered to put him to sleep in his still weakened state.

As he drifted off, he saw through his closing eyelids the puzzled look on Tom's haggard face as Robert's frown became a smile.

There, at the end of a passage, was his blessed, nameless Angel, ready to show him the way.

CHAPTER 15

Walton, recovered but not quite himself, continues with his work.

For the next six days, Robert moved in and out of delirium. Other than a few sips of soup in the morning and at night, he refused all other food that Tom, ever attentive and ever abused, offered him.

One morning, as Tom was readying a tray to take up to his room, Robert came down the stairs, his thin wrists showing at the ends of his loose cuffs as his hands gripped the banister as he gingerly made his way.

"Cor blimey, suh! Ya shouldn't be up an' about!"

Waving Tom away as he exited the staircase, Robert took his Panama hat from a peg and placed it snuggly on his head. "I am going back to the laboratory, Tom. I must not be disturbed. No matter what you hear, no matter what I say or do, I must be left alone. You must promise me, or you shall force me to dismiss you. Do you understand me, Tom?"

Knowing he could do no good if Walton banished him further, Tom nodded, although he could not hide the look of fear upon his face.

"You worry too much, my good and simple son. Has your crouching, stalking phantom returned? If he has, you have not spoken of it."

Feeling as though he had been led into a trap, Tom answered, "'E 'asn't. But that don' mean 'e ain't real an' ain't a concern. Prob'ly bidin' 'is time, clever git."

"As if that makes any sense," Robert answered, pulling on his hunting coat. "To wait until I am recovered. Taking on the two of us instead of just the one."

"The Enfield ain't left my side. 'E knows 'e won't stands a chance against it."

"Speaking of. I want it, Tom. And all of the ammunition for it. Is it in the hall?"

Glancing in its direction in the corner near the breakfront across from where he stood, Tom said, "I don' think that's a—"

With a quickness that belied his frail appearance and slow movement down the stairs, Robert had crossed to where Tom had looked and taken the rifle in his hands. "And the ammunition?" he asked, checking to see if a round had been chambered.

"In my rucksack in the 'all."

"All of it?"

"Aye, suh. All of it indeed."

*****

Twenty minutes later, winded and wiping a thin sheen of sweat from his forehead, Robert locked the door of the laboratory and made his way over to his workspace. Lighting the lanterns, he moved the bookshelf behind him and undid the recently installed lock on the metal box in the recess behind it.

Moving Moreau and Frankenstein's journals out of the way, Robert removed a third from the bottom of the box and took a seat, pulling the two lanterns on either side of him closer. His eyesight had still not returned to its former strength and he strained to see the name and date written in ink upon it.

Placing the thick journal on the table before him, Robert opened its cover. "And now, the final book. What a treasure trove of secrets its scribbles and formulae hold! You have shared with me, across the decades, Doctor Jekyll, how you released the shadow being known as Edward Hyde. Through your careful use of codes you tried to hide from lesser men the details of the tinctures and powders you used. But my nameless Angel has whispered to me in dreams and taken me to dusty rooms of the mind to share with me alone all of the things I need to know to crack your codes. And so I finally shall. And once I have gathered the particulars and readied the sacred recipe, I shall drink your tonic… I shall ultimately triumph where you so badly failed."

Hour upon hour passed as Robert flipped the pages, making notes at a furious, scribbling pace into a separate journal, drinking in the coded knowledge that had so long eluded him. Jekyll's carefully columned and neatly tabled ciphers rose up before him in an extra dimension that twisted and swirled before his eyes.

As the information bled out from the page, gathered and catalogued by the magical wand of his pen, Walton smiled as his third eye opened and his natural ones fluttered, rolled, and closed.

He was no longer in the island lab.

It was Henry Jekyll's lab, on the final, crucial night.

It was he now called to witness.

It was he now called to see.

CHAPTER 16

Regarding the final evening of Henry Jekyll's life.

On the final night of Doctor Jekyll's life—for the events of the past many weeks, including the brutal slaying of the MP Sir Danvers Carew and mounting evidence of Hyde's other atrocities had left him no choice but to take the most drastic of measures—he entered his laboratory soaked to the bone by a cold, relentless rain.

Throwing home the lock but leaving the key in the door, Jekyll flung himself on his reading chair, staring at the stained-red cuffs of his shirt and the last traces of a hard truth on his hands that the rain had failed to wash away.

"Hyde!" he yelled, determined to have his horrid, hellish demi-twin hear him above the thunder and the rain, "Hyde, you goddamned devil—What is this you've done? My hands are covered in blood... Listen to me. We have reached the end of our... partnership. The vials are empty. I will place no more orders with the apothecary. I shall endeavor no more to protect you at the cost of my reputation and my fortune. Hear me well, Edward Hyde—I shall bring you forth no more!"

Jekyll felt his skin chill and blood turn to ice as Hyde made his answer with an asp-like, whispered laugh.

Gripping his walking stick in his slick, wet hands, Jekyll rose from his chair. "There is no place for you to flee to, Hyde. I shall cover for you and your villainies no more. You were a mistake—an abomination. The blasphemies you have scrawled in my journal, the desecration of my father's portrait, the atrocities you have committed with these hands, *my* hands, and with no more remorse than the worst of the criminals who climb the walls of the madhouse—I will undo what I have done. I will make our recompense. I swear this to all of those you—that *we*—have hurt."

Again he heard the spectral laughter. Closer now. Almost in his ear.

Then it came again, from all too deep inside him.

"I feel you moving within me, Edward—seeking your way out. How can this be? I have refrained from drinking the elixir. You cannot exist unless I will it!"

Making his way to the last of the mirrors left unsmashed in the lab, Jekyll saw his deep blue irises change from his own to Hyde's steel grey irises and back again.

"'Ennnn-rrrry. 'Ennnn-ry Jehhhh-kyllllll…" This he heard in a ghoulish singsong, like that of a violent, demented child at a game of hide and seek.

"Do not taunt me, Hyde! Leave me to my future, I beg you!"

Then the killer was there, apelike and deformed, laughing at him in the mirror.

"An' whatta *my* fu-cha, 'Enry Jekyll? Woulds ya leave me ta the ether, ta the mist? Wouldya damn me ta some 'Ell? Orphan me like an un-committed fatha would 'is troubled, bahsta'd son? Would that makes ya clean? Would that soothe ya soul an' fully pay our debt?"

"Once I have removed you, the price will have been paid."

"Ya think it's all so simple? While I'm torcha'd in 'Ell fer my sins, do ya think God will forgive ya yours? As much as Satan wants ta bring me 'ome ta a spot near ta his throne, where he can dine upon my bones, I 'ave work 'ere stills ta do."

Shaking his head to try to clear the vision that loomed within the mirror, Jekyll screamed, "Why must you torment me?"

Hyde leaned forward with force, as if to break the plane of the mirror and enter the world for the first time as his own separate entity. Thankfully, the mirror held. "Yer fancy clothes an' prim, pristine home do not makes ya clean. You are as guilty as I am, Doctah 'Enry Jekyll. I 'ad no choice in the matta. You called me an' I came. This is who I am, because it is who *you* are, stripped a' all pretense! Right ya are that yer no fatha a' mine, but ya coulda been my friend. Come ta that—yer total an' complete dereliction a' duty—do ya think yer God will grant ya forgiveness fer what ya 'ave done? 'Is angels might slake their lust as I am tortured night afta night… but what about you? Ya think yool get off so easy… Huh?"

Henry shook his head. "I was never meant to sacrifice my soul. I was meant to remain the master. I never guessed how you would rage…"

Hyde let go another laugh—enough to shake the frame that held the barrier of glass. "Come on now, 'Enry… All those years ya suppressed me… Denyin' me my rightful existence. 'Ow could I do othahwise?"

Dropping the cane and pressing his hands to the wall for support, Jekyll hung his head and cried. "It is all as you have said. My denial of the bottle, of the comforting flesh of a female, it drove me to suppress you. But I must atone. I will see things made right. This death-dealing dance between us shall end."

Knocking on the glass with his hairy, simian knuckles, Hyde replied, "Ya should 'ave 'ad more than a father's passin' int'rest."

Slapping the glass with the flat of his hand, Jekyll answered, "And you should have had more than a son's undo indifference."

Tilting his head back and letting loose a howl that could be heard by Jekyll's butler Poole and the rest of the staff huddled in the main house, although they knew not what to make of it, Hyde said, "'Tis too late fer all-a that. I shall live inside a' ya now, fer the remainder a' yer days. My benefacta ya are, an' shall continue ta be. As I said, I 'ave work 'ere still needs doin'."

Prior to that moment, Jekyll was unsure as to whether he had the strength to do what needed to be done. Now there was no question. Hyde's repeated declaration of further nefarious actions left him without choice.

If he had to pay the price eternal, he would do it with a grin.

Crossing the room while removing his rain-soaked, all too inhibiting opera cape, Jekyll yanked open a drawer in his desk, pulling from it a Colt Cloverleaf revolver, which he cocked as he turned with determination back toward the mirror.

The fear in Edward's eyes made Jekyll want to smile.

"'Enry... Would ya really end yer life ta rid yerself a' me?"

Moving closer to the mirror, Jekyll answered, "I would breathe my last breath to deny you the means for your hate."

Leaning once again against the mirror so his Neanderthal forehead actually flexed it as it touched, Hyde said, "Everythin' I did was because you were far too much the coward ta do it yerself! An' still ya insist on thinkin' yer a God!"

Raising the pistol to his temple, Jekyll whispered, "I am not a God, Edward. I am just a man."

Struggling to keep Jekyll's finger from pulling the trigger, Hyde flailed and jerked within the confines of the mirror. For one eternal, mistaken moment, as it at last gave way and cracked, he thought that he had won.

But Jekyll then prevailed and sent the bullet home.

As Poole and the others huddled in the parlor of the main house, they heard a last ungodly scream before it all fell silent—the voice of Edward Hyde, furious at his demise.

CHAPTER 17

Walton continues his work.

As Walton awoke from his vision, he found himself in the dark. He must have been out for hours for the lanterns to exhaust their supply of oil.

Navigating carefully to the laboratory door, he pulled the cloth from the broken window, letting in just enough light that he could locate a stash of candles and get some illumination into the room.

He would have to ask Tom to bring more oil from the house.

Pulling a number of anatomy books from a shelf in a darkened corner, Walton retrieved the box of tinctures, salts, and chemicals he had taken the precaution of hiding behind them. Countless times he had wanted to see if any were broken in the journey to the island, but he had resisted. Bad news would only slow him on his path.

Cutting the string that held the lid of the box securely in its place, Walton said a prayer to his nameless Angel and looked inside. *Excellent!* The straw had done its job and all the bottles were intact.

Lining them up, one by one, on his work table, Walton compared their labels to lists he had made from the journals of his dead colleagues, ticking off each one with a flick of his pencil as he went. Jekyll's were, of course, most important of all, although he had found additional chemicals in the writings of Frankenstein that would aid in ensuring success.

Then there was Moreau. How well stocked he had kept his shelves.

Grasping a candleholder that held two pairs of sticks, Walton made his way to the storage area where dozens of jars, bottles, beakers, flasks, and other containers were all neatly arranged. Again attributed to Walton's nameless Angel, the beast that Tom had shot had not gone anywhere near this area.

Pulling what he needed from the shelves, Walton returned to his workspace, placing the additional supplies in rows with the others and ticking off more of what he had written on his lists.

Just one item was missing. *Heliotropium arborescens*. Heliotrope, whose relationship to the sun was part of the mystical rituals he had decoded from Jekyll's journal, although Moreau and Frankenstein had each mentioned it on several occasions as well.

He would need to find it in the jungle—a shame he could not trust Tom with the task—and then distill its oil.

Putting on his Panama hat and field jacket and grasping the Enfield, Walton unlocked the door to the laboratory and—careful to relock the door—headed toward the jungle as the last of the sunlight shone down.

As with all well-paced adventure stories, the lack of any activity applicable to the outcome of our tale necessitates foregoing the details of his walk, which was pleasant despite his still weakened state and lasted no more than an hour and a half, start to finish.

Heliotrope in hand, he reentered the laboratory, admonishing himself for having left all of the candles burning. Making his way to the box that held the replacements, he lit one with a match from his pocket and looked around the room.

Nothing appeared out of place.

Lighting a Bunsen burner and placing a flask full of water upon a stand above it, Walton laid out the bunches of heliotrope he had gathered beside the burner to dry as he gathered the rest of the parts and pieces he needed for the distillation process.

As the water in the flask came to a boil, he filled a tube with the heliotrope, affixing it to the top of the flask. To that, he affixed a copper condenser coil and placed a copper bowl beneath it to collect the precious oil that the still would force from the plant.

Fetching cold water from a barrel outside the laboratory door, Walton silently cursed as Tom exited the main house and headed toward where he stood.

Ducking inside the lab, Walton slammed the door and locked it.

Placing the cold water in a bowl that he placed by the condenser coil, Walton adjusted the flame on the burner and waited patiently as the first drops of precious oil began to appear.

As the distillation process continued, Walton turned his attention to the assortment of ingredients on his worktable. Consulting his notes as he began to prepare them, he said, "You were a fool until the end, Doctor Jekyll. Too proud, too ignorant, too full of your own piety to truly own the fact that there *was no* Hyde—

Jekyll *was* Hyde and therefore Hyde was Jekyll... the pious doctor, the quintessential gentleman... Why not admit you *enjoyed* every minute of every bloody, evil thing that Hyde was doing because you so badly wanted them done and hadn't the guts to do them yourself?"

Working away with measuring spoon, penknife, and mortar and pestle, Walton was in his glory.

Then Tom was at the door, spoiling his reverie.

"Go away, Tom! I am in the midst of the final preparations—all I have worked and sacrificed for these many, many years. I shall be along in the morning."

This was a lie. Walton knew full well his work would take him far into the night.

Through the door he heard Tom spouting the usual complaints... a human form crouching in the kitchen, concern over not having the Enfield, worry over Walton's fever—which he knew had not abated... On and on he babbled as Walton did his best to ignore him and continue with his mixing, all the while monitoring the still, which was yielding steady and well.

It was as if Time did not exist. The candles needed replenishing at a surprising rate, so enrapt was Walton in his work. It was as though he were a passenger in his body, observing the work of the others. Yes! He was the vehicle, the vessel... the space in which all of their geniuses combined alchemically with his own!

On and on he went, not questioning, not caring about the din outside his door.

Then, finally, most likely frustrated or frightened of the dark, Tom fell silent, his monologue replaced by a furious, wall-shaking storm.

Walton did not hear it, so fully was he in the work.

*****

Staring at the single flask of reddish-purple liquid sitting beside him, Walton did not know nor care how long it had taken to produce it.

He had accomplished his task and was ready to drink his fill.

Grasping the half-full flask by the neck and placing his other hand beneath its base, Walton raised it slowly towards the heavens as a priest would the chalice and consecrated host.

"Divine providence is smiling upon me!" he intoned, his hair and eyes wild with the madness now upon him. "The storm has passed and the sun begins to rise. In order to go to the places that I must, in pursuit of all that my predecessors touched but could not grasp, I must bring forth my own dark child, my own adopted offspring of the shadows. Called out of my soul and full of all the fury and bestial avidity required of the one who will open up the graves and steal the beasts I need to do my work from the zoos and farmers' fields once I return to London. I shall have full control over him. I shall give to him my bidding and he shall heed my words."

Then Robert Peary Walton drank the elixir down.

And all the world went dark.

CHAPTER 18

Discoveries abound.

It had happened again.

Raising his head from his worktable, Robert found himself in a pitch-black space. Inside his mouth, a taste like cotton and acrid chemicals made him wince as he tried to swallow. His hands were stiff and sore, as though he had been gripping small instruments for hours on end while doing precision work…

Had he?

Fighting a pulsing headache that was settling into his eyes, producing a dull ache just behind them, Robert fumbled in the dark for matches, a lantern, and a container full of oil—items he had been sure to keep nearby as the blackouts had increased in frequency and length.

Gripping the table against the growing pain in his head, Robert let out a guttural groan as a torrent of images began to flood his mind, seen through his eyes and felt with his hands. Tasted with his mouth and smelled through his nose. Images of dim back alleys full of the homeless and the whores, the gaps in their teeth and droop to their eyes indicating a vast of array of disease and deterioration. Dancehall girls with gartered legs and generous cleavage, such a pretty sight at present but destined to replace those in the alleys when the next batch of daughters their laid-off fathers could not feed came along to join the ball with thinner waists and brighter eyes.

Pestilence and perfume. Vomit and violets.

And violence. Such incessant, horrific brutality was he witness to and at times participant in on these nightly strolls in a madman's tilt-framed hellscapes! The slitting of throats, battering in of brains, stomping of stomachs down by the docks and at the back entryways of warehouses… sailors and soldiers, pickpockets and mountebanks—even the policemen, sometimes so kind, taking out their frustrations on the rabble, guilty or not.

He would be their savior. He now had the cure.

So terribly thirsty he was. So in need of strong relief.

Each time he awoke, four times in the past seven days, he had craved the elixir that had been the sum of the work of the three men whose journals he no longer needed to light his way. And each time, a beaker sat beside him, the level of amber liquid a little higher than before.

He was building up a tolerance and paying a greater price in side effects, such as the blackouts, lack of memories upon waking besides the details of the nightmares, and various aches and pains.

It was worth it, he told himself. *I feel like a God for several hours after*.

Filling and lighting the lantern, he turned his gaze to the stand above the burner where the beaker always sat.

The beaker was not there.

Instead, balanced on the stand, was a bloody kitchen knife.

What use would he have, surrounded by scalpels, Valentin and Liston knives, and surgical saws, of such an imprecise and clumsy blade?

Then, through the fog, a memory.

A human form crouching in the kitchen.

That is what Tom had said.

My god… Robert thought.

Grasping the bloody knife and stumbling to the laboratory door, which he unlocked and threw open while choking down a throat full of bile, Robert fell face-first into the rain-soaked soil, having stumbled over a mass just outside the door.

Wrenching his legs to the side as he realized they lay upon what it was he had stumbled over, Robert gripped the knife tighter, spinning himself around to look at what it was.

A once-human body in lurid disrepair.

If it were not for the bright red bandana around its neck and the now blood-soaked, but still clearly light blue Henley shirt Tom always wore while working, Robert would not have been able to identify it, such was its condition.

Something had deeply slit the throat, a gash from ear to ear, the flesh having separated to the point that a portion of the trachea clearly could be seen.

But that was not all. The corpse had no hands.

Nor did it have a face.

"Tom," Robert whispered, cradling the back of the head with a free hand, though the hair was sticky and knotted with clots of tissue and blood. "Tom. I should have listened. Who was it could have done this? Tom… my faithful servant. My friend. How unfair it is that you shall not be witness to my triumph."

Be witness to my triumph.

With those words, Robert remembered.

He had been working at the surgical table for hours. How his hands were cramped—Yes! The cramped hands... another memory, another explanation retrieved!—when he had realized he could proceed no further without the assistance of good Tom Paris.

Moving excitedly to the door, he had called across the distance between the main house and the laboratory, "Tom! Come here and be my witness. You will write down all you see and hear as it happens. Only then will the doubters truly understand the triumph of my moment as I work to make it unfold."

Tom had come. He must have... Of course he did! Faithful to the end!

What had happened next?

Pulling his hands from Tom's tangled, gore-draped hair, Robert reentered the laboratory.

The surgical table!

There upon it was his triumph!

Memories flooded back. Unburying the beast that Tom had shot. Dragging it under cover of darkness back to the laboratory, sure that Tom was sleeping. Hoisting it onto the surgical table.

Then the settling into the work—removing the tusks, replacing from the jars of preservative all he had removed from the jaguar-boar's torso, using all of the knowledge he had gained, guided step by step by his nameless Angel whispering in his ear.

Such brilliance and precision in the work.

But the snouted and de-tusked, hybrid, malformed face... And the paws—so clumsy, so inhuman...

They simply would not do.

Who could blame him for fixing the problem as best as he could?

Tom came willingly. He always had. Like a dear, devoted son. Now he would live on in this marvelous creation.

Bringing the lantern close, Robert stroked the Tom-beast's face, his fingertips lingering with a father's deepest love over each suture, each bandage, each surgically wrought improvement.

As he kissed the Tom-beast's forehead where it met the coarse hair of the boar it once had been, Robert heard a laugh. Soft and sinister, from the far side of the lab.

"Come forth, my nameless Angel," he whispered, peering into the darkness. "Do not laugh as I make my revelations. I know we had our reasons for slitting poor Tom's throat. He gladly gave his life. And he soon shall live again."

Once more he heard the laugh.

And he knew it was no Angel.

A human form crouching in the kitchen.

"There is no need to be afraid, my son," Robert said, suddenly understanding. "Your father's love awaits you. My guidance is yours to use. I know that you have helped me. I have seen the things that you have seen. Felt the things you have done. I will not be like the others. I know you had your reasons. Come and meet your beautiful brother."

As he spoke these words, Robert crept slowly sideways to where he kept the Enfield.

Like the beaker full of elixir, it was missing.

Yet again the laughter came.

Louder.

Closer.

And then it was upon him.

Clutching his stomach as it cramped, he said through gritted teeth, "I feel you moving inside of me, seeking your way out. Do not be afraid. I know you have been suppressed. I know you have been ignored. How well I understand it! I will give you all I have, if only you will obey me."

Instead of a laugh, a singsong whisper: *"Rahhhhhhhh-berrrrrrrrrt. Rah-berrrrrt Walllllll-tonnnn…"*

Suddenly terrified and revolted by the unholy mass of sutured flesh on the surgical table beside him, Robert dropped the lantern and ran hard for the house.

CHAPTER 19

At long last, Walton meets his nameless Angel.

Despite the blinding pain radiating from the center of his brain, Robert managed to cover the distance from the laboratory to the house as though he were being chased by a winged demon intent on eating his soul.

Perhaps that was the truth.

Entering the house, Robert felt his heart jump a little farther into his throat.

There were clear signs of a struggle, which triggered another memory.

Tom had not come. Robert had come to get him.

His once-faithful errand boy must have refused with all his might, judging by the overturned furniture, broken glass and crockery, and smears of blood on the floors and in doorways as he went from room to room.

Still the missing Enfield was nowhere to be found.

Compelling his jellied legs to take him up the stairs despite the groans of protest from his cracking knees and calves, Robert peered into his bedroom as he reached the top of the landing, hoping the rifle was there.

It was not.

Proceeding down the hallway, Robert came to an ornate mirror two feet long, outside of the room that Tom had claimed for his own.

Glancing into the glass, he choked down a silent scream.

The face there, leering and laughing, was undeniably not his own.

It was a visage produced by a nightmare and trapped beneath the glass.

Trying to turn his eyes away, he found he could not move.

Again he heard the monster's mocking laugh, followed by the whispered singsong: "*Rahhhhhhhh-berrrrrrrrrrt. Rah-berrrt Wallllllll-tonnnn…*"

Touching the glass tenderly with his fingertips, as though it were a schoolboy's cheek, Robert asked, "Why do you mock me, my child?"

The ape-like half-thing, dressed as though it were an English earl on his way to a night at the opera, let loose a laugh that sounded as though a thousand rabid bats had begun to flap their leathery, Luciferic wings in Robert's ear. "Yer *child*?" the simian demi-man hissed back. "You *'ave* no child! Yer mind's womb is filled wit' the piss-drenched ash a' yer pride. The splintered bone an' rotten flesh a' yer hubris. Ya 'aven't the brains ta unnerstan' this, Walton. Yer anotha poor purveyor a' scientific blasphemies. Anotha withah'd minion seekin' salvation in the mystical, transcendental promises a' things ya cannot hope ta fathom or control. Yer jus' like Moreau, an' Frankenstein, an' that waste a' flesh Jekyll. Ya sicken me. Ya sicken us all!"

Slapping his hand against the glass, Robert yelled, "Stop this! I command you!"

Leaning in, its terrible red-tinged eyes aflame with anger, the thing in the mirror replied, "You do not *command me*, Walton! If I so choose, I shall make commands a' *you*, an' you shall obey me like the castrated mongrel ya are."

Stepping away and shaking his head, Robert replied, "You ungrateful cur! I am the one who gathered up the books. I am the one who found the island!"

Again the horrific homunculus laughed. "Do ya think ya came 'ere a' yer own accord? Through yer own blindin' brilliance? Ya prattle on about the guidin' 'and of ya nameless Angel. It was no *Angel*, Walton! An' I am full amazed ya 'aven't guessed it. It was I, *Edward Hyde*, who led ya ev'ry step a' the way."

Unwilling to accept what his mind had been trying to tell him for the better part of an hour, Walton placed his hands against his ears. "That is a lie! Like all demons come from Hades, you deceive me!"

"Please," Hyde said, drawing the word out through his serpent-like slit of a mouth until a thick stream of spittle spilled down his bristled-haired chin. "The mornin' ya awoke from a dream an' explored yer gran'muthah's attic… The article 'bout the Uttahsons in the paypa… The findin' a' the map that led ya ta this island after so many months a' failure… Do ya think these all coincidence?"

"Stop this talk, I beg you! What is it you want of me? If we are not to be father and son, perhaps we can be colleagues! Collaborators!"

"Almost everythin' I needed from ya I now possess. You 'ave brought me the journals, drank the elixir that brought me back ta life, an' soon enough ya git, yool be finishin' up yer service."

Afraid of the answer but unable to refrain from asking the question that would bring it, Robert whispered, casting his eyes at last away, "What am I to do?"

Drawing his servant's eyes back up to his own with a wave of a hairy, long-nailed hand, Hyde shook his head in amusement. "What are ya ta do? Yer ta put my essence inta that beautiful beast ye've assembled in the lab so I can go about my bloody bis'ness unimpeded."

"What you ask of me is impossible," Robert said, finding a bit of relief in the truth of it. "I have not the equipment it would take, if such infernal machines exist. If you need a vessel, I will have to do."

Hyde shook his simian head. "Not possible. Not after what 'Enry done ta me. Takin' 'is life while I was defenceless insida 'im, leavin' me ta float around in the etha like I 'ave these many years. I need a body a' me own. The one in the lab'll do. An' you will make it 'appen, an' right as rain it'll be."

Leaning his head on the glass as tears spilled down his face, Robert felt himself submit—exhausted and humiliated, his spirit utterly broken. "Tell me, Edward—how?"

Putting his hand to the glass with such force Robert could feel it on his cheek, Hyde whispered, "First, we need the transmittah."

CHAPTER 20

More of what Walton remembered.

*F*irst, we need the transmittah.

There was a moment, as busy as he had been with so many other things—how much of it not yet remembered?—that Robert had no idea about what it was that Hyde was wanting.

Then, like a flash of insight, there it was, in the center of his fuzzy-edged mind. The radio he and Tom had brought with them to the island.

How they had fought over whether or not to use it in recent weeks. Tom so insistent... Robert full of resistance.

Navigating through Tom's bedroom, not allowing himself to look at the dead man's few effects scattered about the room, Robert unlocked the window, stepping out onto a small covered balcony where they kept the radio transmitter, the tower Tom had cobbled together from materials he had found in the island's workshop bolted to the roof above it. Flicking the switch to turn the radio transmitter on, Robert felt his breath catching in his throat.

Not a damned thing happened.

"Ya decrepit little dotterer," Hyde whispered in his ear, "ya gots ta put the valve tubes back innit. They are 'idden beneath ya bed."

Reentering the window, passing through Tom's room and entering his own, Robert found the five valve tubes wrapped in a shirt and shoved between two supports in the middle of the frame.

"Ya oughta remembah," Hyde whispered, his dismissive hiss a lizard's tongue lapping Walton's inner ear. "Twas quite the tuchin' scene."

Closing his eyes tight to keep the memories from coming, so afraid was he of what it was that Hyde had meant, Robert found himself utterly helpless.

It was the night before Tom had given his life for Robert's grand pursuits. Robert had come upstairs to change his shirt when he heard Tom on the balcony, speaking slowly but insistently.

"Tom," he had said, sneaking into the room and poking his head through the curtained window. "What do you think you are doing with that transmitter?"

Continuing to adjust the receiver, Tom answered, "Yer not right, suh. Nor is this place. An' I saw that thing downstairs again. I am gettin' us off this island, suh. I havta, ya see."

What he next remembered filled Robert's eyes with tears. He had placated Tom, asking for a single day's reprieve. "One more day, and then we will do just as you say. I am so very close now. And when I have finished, we can go back home. I have accomplished nearly what I need to. London shall embrace us, Tom! Oh, the long list of naysayers and cynics who shall line up before me to make their apologies! I shall finish my degree and take an appointment as professor of surgery at Royal London Hospital. Why, I might even contact Katherine. Try to make amends…"

How Tom's heart had leapt at these dreams of amends and reconciliation, girded by the proof in Robert's eyes, which gleamed with a brilliant, hopeful light.

Robert had suggested Tom go and make their supper, to which his smiling manservant readily agreed.

The moment he was gone, Robert had removed the line of valve tubes, replacing the back of the radio transmitter so Tom would never know.

Had Robert known what he would have to do the following day? Had he cared?

"It ain't no matta now," Hyde grumbled. "Reassemble it so we can call the ship."

Robert, removing the back of the transmitter and replacing the valve tubes as instructed, raised a brow. "What ship?"

"Damnitall, the things ya can't remembah, Walton." Hyde's frustration was making Robert's muscles tense. His heart began to race. This was how deeply, how thoroughly the beast was now a part of him. "The *Boa Sorte*—yer ole mate Cap'n Costa. 'E should be jus' off shore, waitin' on our summons."

"Captain Costa… He would never—"

Hyde growled, sending reverberations up Robert's spine and into his throat, forcing him to gag. "Knock that off, ya blighta! Fer the right amount a' coin it is unlimited whatta man'll do. An' our new benefacta has plenty a' coin. Now, focus. Set the receiver ta—. Ah, ya remembah somethin' afta all! That's right…"

As Hyde spoke, Robert remembered more. He had not immediately taken the valve tubes out of the transmitter that night. First, he had made a call. As he must have done on other occasions too, since Costa was awaiting further instructions.

Unable to recall the details, Robert asked, as the signal began to whistle before clearing with a crackle as the radio made contact, "What am I to tell Captain Costa, Hyde? I do not know. Tell me what to say and I will say it."

As Costa's thick Portugese accent came over the speaker, Hyde said, "Tell 'im we will be waitin' on the beach at first light. Send three men in a longboat fer supplies an' poor Tom's corpse. Succumbed ta fevah, 'e did. But not ta worry... 'E's all wrapped up safe an' tight fer transport."

Having delivered the message verbatim, as much as it hurt his heart to concoct another series of lies, Robert asked, "Anything else?"

"Yeah there is," Hyde said, licking his blood red lips. "Tell 'im we are most anxious ta get ta Orkney as fast as 'e can manage."

CHAPTER 21

What transpired the morning they left the island.

Having read the journal of Victor Frankenstein as many times as he had, Robert Peary Walton knew exactly what a journey to the Orkney islands meant.

They were going to Victor's second lab—the site of his self-aborted attempt to make his Creature a mate.

Lying down for a few hours of what would no doubt be a begrudging, restless sleep, Robert replayed the events of the past years repeatedly in his mind, castigating himself for not putting the pieces together. Then again, Hyde had done a masterful job of hiding his true nature. Who would not have believed that his nameless Angel meant him—and all of mankind—well? Despite the horrors revealed in the past thirty hours, he still had faith that his work had the potential to save the world.

First and foremost, however, he must deal with Edward Hyde.

The laugh he heard at the end of this thought coldly confirmed what Robert feared the most… that Hyde was with him now.

Part of him forever.

A cancer of the soul.

And making matters worse, he was thoroughly unafraid.

In the middle of the night, as Robert walked the strange darkened roads between the sleep and waking states, he heard the voice of Edward Hyde telling him he needed to get prepared—the longboat was arriving near dawn, and they must be packed and ready.

Although first, there'd be more sewing.

As they entered into the lab, Robert felt his fingers begin to twitch as Hyde took first his left hand and then his right one under his control. Although Robert was still conscious, still aware of the input his brain was gathering second by second through each of his senses, he no longer moved of his own volition. He was a marionette manipulated by a madman.

A madman who whistled vile chanteys like "My Donna a' the Pox" that only motherless sailors sing in shadowy sections of ships amongst the rats in the filthy bilge as he worked on the amalgamation of boar, jaguar, and human on the liquid-slick surgical table, making improvements to the face so it was not quite so horrific.

A madman who concocted elixirs in the oddest of combinations, combining them with the blood of the Tom-beast, which he ran through a complex series of tubes and crude filters before injecting it back into the body.

When he was satisfied—or, more accurately, had gone as far as he could go with the materials that he had—Hyde retreated, leaving the apprentice work to Robert.

He worked in the lab for hours, packing up the tonics and tinctures he and Hyde had developed. He carefully packed away in dried grass the distilling mechanism and made sure he accounted for all of the journals before buckling up his haversack.

He wanted nothing from the house. However, Hyde had insisted, before they left for the lab, that Robert remove the valve tubes from the radio transmitter and smash them each in turn beneath his heel.

What reason could he have? They were now alone on the island.

"Lead thee not inta tem'tation, mate," Hyde had said as the last glass bulb exploded into dust. "Cannot take the chance ya might try ta alta the plan…"

The last task before heading to the beach to meet Captain Costa's men was the wrapping of the Tom-beast. Robert tried and failed three times to approach it, so repulsive had it become to his sight.

"Wundaful!" Hyde spat out, his mental saliva trickling down the back of Robert's throat and into his chest, where it sat like toxic bile. "Now yer jus' like Victah. Repulsed by yer own creation!"

"Not mine!" Robert replied, slamming his hands against the Tom-beast's breast. "It was you alone who did this! I would have never severed the hands and face of good Tom Paris… Never would have sewn together such an abomination!"

"Tell yaself that as much as ya need ta," Hyde whispered. "We both know itsa lie. Now wrap it up wit' care. I shall occupy it soon enuff. Whatta wunda I shall be!"

Too exhausted to argue, too confused to discount completely Hyde's reply, Robert tried his best to hide his revulsion as he prepared the body for transport.

As he worked, stitch by stitch, to sew the corpse in tight—and a corpse was what it was—Robert felt his head begin to swim as a new wave of fever and disorientation threatened to overtake him.

Leaning into the surgical table for support, he heard a montage of mumbled voices, their whispers overlapping into a crackling static half a dozen times before separating out into individual voices:

First, the Sayer of the Law: "Father, am I not five-man like you? Why must you give the others and I the Pain?" Then it was the Creature: "I am shunned and hated by all mankind! Shall I not hate them that abhor me? If I cannot inspire love, I will inspire fear." Again, the voice of the Sayer: "The Pain you make on us, Father, is a kind of Hell." Then again the Creature: "You are my creator, but I am your master; obey!"

Then, loudest and ugliest of all, the awful voice of Edward Hyde, murderous and mocking: "Woulds ya leave me ta the ether, ta the mist? Wouldya damn me ta some 'Ell? Would that makes ya clean? Would that soothe ya soul an' fully pay our debt?"

Then the infernal trio started in again:

These are "big thinks," Father. They hurt me in my heart.

Why should I pity man more than he pities me? I am fearless and therefore powerful!

Orphan me like an un-committed fatha would 'is troubled, basta'd son?

"Stop it now!" Robert screamed, as the voices started over, louder and more insistent. "I shall do all that you ask! I will make this right, as was always my intention! I shall be father to you all. I have so many questions... So very many questions..."

"I know them well enuff," Hyde answered. "Costa will be loyal... not like last time. 'E 'as 'is instructions, an' 'e shall obey. 'E won't bat a lash at the body bein' Tom's, succumbed ta fevah, the poor, poor blighta. An' as ta the funds fer the work—a descendant a' Victah's benefactah, name a' Ravenskald, 'as it all in 'and. Anythin' we need, 'e shall provide. 'E's anxious the work should progress."

An hour and a half later, after several trips to the beach, including the carrying, then dragging, of the corpse, Robert collapsed in the sand as three sets of sailors rowed the longboat from the *Boa Sorte* into the shallows and three of its passengers waded their way ashore.

To Robert's surprise, Captain Costa was amongst them.

Tipping his hat, Costa forced a smile. "I hope I have arrived at the proper time, Senhor Walton. I wish to do nothing but serve you for the duration of the trip."

Staying in place as Costa instructed while he and his crew brought his belongings to the longboat, Robert felt a smile start to spread across his face.

Finally, Christ be praised, he would be treated with respect.

CHAPTER 22

On the journey to Orkney.

xcerpts from the journal of Captain Gonçalo Costa, of the tramp steamer *Boa Sorte*.

—4 June 1929

Ah, my beautiful wife Mariana... To write these notes to you whenever I can is the great joy of my life. A life that is no longer mine, though I must not dwell upon the details. I cannot begin to express what it is that has kept me on course beyond my love for you and our three little wonders. How fares our little Beatriz? I imagine her working in the garden with her *mãe*, and learning to cook for her brothers, Agostinho and Aleixo. I hope they are behaving for their *mãe*.

And what of Renata? I trust the money I sent for doctors and medicine has been well spent, bringing the wished-for result, and she is back at work with the household staff teaching the children of Baron Riviera. She has a future there, Mariana. Perhaps even marriage to one of the baron's handsome heirs.

I dream, oh yes! I do. What is a father to do besides?

With abundant blessings of *meu Deus*—which I hope I have not squandered by agreeing to this task—I shall be home to see you by the second week in July. Yes! Our errands, a list of which runs long, includes our docking in Lisbon for several blessed days.

How I wish I could stay. It is time to extend our family, and I shall have the funds to do it after this.

This is why *I engolir sapos.* Why I swallow frogs.

Ai, Mariana... this is a nightmare from which I struggle to wake.

As we make our way tomorrow through the Panama Canal on our way to the Bahamas—New Providence being the first of our ports of call—I shall be tempted as if by the very demons who tortured San Antonio to relinquish command of the *Boa Sorte* to some hired man and make my way home to you, though I know I shall resist.

The events of these past weeks are beyond description—and the deal I have made with the *demônio* that calls himself Ravenskald, the source of my fee, prevents me from saying all that I might wish.

Do you recall this name, my *flor bonita*? A name uttered with vitriol and bile in my family for many generations... for it was a Ravenskald, in October 1716, who brutally tortured and murdered a fisherman name Costa—my ancestor—who had settled in a place called Beaufort in the Carolina colonies.

And for what? Information about an object pursued for power. A Holy Relic, the family stories say.

Deus has a strange way, my love. To cross our paths like this, a Costa and a Ravenskald, more than two hundred years after the bloody fact...

Ai... Suffice to say until I can whisper to you the totality of this current tale with only a pillow's edge between us in our bed, that there is something in the hold of this ship that I fear is most inhuman. My guest—how he has changed since I allowed him to leave for the island—has told me that it is the body of his assistant, Tom Paris, whom I liked very much... a man of reason... He succumbed to a fever, so I'm told...

We have packed him in salt and ice. We are taking him to the Orkney islands, just above Scotland—that is the terminus of this journey—where I am told his family is from. Why I do not believe it, I cannot say. They do not yet tell me which of the islands. Their utter lack of trust is foul food for a captain of my years.

Ai, my Mariana, I wish I could share the details of why I do not believe the boy was from the Orkney islands. But do I dare? I must confess, I have indulged in more than my share of *ginjinha* this evening and my hand—this, my silent tongue—is looser than I would like.

Perhaps it was its shape as it pushes against the canvas. Of a man, yes, but more. Odd shapes where they should not be—those are what I saw, what I felt, Mariana, I swear!—as we first placed the corpse into the longboat and then as we transferred it to the hold.

And Walton—so gaunt, so hunched. And always with those infernal journals! My *avó* always said it, Mariana—and I say it to our boys, although you become sore with me for doing so—*queimar as pestanas*—to burn one's eyelashes, that is what so much reading is good for and nothing else besides! I see him sometimes, when he thinks no one is looking. You may think me unfair, that I am obsessed with fleas and monkeys, as was my distrustful father, but I tell you, Mariana—I have *pulga atrás da orelha e macaquinhos na cabeça* for good reason!

I have seen a change. A look in the eye, or a shadow over the face. In that moment he looks as though a *macaquinho* lives inside him. A violent, ugly monkey bent on tearing us apart and devouring our intestines. I have heard him laughing, as he dreams of eating souls.

Ai, Mariana, yes... Superstitious I am, I know. A good Catholic, though, who believes that demons are real, as are angels.

But no angels watch over me now.

And so I am afraid.

—23 June 1929

To my *flor bonita*, my precious Mariana.

It has been weeks, and I have had no time to write. Perhaps it is just as well, for Walton watches like a hawk. Did I see his eyes turn a different color? A cold and heartless grey? Was there a flash of a sharpened tooth? I do not know... I must be brief, as dinner will soon be served—how it makes me miss you, to sup upon *bacalhou* and *enchidos* without my beloved family around me.

We passed through the Porta of Balboa, where we stocked up on provisions and then the Panama Canal without incident. Questions began to be asked, and Walton whispered in the ear of an official some secret thing and they let us pass without checking our holds. Can you imagine such a boon for an insignificant steamer?

For six days, we plied the Atlantic waters until we reached Nassau in New Providence, the Bahamas. Such a beautiful place, Mariana. It always does my heart good to see the Atlantic! And the beaches of the Bahamas, *meu Deus*! Blinding white sand and crystal blue water. The crew was allowed to visit the fort, which is much in disrepair, and the taverns in town while the sun was in the sky, but they were confined to the ship in the evenings, where they passed the time in drunken revelry. Many sought comfort from the *putas* in the inn. Walton, after his first day somewhere on the island, had sent back ample money for seeing to their needs.

Whom it was he has met with, I cannot say. I cannot say for I do not know. Walton tells me nothing. Last evening, as we gazed upon the stars from the deck, he said that I was lucky. One day I would thank him.

As to what he had been doing, why we were there, I can tell you only this—he returned after a little over a week with a strongbox he took to his room. Whatever is in that box was the purpose of our stopping. Perhaps he had to learn to use whatever was inside.

We have been back at sea for nearly nine days. If the weather holds and all remains well, we shall dock in my beloved Lisbon the first day of July.

Until then, I shall hold you and *as crianças* in the center of my heart. Bestow my love on them—Beatriz, Agostinho, and Aleixo. Their father fights for their future every passing day.

—9 July 1929

My precious Mariana.

I cannot imagine the agony, the dreadful pain to which you and *as crianças* have been subjected because of my carelessness, my foolishness!

To watch your faces as I was dragged from our home, the soldiers' heavy boots trampling the flowerbeds as they brought me back to the *Boa Sorte* after our hurried dinner that first night I was in Lisbon, to be made a prisoner on my own vessel!

I had thought of nothing for weeks but to lie with you in our bed after kissing the foreheads of *as crianças* as we wished them all goodnight. Never would I have guessed that Ravenskald's agents would track me from the Porta of Balboa. They were no doubt watching as we approached, as I paid the fees of the harbormaster, as we secured the ship at dock.

And, most grievous of all, trailing in the shadows as I followed Walton to the cottage of the *curandeira*, the deceitful Senhora Martinez! That same demonic hag who had taken my coin to tell me she had seen *nada*! When, in truth, she had seen *everything*!

What vile substances, what tinctures and tonics has she supplied to Walton for his monstrous work? He returned to us by wagon three days later, and the men spent an hour stowing his ill-gotten cargo.

My mind is aflame! I must wonder now, my love, if Renata's fever was not a game the puppet masters played. I have done some digging… who is it that partners in exports with Baron Riviera, our daughter's employer? The Ravenskalds! If that terrible witch had told them I was wavering… that would surely have been their game. I have been played, my dear Mariana! Played from all sides! Played by *Deus* himself!

I have sat here in my cabin, or attending to the engines, day after day, although they have allowed the crew access to the market streets and a single tavern that they very closely watch. They must return before evening. Such restless men my crew have become. I do not doubt they will abandon me upon our return.

Ai, Mariana, it all is coming clear... I know you tried to come to me—I know you were turned away by the harbormaster's thugs, his *rufiões*... It was all I could do to restrain from charging onto the deck with my revolver and laying all of them low.

I should have... they took my revolver from me as I was cleaning it not more than an hour later.

We prepare now to leave for Ireland. The port of Wexford. We shall arrive in a day and a half. What further horrors there await me I cannot begin to imagine.

Walton, that ugly home to a brutal *macaquinho*, is banging at my door. Ai, Mariana, my eternal *flor bonita*, watch over *as crianças*. When I am paid, we must rescue our Renata from that *vilão* Baron Riviera, who has betrayed our trust.

I will protect our family.

Even if I must die.

—*15 July 1929*

There is a *demônio* on the *Boa Sorte*! Do not laugh, Mariana—I have seen it!

We sit here docked in Wexford, Ireland, while that arrogant bastard Walton meets with more of Ravenskald's agents. Several days have passed. Liquor and *putas* are brought aboard for the crew. They are forbidden to disembark—further punishment for my mistaken actions in Lisbon.

And now I know, my Mariana, the full extent of my lapse in judgment. Yes, I confess, I know the truth of it—during dinner while steaming on to Ireland, Walton told me the terrible news... our Beatriz has been transferred to the mansion of Baron Riviera, where she and Renata work as servants in the kitchens... scullery maids! One barely ten and the other a talented schoolmistress. Apologies, my love! My poor *flor bonita*! It was only my love for you and *as crianças* that led me to follow Walton. To end this madness I have aided in bringing to the world, if only I could find the means...

Now I know that I have failed. But do not despair... I shall do as they ask, in every way, to ensure our daughters' return when I finish and come home.

We depart soon for the Isle of Man... shall we dock there? They tell me nothing now... and then on through the North Channel, past Skye and finally the Orkney islands.

Soon to be rid of these slaves of Satan's will.

—*17 July 1929*

I have seen the monkey-monster, Mariana! I have... you must believe me!

It was the night before we arrived in Wexford. Determined to assure Walton of my loyalty... nay, my pliability, the breaking of my will, I went to his cabin, where I stood at the door, which was slightly ajar, while he talked to himself—so I thought—in the mirror. But the face reflected back *was not his*! Ai—I, a man of faith, devoted to *meu Deus*, to have seen that hunched and laughing *macaquinho* in the mirror. Hair and eyebrows course, forehead bulbous and low, like a Paleolithic visage! For a moment, I thought he would come through the glass, so violently did he press against it—an unangelic symphony of hate his tapered nails were tapping upon it.

And Walton, weeping like a child, pleading to be left alone! To be released from his bargain. Ai... such dark doings on my once peaceful vessel, now most mockingly named *Boa Sorte*!

The sound of the laughing man-thing... I cannot wrench it from my head, though I pickle my brain in *ginjinha* every evening, as we wait here, hour upon hour, as he is off on his evil errand.

I must try to sleep, my love. I wish I could be with you, with *as crianças*. Are the boys all right? Their papa misses them.

And I miss you most of all.

—*19 July 1929*

Mariana, Mariana. Your name is water upon a dying man's parched and aching lips.

I must be mad indeed to speak of death as metaphor, all the while I am surrounded by its stench.

I write this passage in my journal, hurriedly scribbled, from the Isle of Skye, in the Inner Hebrides. We have docked just off Portree. Walton has graciously allowed me to leave the ship to visit the medieval castles and fishing villages of this picturesque place.

Graciously I say… more to the truth, I am sure he fears I will go mad if I am forced to stay there alone.

Three of our crew have died since last I wrote you. In each case, a boy in his twenties in the prime of life and health. They complained of a headache, collapsed at their station, soon developed a fever, and died of horrid convulsions, all within hours.

I believe that they were murdered, chosen for their physique by Walton for whatever nefarious purposes he has sold his soul to pursue.

And that is what he has done… think of the ape-thing in the mirror, Mariana! You must know that I am right!

I wished of course to bury them at sea, as their families would wish, to drop them in the North Channel sewn into the sheets, but Walton would not allow it. Although sewn into sheets they were— and then stored with the body in the hold! I know not the reasons why—so in control does Walton feel, so entitled to make decisions on my own ship though I am its captain that he does not bother to offer any.

The name of Ravenskald is all he must speak in order to get his way.

So, once again, I acquiesced. What will I tell their fathers? Their mothers? Those who entrusted the lives of their sons to me? I have failed as a father all around. And my failure causes death.

Just prior to this trio of tragedies, we docked for a day and night on the southern end of the Isle of Man, so Walton might meet God knows who in the imposing Castle Rushen, a walled fortress of towers and keeps that calls to mind the stories of monsters and their makers my *avó* told me as a child. Such *pesadelos* they gave me, such sheet-soaking nightmares, as does this all too truthful story that I am living now.

Although I have never been there, the castle I know to be a holding of the Ravenskalds, who used it to their advantage during the time of Robert the Bruce and again during the English Civil War. I cannot tell you how I know this. Not now… but soon. Our journey is nearly ended, Mariana. God willing, I shall be home to you by July's end, pockets full of coin and full determination to retrieve our daughters. Renata will find another position—she is as bright as she is beautiful!

We shall arrive at Orkney on the 21st and I hope to leave for Lisbon as soon after as we can unload Walton's unholy cargo and be rid of him.

As I try to sleep tonight, that shall be my sole and only thought.

A Note from Your Narrator

What is it about a journal or diary that compels us to read its entries? That fills us with such interest? Walking along the rows of wares and trinkets in a bustling market bizarre or flea market in an exotic, far off city, how the eyes light up when a book of one's thoughts is discovered. Like Walton in an attic, the hand clutches the treasure of letters, the collection of punctuation and ink notations. The pupils grow wide as the initial page is turned.

In the months since I obtained it, the journal of Gonçalo Costa, father of four and late captain of the tramp steamer *Boa Sorte* out of Lisbon, Portugal, has fascinated and haunted me in equal measure. The clear deterioration of his mood and faith, replaced by madness and fear, is evident with each sentence, each paragraph, each newly dated entry.

How he clung to the love, to the memory and promise of his beloved Mariana, from whom I obtained the journal well after his death.

I must, as a storyteller, tread carefully here, Curious Reader, so that I tell you only what you need to know before you again encounter Walton and Hyde as they take up their work in the laboratory in Orkney. There are thirteen months between Costa's last entry and my two-day train trip to Lisbon to meet with the widow Costa and her four fatherless children.

I shall save the details of what transpired during that time for further along in the narrative.

The purpose of this interlude is to share with you the details— as I have pieced them together from a variety of sources and interviews—of how the good man Gonçalo Costa met his death and how his journal was preserved.

The last entry, dated 19 July 1929, and Costa's death being reported by a credible witness as occurring three days later, lead one to surmise that, either as they approached their destination, which I have discovered to be Rousay, on the Eynhallow Sound in the northern isles, or soon after docking, Costa realized his life was in danger. Having come to this conclusion, he then took the bold step of paying a local boy to send the journal to his wife.

How wise he was to keep the journal separate from the steamer's official logs, which reveal only latitudes, longitudes, weather conditions, supplies on and off loaded, and notes on their various ports of call. In other words, Costa brought nothing to light of the horrific events unfolding in his official record, which remains with the new owner of the *Boa Sorte*, Costa's former navigator—who shall remain nameless, as I am convinced that he played a part in his captain's death in return for ownership of the steamer.

So functions greed as the powerful corruptor of the lives of simple men.

The boy Costa chose to complete his errand nearly undid him. In fact, as the boy, now nearly twenty, himself reported to me from where he currently resides in the south of Scotland, he had decided to turn the journal over to the groundskeeper at the laboratory. His motivation for betrayal? A promised reward in addition to Costa's payment. Again we encounter greed as the vicious corruptor of souls! It was only when he witnessed Costa being brutally attacked with an axe handle by a short, hunched, and hairy humanoid—that the boy reported as laughing with delight as it reduced Costa to a mass of gore and pulp—that he decided to do as Costa wished.

I say "it" because it was no doubt the evil Mister Hyde taking up temporary residence in Robert Walton to do the damnable deed himself.

This is all that I should share at this point in the narrative regarding Costa, his journal, and his family.

We shall return to them later.

And far more pleasant company do they make than the villains to which I now return your attention.

CHAPTER 23

Walton and Hyde resume their work in Orkney.

As July became August in that fateful year, 1929, all the world teetered on the brink of a catastrophic economic collapse. In Munich, 60,000 SA and SS storm troopers prepared to march while the Graf Zeppelin readied to leave Lakehurst, New Jersey, for a trip around the world.

None of this mattered, however, to Robert Peary Walton and Edward Hyde, as they unpacked their tinctures, potions, and equipment in Victor Frankenstein's abandoned lab on the isle of Rousay.

Prior to their arrival, their benefactor, Simeon Ravenskald, had arranged for local laborers and technicians to clean and prep the laboratory, outfitting it with the latest apparatus.

A titan of shipping and the burgeoning air transport industry— he was the primary investor in Luftschiffbau Zeppelin as well as in Transcontinental Air Transport, which had begun making regular flights between New York and Los Angeles—Ravenskald had sent his regrets that he could not meet them in person due to demands on his time in London and Berlin.

"All fer the best," Hyde had whispered as Robert unpacked his surgical instruments. "Gives us time ta propa'ly prahpare."

Robert remembered little of his final few nights on the *Boa Sorte* and even less of the hours before and after Costa's brutal murder at the hands of Edward Hyde. He had tried to prevent it, he remembered well enough, and had suffered Hyde's prolonged derision throughout the following day.

It was on the Isle of Skye, in the crowded, dusty basement of an obscure apothecary shop, that Hyde had insisted Robert obtain the final ingredient needed to create the mixture that would allow Hyde to once again fully inhabit Robert's body. The relief from this foulest of intrusions was a blessing Robert had been enjoying since leaving Moreau's island weeks before.

If he would have known what Hyde had planned—the beyond-brutal murder of Gonçalo Costa—he would have tried all the harder to refuse him his vicious wish.

He had cared far less about the poisoning of the three members of Costa's crew using an African plant extract obtained from the *curandeira* while the steamer was docked in Lisbon.

As Robert familiarized himself with the equipment in the lab, both the original items from Victor's aborted work as well as the most newly installed and complicated, he played over and over in his mind the events of the voyage from the South Pacific to the Orkney islands.

Wherever they stopped, his hosts had treated Robert like the man of the hour, insisting he attend long, lavish lunches by day and high-class soirees in the evenings. Like Frankenstein on his European tour, it was all of little interest, although Robert knew well enough to play along. At each port, Ravenskald had arranged private meetings for his other investors, the most important of which, in Lisbon and Wexford, had listened for hours as Robert talked of his work. One in particular, an Irish surgeon who had made recent breakthroughs in organ transplantation, had obtained permission from Ravenskald to see the journals of Jekyll, Moreau, and Frankenstein, although it pained Robert no end to allow it.

The unfortunate incident in Lisbon that resulted in Costa's forceful removal from his home and further sad situation for his two daughters at the hands of Ravenskald's associate, Baron Riviera, had not concerned him at the time. The idiot well deserved it for his trespass—but thinking of the dead captain's now widow and orphans waiting in vain for him to arrive back home had worked on Robert's nerves since his murder.

The news that Ravenskald had agreed to pay double Costa's original fee to his widow, in addition to securing the return to their home of his two daughters, was a minor consolation. At least they would not suffer needlessly for the stubborn captain's indiscretions.

Perhaps, in time, they would see his death as a blessing.

Sending away his two locally hired lab assistants for the evening after his third day on the island, Robert sat at his new workstation—set up exactly as the one in the laboratory on Moreau's island—with the strongbox he had obtained in New Providence before him.

Unlocking it with a small golden key that had hung around his neck since the object was in his possession, Robert slowly opened the lid and looked inside at what the seller—a magician and alchemist with the last name of Abriendo, who was purported to come from a long line of wizards—had called the Ezekiel Wheel.

How apt a name—had not Robert's own visions rivaled those of the Old Testament prophet? Surpassed them, even!

Fairly unremarkable in its design—although featuring exquisite bas relief images of Biblical man, as well as an ox, a lion, and an eagle—the Ezekiel Wheel reminded Robert of the Antikythera mechanism, found in 1901 in a shipwreck off the coast of the Greek island that gave it its name. Although the object before him was much more powerful than a mere astronomical calculator, it shared a basic design with the Antikythera mechanism and sketches he had been given of ancient machinery built by Archimedes in Greece and by the priests and scientists of Byzantium and Persia.

Using a jeweler's screwdriver, Robert examined the various gears, counterbalances, and other components comprising the strange device, which was capable of providing the immense amounts of energy that Frankenstein had no other option but to harness from lightning itself.

Although he could not discern exactly how it worked, or from where it derived a power equal to that of lightning, Robert had faith that Abriendo's word was good.

When the time came, it would do its job.

As would he.

It would take some time for Robert to wire the device safely into the much-improved electrostatic machine that Ravenskald had supplied. His pair of lab assistants, newly graduated from the University of Edinburgh in chemistry and engineering, would no doubt be of assistance in the matter, and in many others.

Their mutual employer had guaranteed their cooperation and discretion.

Closing and locking the box, Robert crossed the room to the operating table where the Tom-beast's still-wrapped body lay in wait for the demonic work to come. Just beyond it were a series of long tables holding the also still-wrapped corpses of Costa's three young crewmen.

To what uses Hyde would put them, Robert did not know.

With any luck, he would be safe in a deep and dreamless sleep as Edward did his work.

The barely recognizable face of Tom Paris sewn onto the beast was something Robert wished he would never encounter again.

CHAPTER 24

An unexpected visit.

"**M**ister Walton. Are you quite all right?"

Robert had just burst through the doors and out of the laboratory, barely making it into the high grass at the perimeter before losing his breakfast of poached eggs and toast.

Ignoring the speaker behind him, whose voice he did not recognize, Robert sank to his knees as another wave of sickness overtook him.

For nearly a week, he had awoken each morning to examine the work on the Tom-beast Hyde had done with Robert's hands the previous evening. Hyde had made refinements to the elixir that made it impossible for Robert to remember anything of what the ape-man inside of him had done. Here and there he heard snippets and stirrings amongst the groundskeepers, meager staff, and handful of villagers hired to help around the facility and nearby cottage that Hyde had been in the pubs for several hours each night, buying drinks for the locals and taking a few of the barmaids to the private rooms upstairs. His money was welcome and no one made a fuss.

Until a barkeep found one of his girls in an alley, her neck so badly broken it had turned her head almost completely around.

This was the very day Hyde had begun experimenting with the corpses of Costa and his crew.

Admittedly, it was Robert who had first opened them up, applying what he had learned from the surgeon in Wexford to their hearts, kidneys, livers, and lungs, but this was nothing compared to the dis- and reassembling Hyde had gotten up to.

Just this morning, Robert had come into the laboratory from a deep, dreamless sleep, fringed nonetheless with a sense of foreboding and ill intent, to find Costa's battered head sew onto one of the crewmen's bodies and parts and pieces of the other two attached along the torso. Lying beside this effrontery to the human form, Robert had seen a sight that had precipitated the regurgitation of his breakfast.

Upon Costa's body was sewn the half-rotted head of a goat.

This was not science! This was mocking God, Nature, and Robert himself.

To be used as a tool for such meaningless sport... "I ask again, Mister Walton. Are you quite all right? Have you gotten a bit of a bug?"

Certain the last of the toast and egg was out of his body and the waves of nausea would not return, Robert slowly stood, turning to face the source of the voice behind him.

"I am fine. Thank you for your concern. Something I ate must not have agreed with me. I will have to speak to the cook." Wiping his mouth with his shirt cuff, Robert tried to smile. "And you are?"

"Simeon Ravenskald. Did you not receive my telegram, indicating my arrival from Switzerland this morning?"

Damn you, Hyde, Robert thought. *Such fun you are having at my expense.*

"Oh, yes. Yes of course," he said aloud, tapping the heel of his hand lightly against his forehead. "With so much to do, it completely slipped my mind. Have you had breakfast? Freshened up? I can take you to the house to settle in. The laboratory is in a bit of disarray ... It will take me some time to make it presentable..."

"Nonsense," Ravenskald said. "I am most anxious to see what your brilliance—and the help of your companion—has yielded you thus far. Your work is fully fascinating to me, Walton. I had such high, high hopes for Moreau, as did my ancestor for Victor Frankenstein—in this very place. And yet they disappointed us..."

Fighting off another wave of nausea at Ravenskald's unwillingness to agree to a delay, Robert shook his head. "Really, sir. It was a long night of vivisection and my assistants are not yet here to help me dispose of the waste. If you would kindly give me an hour..."

"I have given you ten days. Show me. *Now.*"

The voice coming out of the richly dressed and jeweled man before him was suddenly more street thug than gentleman.

All the rumors he had heard about the ruthless Ravenskalds were without a doubt the truth.

Leading the way to the row of operating tables, Robert wracked his brain for an excuse for what his benefactor was about to see.

He never got the chance to utter even a word.

"Ah... I see our Edward has been playing!"

The pure joy in Ravenskald's voice recalled to Robert his father's pleasure midday at Christmastime when his son had put together some puzzle or building kit that his parents had gifted him that morning.

"He is quite the agent of chaos, is he not?" Ravenskald continued, leaning in to examine the sutures between the head of the goat and Costa's neck.

"Ah—I know this tattoo," he said, his eyes focusing on Costa's left forearm. "Costa was proud of it. Saint Anthony of Padua, patron saint of Portuguese sailors. Born in Lisbon, you know. Perhaps Saint Anthony of Egypt would have better protected him from the demons with which he trafficked, eh?"

Robert did not know how much more he could withstand. Again, his stomach began to churn as a fat white maggot emerged from the socket of the rotting goat's right eye.

"I see the apparatus is all in order. All state of the art, Walton. If Moreau had access to these devices, his story would have been different." Ravenskald had thankfully moved to the far side of the laboratory. Robert quickly followed.

"This is the reason I have come."

Simeon Ravenskald, one of the wealthiest and most powerful men in the world, did not strike Robert as one to stoop to reverence, and yet that was precisely what the look in his eye and the gentle touch of his fingers on the Ezekiel Wheel conveyed.

"Have you tested it?"

A whispered prayer by either of the Anthonys would not be half as holy sounding as was this simple question.

Robert shook his head. "We are not quite there yet. I have spent several hours each day pouring over the schematics and assessments you sent—some of them are undoubtedly hundreds of years old, perhaps more—and I have figured out how to turn the thing on, although it is impossible to know what will happen when I do. The documents are filled with all manner of poetry and exaggeration. 'It shall be as if day swallowed night.' 'As if all the energies of the Great Pyramid and her brothers were gathered together in a single sacred space.' Meaningless romanticism to a scientist. I still have research to do. In the meantime, the Tom-th—. I mean, the vessel we are preparing for Edward Hyde to inhabit is near to completion. Just another month of refinements…"

Now it was Ravenskald's turn to shake his head. "Nonsense. I have provided you two very bright assistants. And Hyde is highly motivated, his time at the taverns aside. I want you ready for the transfer in a fortnight, when I shall make my return. You must be getting low on ingredients for the elixir…"

"How could you know that?"

Ravenskald smiled. Robert was surprised. It was bright and full of life. "It is my business to know how my money is spent and what dividends it brings. This project is no different from my shipping and transport concerns, nor any other of my family's myriad holdings and investments. It is a means to an end, Walton. A rather important one. One that is holding my interest step by step."

Ravenskald's hires were more than just assistants, Robert realized.

They were spies.

"Now," Ravenskald said, placing a monogrammed handkerchief to his nose as if he were suddenly aware of his surroundings. "Let us leave this dark, dank house of necessary horrors and take a walk. Have you made time to visit the Midhowe chambered cairn and the brochs and crannogs that surround it?"

I am trying to bring life from death with the soul of a madman inside me and he asks me about walking tours as though I were on holiday?

Robert was careful not to let his face betray his thoughts. "Work first, sir, as I surely would think you would want it."

"You must not think you know what I want," Ravenskald said, exiting the laboratory and assessing the sky. "We should take advantage of the weather. A Viking ancestor, an ally of the great Orkney jarls Sigurd Eysteinsson and his son Sigurd the Mighty, died in battle near the cairn. Let us pay our respects. It was during the Iron Age, the time of the monuments we are heading out to see, that my family truly embraced its destiny. To this day, we give the head of the family a Viking funeral, exact in every detail to the one given our ancestor, Jórkell. Shall we go?"

As they walked to their destination, Robert attempted to process all that Ravenskald had said. Fascinated by the stories of the Norsemen of Scandinavia, the fabled sailors known as the Vikings, from the time he was a boy, Robert was well acquainted with the details of their funerals, including the human sacrifice.

Somehow, Ravenskald had known that he was. This little stroll through history was all a part of further establishing his pedigree and dominance over Robert.

After all, how powerful must one be, in this enlightened age in which they were living, to have around them those willing to die to serve their master in his everlasting life?

As they approached the chambered cairn half an hour later, Robert began to understand Costa's regret about the terms to which he had agreed.

CHAPTER 25

Another unexpected visit.

Hyde was getting stronger, and ever more impatient. His restlessness was starting to cause Robert considerable physical pain as his guest's essence, increasingly more viscous, paced like an expectant father up and down his reluctant host's spine and kicked and whirled through his ribcage and around his pelvic bone.

His outbursts and ugly behavior in the local taverns had necessitated a deal be made to bring girls from other islands to the laboratory each evening for Hyde's personal pleasure. Some left. Others did not. The sound of a small prop plane approaching the island around dusk each evening made Robert's blood run cold. It had not only served to start the fingernail-pokes and tongue-flicks that signaled Hyde's awakening—it was a daily reminder of just how far astray Robert's once-holy mission had gone.

Robert never knew what to expect when he opened the doors each morning. On a good day, his gaze met nothing more than empty bottles, the odd used syringe, various articles of silky, lacy clothing, and the stray, lifeless feathers of cheaply dyed boas. On the worst days there were bloods stains, discarded parts and pieces, and new experimentations with, modifications to, and further graftings onto the now thoroughly grotesque forms of what were once Costa and his crew.

As the days went by in the quiet and solace of testing the machinery and preparing the plasma, saline, and other fluids that would need to be infused through the Tom-beast prior to Hyde's taking possession, Robert kept careful note of the procedures in a new journal Ravenskald had gifted him prior to his departure.

Ravenskald. He had said again that he would return in a fortnight to witness the transference. That was thirteen days ago. The next day's plane would not bring some semi-drugged showgirl from London or Glasgow or homeless, bound-and-gagged teen. It would bring the villain who made the debauchery possible.

Instructing his assistants to lock the door of the laboratory in the late afternoon, Robert placed a pair of goggles over his eyes and pulled the adjusting strap tight. Raising a soft cowhide mask over his nose and face, he signaled for his assistants to employ their own protective gear and stand well away from the Ezekiel Wheel. Satisfied that they were reasonably safe—after all, he was not positive what was going to happen—he slipped his surgeon's hands into a pair of thick welder's gloves, and took a breath to clear his thoughts so he could apply the full power of his concentration. Moving from one to the next with care, he checked the connections between the ancient device and the various collectors, conductors, and cathodes the energy it produced would pass through before being harnessed by a complex capacitor the engineer had been constructing, testing, and refining since the day that he was hired.

Satisfied that all was in order, Robert placed his gloved hand upon the outmost gear of the Ezekiel Wheel. If he had read the schematics correctly, a quarter clockwise turn would be all it would take to activate it.

Gripping the gear tighter in anticipation of the turn, Robert felt Hyde's cold hands pressing up into his throat as he jockeyed for a view.

Settle down, Edward, Robert whispered in his mind. *This could be the end of us all*.

If he remembered how to pray, if he were not fearful of God's response were he to try, Robert would have done so. Instead, he closed his eyes tightly and turned the gear, which groaned a little in protest before doing what he asked.

Beneath his fingers, Robert felt a subtle vibration begin to course through the teeth of the gear. He gripped it even tighter to better feel the sensation, which was not at all unpleasant, as the energy entered each of his fingers, moved across his palm, and up into his arm. He heard Edward groan with pleasure.

"Ah, yes… Yessss… You 'ave done it, Rahbert, it seems. Best step away tho', 'fore ya kills us both."

Robert hesitated. Hyde had offered a solution. Was he requesting it? Did Robert have the courage?

Before he could consider the question completely, the Ezekiel Wheel began to hum, the gears and tiny components to which they were attached all beginning to move. Robert pulled his hand away as the top gear started to spin counter to the ones below it. The wheel gave off a glow—first a pale purple, then green, then a rich blue, as from the flame of an acetylene torch. It began to give off heat.

"Keep well away now, lads!" Robert cautioned his assistants, as he took several strides away from the wheel. Placing his still-gloved hands over his eyes to protect them further as the rich blue light went white, Robert saw the cathodes begin to glow as the collectors and conductors did their work. As the energy gathered into the capacitor, Robert moved a small lever on the edge of the Ezekiel Wheel and it proceeded to power down, the machinery all around him sparking and smoking but holding together against the strain as the energy diminished.

"Success!"

He and Hyde had said it together.

"Well done! Well done indeed!"

This came from neither of them, nor the assistants.

Ravenskald had slipped in during the test—he no doubt had a key—and was now standing at Robert's side. In his arms was an oval wooden case that looked as though various owners had subjected it to hundreds of years of travel on both the sand and sea.

"Ah… I see you peeking at my surprise. Let us move over into the better light of your work station and I shall show you what it is."

Pulling his gloves from his hands and removing the goggles and mask, Robert followed Simeon Ravenskald as instructed. Turning up the wicks on his work lanterns, Robert watched with bated breath as his benefactor undid the trio of latches on the case, lifting the lid to reveal a beautiful mirror with gold-gilt frame and a surface of highly polished obsidian.

"Gorgeous," Robert said, in spite of himself.

"Indeed. And such pedigree," Ravenskald answered, lifting it carefully out of the case. "Though its origin is uncertain, it is thought to have been crafted in the time of the carving of the Sphinx by a pair of Egyptian priests that they might better speak to Heru-Khut, spirit of the Rising Sun, of which the resplendent lion–man is the glorious embodiment. As you can imagine, such a powerful object was highly in demand, ownership contested from everyone from the Israelites to the Mesopotamians. It was complicit in the downfall of a Meso-American god-man. Wars have been fought and dark bargains struck so that emperors and queens could possess it. The alchemists made perhaps the best use of it, from Albertus Magnus to Agrippa and Paracelsus. Then came the scientist-philosophers and conjurers—Sir Francis Bacon, Doctor John Dee, Abraxas Abriendo, Emanuel Swedenborg… Men who wanted to speak to God… and to the angels. You understand that well enough, Walton, eh? The desire to converse with angels?"

Ravenskald's tone was subtle in its mockery. Edward's accompanying laughter was not.

"What is its purpose here?" Robert asked. "Surely not God nor his angels want any part of this madness."

"My word, how you have changed," Ravenskald said, shaking his head while putting the mirror back into its case. "My agents in England spoke so highly of you. For a man with considerable imagination you have so little stomach for the things that bring its visions to fruition. As to your question... I acquired it some time ago for another of my ongoing projects—far too imaginative for involvement by the likes of a limited heart-mind such as yours, though I initially had thought it otherwise. Then again, it does have varied uses, equally valuable, and perhaps applicable here—once the transfer of Hyde is complete. But enough of that for now. I have not eaten. I hope your cook has something fine prepared."

Robert, his mind racing about the history and possible uses of the mirror, shook his head. "We were not expecting you, so..."

Rolling his eyes, Ravenskald said, "How you deign to live like a savage when wealth is all around you, I cannot understand. I shall have a bath while you put the cook to work. Fresh fish and plenty of vegetables, yes? There is an excellent Madeira in my luggage. Make sure he lets it breathe."

Instructing his assistants to secure the lab for the evening, Robert followed Ravenskald out into a light but steadily strengthening rain.

Hyde would stay put for the evening; Robert could sense it. Furthermore, he believed that Jekyll's evil creation was pondering the mirror as well—its possible uses, especially if the Tom-beast was not sustainable.

After all, if a simple hallway mirror almost let him through, what might the ancient creation of two Egyptian priests ultimately allow?

CHAPTER 26

A first attempt at transference.

To one who does not give himself naturally over to deep thought, the solving of complex problems, and a mission so consuming one must term it Religious Fervor, the seemingly ludicrous revelations that dawned on Victor Frankenstein, Henry Jekyll, and Robert Peary Walton in the course of their scientific pursuits speak to weak character and an absence of self-reflection.

While I, your narrator, to a point, agree, we must also consider that, far from a flaw in character—and we must agree that each had plenty of those—this sudden shock into the *now* of things speaks to a certain level of Genius, of Nietzsche's Übermensch and Dostoevsky's Superman. Of men whose minds do not work like those of the busily grazing, happily ignorant masses.

Not unlike Walton's abrupt realization of the horror of his work as he viewed the Tom-beast on a single fateful morning, his reaction to the moment he was due to be strapped into an operating table and hooked up to the machinery and the Tom-beast's body in preparation of the transference of Hyde's mind into his new vessel was beyond the average man's comprehension.

"I cannot go through with it," he protested, as his two assistants began switching on the powerful surgical lights and the machinery according to a clip-boarded protocol they had spent days with Walton devising, practicing, and refining.

"Nonsense," Simeon Ravenskald answered, taking him gently by the arm. "To be nervous is understandable, although I find it laughable that in all the years you have spent cutting into and reassembling human and animal forms that you never once imagined yourself in their place."

"Why would I?" Robert asked, stepping away from his designated operating table, only to find himself blocked by the assistant with the degree in engineering. Another abrupt insight—he was tall, broad-shouldered, and made of considerable muscle.

"It is hubris," Ravenskald said. Turning to the assistant with the degree in chemistry, he asked, "Is the elixir prepared?"

In order for the transference to have its best chance of success, it had been decided, by Ravenskald and Hyde, with Robert having not even the dimmest recollection of it, that a massive dose of the elixir—double what was normally imbibed—was called for.

Robert saw the chemist nod and move to the table where they had already arranged a variety of spotless surgical tools and other supplies. Instead of returning with a beaker, he held a large syringe.

"You do not mean to *inject* the elixir into me?" Robert asked, feeling in answer the engineer's powerful hands envelop and restrain his tensing upper arms.

Ravenskald laughed. "That is precisely what we'll do. Stay still now, Robert. I would hate to have the needle snap inside your arm." Nodding to the chemist, who sent a short spray of the purple liquid into the air to clear the syringe of air bubbles, Ravenskald smiled wide as he inserted the needle into Robert's left forearm and emptied the contents into his vein.

"Secure him onto the table," he ordered.

The assistants had secured the four buckles attached to the table around his ankles and arms when Robert felt a flash of fire where the chemist had drained the needle. It quickly spread to his shoulder and through his neck and torso. As the engineer pulled tight a strap across his chest, his body began to convulse. His tongue began to thicken and as his head began to swim and eyes go dim, he heard the duel laughter of Ravenskald and Hyde. Fighting the contradictory feelings of wanting to be unconscious due to the pain and to be awake to witness what was about to occur, Robert craned his neck as he heard the gearing mechanisms in the Ezekiel Wheel begin to fire up as an oxygen mask was affixed over his face and various probes inserted into his arms and neck.

As the machinery whirred to life and Hyde began to stomp on his bladder and shout with glee within him, Robert's eyesight failed. With a scream of pain as Hyde climbed upward, ready to emerge, his finger- and toenails digging into his organs and muscles for leverage, Robert said a prayer of thank you to a God who had forsaken him as he finally lost consciousness.

CHAPTER 27

A final attempt at transference.

R obert Peary Walton awoke to an ungodly growl.
It was not inside of him, but next to him.
Perhaps this time it worked.
Two days prior, Robert had awoken to find himself still strapped to the table. Down in his sternum he could hear the weeping of the frustrated devil who remained still trapped within him.

Focusing his eyes in the dim light of the laboratory, he saw Ravenskald in a tight triangle with the engineer and chemist. Each held one of the three doctors' journals, as though they were comparing notes. As Robert asked softly for water—his mouth was dry, with a taste that made him gag—their leader broke from the group. Robert could see that Ravenskald also held both of his own journals in his massive, manicured hands.

"Robert." It sounded unusually kind. "Of course. Water. Gentlemen... see to it, please." As the chemist moved to a pitcher by the workstation, Ravenskald leaned over. "It did not work. We came close, but it was not quite enough. No worries, my friend. We have another plan."

As the chemist lifted Robert's head, holding a glass of tepid, metallic-smelling water to his lips, he heard Ravenskald whisper, "That's right. Drink it all. All in one go. It will help you to relax. There. Rest now. We shall work again quite soon..."

Opening his mouth to release the first of a dozen questions, Robert felt himself losing consciousness.

They had drugged him yet again!

As he faded into an admittedly blessed oblivion, Robert heard Edward's sobs turn to cries of anger. He felt an immense pressure on his heart, as though the bastard were trying to hold it so tightly that it would cease to beat.

Though why would he? To kill himself when they were so close... Or was Ravenskald deceitfully placating him?

Had all of the effort and the death of Tom and Costa and the rest come to nothing? How could that be?

As Edward railed and raged inside him, Robert let the sedative work.

According to Simeon Ravenskald, twenty-four hours had passed before Robert again was awake. Still strapped to the table, he saw his own reflection in the polished obsidian mirror, which the two assistants must have fastened to an improvised device that allowed it to be suspended a foot from his face with a pair of surgical clamps. They had arrayed a series of wires and coils around it, no doubt attaching them to the bank of machinery behind him.

What in the world was it for?

As though he was reading his mind, Ravenskald said, "We need you to talk to him, Robert. Talk him through the process. He has become so goddamned difficult since suffering our second failure."

A second *failure?* Robert had not even the slightest recollection of it.

"Edward Hyde," Ravenskald said, his voice like that of a governess trying to get a shy child to come out from under the bed to meet some distant relatives. "Robert is awake. I am sure you are aware. If you want to be free of him, you must cooperate." Motioning for Robert to continue the conversation—the father called in when the governess comes up empty—Ravenskald stepped away.

Gazing into the mirror, Robert winced. The skeleton features of his face and several days' worth of reddish-brown hair along his jawline and under his nose made him nearly a stranger to himself.

"Edward," Robert whispered, his throat swollen, dry, and sore. "Tell me what troubles you. Tell me how I can help."

Of all the nightmares, losses, depredations, and ridicule Robert had suffered for his quest, this was perhaps the worst. As much as he wanted rid of Hyde, once and for all, he shuddered to think what the monster would do with a body of his own. A muscular, carefully crafted killing machine such as the one still strapped to the table beside him.

The mirror started to shift ever so slightly in the clamps as Edward came up from a thick red fog in its center, the child now emerged with the look of an angel to hide his ugly deeds.

"I like it in 'ere, Rahbert. I thinks I'd like ta stay. Cannot take the pain a' anuvver go at a transfuh. We could go back ta London ya know. I 'ave seen yer Kath'rine in yer dreams an' I do likes what I see. A fine bit a' crumpet she is. It'd be a decent arrangement, work out well fer her, I tells ya. You take the days, I take the nights. Tried that once before wit' 'Enry an' a bird 'e was courtin'. An' a cold, propa courtin' it was, 'til I stepped in that is... 'E lacked imagination. An' *oomph*. As fer you... ya won't 'ave no mem'ry an' I won't be a botha. An' I guarantee, Kath'rine won't want fer love."

Robert shook his head. "You shall never spend a moment with Katherine. Not ever! Besides... she is not mine with which to bargain. To divvy up in your mad proposal. Any thoughts I might have had in the South Pacific of reunion were only to placate Tom, to buy me additional time."

Hyde chuckled, vibrating Robert's ribs. "She might not agree straight on, but women are weak. 'Spesh'ly society types like our Kath'rine. You jus' leave 'er ta me. We can make this work."

Did it all make sense? With Hyde still inside of him, Robert could maintain some measure of control. And Edward had helped with the surgeries... he had a perspective no surgeon or scientist could. Perhaps, together, they could make the Perfect Man.

Perhaps...

"I do not understand you, Edward," Robert said. "So rough. So fearless and stubborn and proud. Would you settle for a semi-life, within the confines of my ever-weakening body? The liquor. The drugs. The violence. It has already taken its toll... can you not see that? Feel it? We have come so close. Will you fail to see it through?"

Placing his broad, flat nose against the glass, Hyde sneered. "Stop ya blatherin'. It ain't my first choice, Walton. Yer a sad excuse fer a man, ya are. But the pain... Moreau was a 'eartless bastahd. I sees that clear enuff. An' what if it don't work? What if I get in there, like I did last time, an' sumptin' immediately pulls me out. 'Cause I tells ya, sumptin' did!"

"Is this true?" Robert directed his question at Ravenskald, who managed to lift and drop his shoulders in place of a spoken answer. He was a man unaccustomed to failure. Robert saw how these past several days had served to dull his pride.

"We have boosted the capacitor, added more coils, and our industrious engineer has made some slight adjustments to further strengthen the output of the Ezekiel Wheel. To go any further would be unwise. But I believe it is enough. Worth one final, desperate try. Do you hear me, Edward? Embrace the life that you deserve! Enjoy the freedom Jekyll denied you. One last grasp for the open door, my son."

Robert could not believe the tone of love and caring coming from Ravenskald's throat. In all of this madness, he had never asked Ravenskald why. Why the expense? Why the risk? How could Hyde, once in the Tom-beast body beside him, serve the purpose of the richest man in the world?

He could not bear to surmise the answers.

"Time grows short," Ravenskald said, his usual impatience and edge to his voice returning. "We are ready to proceed."

Looking into the mirror, Robert saw Hyde's eyes brighten ever so slightly.

He was going to agree. His fathers had calmed him. Focused him.

"So be it. But ya best not fuck it up."

With a nod to the assistants, Ravenskald set the protocols in motion. The ignition of the machines, including the modified Ezekiel Wheel, which whined at a far higher, more nauseating pitch. The switching on of the surgical lights and placement of the oxygen mask over Robert's mouth and nose. The pinch in his forearm, followed by the warmth of the elixir as they ran it through his veins.

He was starting to sleep. To allow what visions would come.

Then, from deep within the din of the machinery, Robert heard a voice he had not heard before.

"Psst. Wakey, wakey, Robert Peary Walton, would-be god and colossal failure of a father. We need to have a chat."

Closing his eyes tighter, willing sleep to come as Hyde began to twitch, claw, and groan, Robert heard the voice again.

"Mewling little *bitch*." This, he knew, the voice had not directed at him, but at Hyde. "You were a bore back in London and you're still in the end just a simpleton Cockney git. Now… where was I? Right… Be sure you want this, Robert. I pulled him out of the transfer yesterday, but then I got to thinking… it should be up to you. Like it was for me. Yes—I too thought I could follow in the footsteps of Jekyll and Moreau, extracting evil from a soul like a pimple pinched of puss. To build all around me a cathedral of cathodes and capacitors, of tinctures and tonics. I spoke with Moreau before he fled for the island. I visited this very laboratory half a dozen times. And I *did* extract my evil… or I will, in approximately eighty-four years. Never mind my explaining. This isn't the time or place. But the *carnage*… how that homunculus of mine ripped and raped and raged. A brutal thing he was. Jaldaboath. Taking a cue from Hyde, he scrawled his black blasphemies in Bibles. Took an army of twelve to control him. So be warned. I can stop this if you want. Kill you both. SHUT UP AND

CRAWL NO FUTHER, EDWARD HYDE! I WILL KICK YOUR FUCKIN' FACE IN!"

It was at that moment of such preternatural volume that Robert realized the voice was coming not from the machinery but the mirror.

And there he was… a man in many ways, with shoulder-lengthcurly black hair, brown eyes that glittered with passion and experience, and a face like an angel… although corrupted and more than a little mischievous.

"Guilty as charged," the visage in the mirror replied. Looking just past him, Robert saw Hyde.

Was he *cowering*?

"Hierarchy is everything," the mirror-angel said. "It's up to you, Robert Walton. Let him pass or end it now?"

In the handful of hours in which he remained alive, Robert examined his answer almost without pause.

He never got close to understanding why he said what he did.

"I must allow at least one of our sons to thrive."

What had happened from then until the moment the guttural growl had jolted him into consciousness, Robert could not remember. Ravenskald, beside himself with joy as the Tom-and-Hyde-thing started to struggle against the straps, thought it pointless to describe it.

"It is working! What else matters?"

Turning his face away as the first of the buckles that kept the demon restrained stretched and flexed and broke, Robert saw that the mirror-man had not yet left.

The look on his face was equal parts pain and resignation.

"I knew what you'd do," he whispered. "Ain't free will a bitch?"

Who are you? Robert thought.

"Just an angel falling upward, who is always in the shit."

CHAPTER 28

An expenditure of ink about the "angel falling upward."

Although many months would pass before I would learn the details of this encounter from the lips of Simeon Ravenskald—our families have been enemies and allies for centuries, as circumstances dictated, the former much more than the latter—I am compelled to explain without delay what I know of the dark entity that calls itself the "angel falling upward."

As I mentioned at the opening of this narrative, I was assigned as a young reporter to the series of murders attributed to Jack the Ripper. Since I will save the details of that wholly evil and almost completely misunderstood case for a volume of its own, I can only say that this was my first encounter with the "angel falling upward," who goes by the misleading *nom de guerre* Planner Forthright.

In my limited experience with this demonic presence, he was neither. As you have just read, Astute Reader, he is secretive, sarcastic, and quite possibly possessed of a singularly lunatic mind. Although I have been able to confirm through numerous sources that he did indeed have at least some semblance of relationship with Edward Hyde, and further that he was involved on at least one occasion with the events that led to Abraham Moreau and his assistant Montgomery fleeing London in 1894, his professing to have extracted the Archon named Jaldaboath from within his own demi-body *eighty-four years in the future* after his brief mirror-meeting with Robert Walton is beyond my considerable abilities of comprehension.

I would not mention further this mysterious entity Planner Forthright if it were not for a visit he made to me in hospital during the final days of my pursuit of Edward Hyde and the not insignificant part he played in the ultimate resolution of the narrative at hand.

I will relate those events to you in detail later in the story. For now, let us return to Rousay in the Orkney islands, where four days have passed since the successful transference of Edward Hyde into the hybrid body—dubbed the Tom-beast by Robert Peary Walton.

CHAPTER 29

Revelations abound as Ravenskald is set to depart.

After four nights of nightmares and days when all he could do was put on a fresh shirt, sip some broth, and stare out at the Eynhallow Sound, wishing that the steady wind would increase into a gale and blow his guilt away, Robert exited the cottage, where he had remained since the successful transference. As he gazed up at the sun, he heard the ignition of the triple engines of the Fokker F.VII passenger plane that Simeon Ravenskald used to travel to and from the island.

Making his way slowly to the laboratory building—he had far from recovered from the ordeal—Robert put his hand on his stained and frayed Panama hat to keep the powerful plane's three props from shredding it like his soul.

Four of Ravenskald's bodyguards arrayed themselves around the plane, each with a rifle and sidearm.

As he approached the door to the lab, several islanders Robert had only seen in passing during his weeks on Rousay hurried past him with various boxes and crates, purposely averting their eyes.

All but one, with a long beard and fiery head of hair, who shot him a look of hatred and utter disgust before one of his companions warned him to keep on walking.

Entering the laboratory, he expected to find the engineer and chemist busy doing whatever it was that their employer needed before he departed the island.

Instead, he found Ravenskald alone, sitting at Robert's workstation, his face as white as the monogrammed handkerchief he was using to cover his mouth and nose.

It was merely a second later when the acrid smell of copiously spilled blood and human waste hit Robert like a hammer.

"My God," he whispered, placing the crook of his arm over own his mouth and nose. "Have the Portuguese corpses begun to rot so badly? That damnable goat's head…"

Moving to where the bodies had remained during the days of the attempted and final transference—*should they be needed for parts*, so said Hyde—Robert saw that they were gone. It was then that he realized—

The smell was coming from the other side of the laboratory.

The space where the assistants had worked.

"Spare yourself, Walton. Believe me."

Ravenskald sat with his back to the assistants' workstations, his head forward and shoulders dropped.

"There is very little left that one would call a man. Hyde blamed them for his pain. The multiple attempts at transfer... I have no doubt he took his time. While we were sleeping in the cottage."

Robert resisted the urge to ignore Ravenskald's warning and see just what it was that Edward Hyde had done. Perhaps a month ago, a week ago, but now his tolerance for the spectacle of carnage was gone. He had no clue if he would ever get it back.

"I understand now why you have hired the locals to—"

"You understand *nothing*." Although Robert had become well acquainted with Ravenskald's swift shifts in mood, he was still not used to them. In a flash, the Viking-sized man in the expensive tailored suit was up on his feet, his hands slamming against the worktable so the beakers and lanterns rattled from the force. "I have hired these men to appease them. What I am paying them is ludicrous. Bribe money for indescribable anger and grief. You saw my guards by the plane? They are to dissuade them from making their true feelings known, or worse yet, to act upon them."

"What additional horror has he done?"

Ravenskald stayed standing, although his stance and glare were softening. He was no doubt as exhausted as Robert. "The rooms at the local pub. Up he went with three local girls—one of whom was engaged to one of those men, the lad with the bright red hair. Was it fear? The abundant coin he flashed? The gleam in his eye perhaps, because I tell you Walton, it is mesmerizing. Perhaps it was a morbid fascination with a mysterious stranger in opera cloak, half-mask, and gentleman's hat—an alluring amalgamation of the phantom of the opera and Lon Chaney's disguised Inspector Burke in *London After Midnight*. Substituting your Tom Paris's hands for the hybrid beast's clumsy, impossible-to-hide paws was nothing less than genius. By the time the girls began to scream, it was all but over. Why his fascination with the dashing in of brains? Sir Danvers, all those years ago... an ally of my father's. I met him more than once."

Robert moved toward him, careful to keep more than an arm's-length away, sure that Ravenskald was capable of doing considerable violence even without a weapon. "If you knew of what he was capable…"

"It was business. As it must always be." Reaching below the table, Ravenskald produced a set of six journals—those of Jekyll, Moreau, and Frankenstein and two of Robert's and one he did not recognize. "I am taking these. They are of no more use to you, but I have meetings with several wealthy financiers and corporate laboratories. The applications for your work, Robert—so extended from that of your predecessors, a feat for which I commend you—are innumerable. Military. Scientific. Governments will line up to go exclusive. We have learned an enormous amount about the Ezekiel Wheel. Before last night's carnage, I had planned to take your assistants with me… together they would decode all it still keeps occult. No matter—I will hire others. There are always others…"

"And what of me?"

"You, Robert? You still work for me. This laboratory is yours. I have taken some items, yes. But you shall have anything you require. Upon my return to Zurich, in a few weeks' time, I shall deposit a considerable sum in a bank account to which only you shall have the code. My agents will keep you supplied and I have arranged for local builders to make vast improvements to the cottage. You shall want for nothing. This is an idyllic place for you to raise a family. In time, the locals will forgive and forget. My money shall see to that."

Robert shook his head in confusion. "Continue to work for you? What could I possibly offer? I am broken. Just to breathe takes all my effort. I do not see what you could possibly think I—"

Placing the journals on top of the boxes with the Ezekiel Wheel and mirror, Ravenskald took Robert by the shoulders, making him feel like a child. "There is much still to do. Improvements to be made. I will send detailed instructions after my meetings. The richest bidders for this information will surely have their requests."

"And should I refuse?"

"Robert." How like his father Ravenskald sounded! "You have nothing else. You have forsaken your fiancée. Your reputation in London is destroyed. And, my silly friend, you are guilty of the most heinous of murders. With my power, my connections, I can make the case utterly convincing. Not only Tom, but those two over there. The crew of the *Boa Sorte*. Because, with Hyde now disposed of, there is only you. There was *only ever you*. Countless witnesses will swear to it. You truly have no choice." Taking the books and boxes in his sizable arms, Ravenskald again shifted tone. "Now, you have some time to rest. I would stick close to the cottage for at least a week. Then you can venture into the village. Be polite. Engage with none of the women. Not long after, I will begin to send you your tasks. Understood?"

Not able to bear vocalizing his assent, Robert nodded. As Ravenskald barked a few orders at the hired laborers, who dared not look either him or Walton in the face, Robert called out, "You said Hyde is *disposed of*. How do you mean?"

Turning toward him with a huff of frustration, Ravenskald said, "Naiveté does not become you, Robert, although I shall indulge you, knowing what you've endured. I took the liberty of sending for two hunters several days ago. A precaution against Hyde's further mayhem. I prefer to be prepared. They are arguably the best in the world. Trained by Colonel Sebastian Moran. I am sure you've heard of him."

Robert did indeed. He was, at one time, after Professor Moriarty, the most dangerous man in London. He had killed one wealthy son of an earl that had caught him cheating at the card club and had nearly succeeded in killing Sherlock Holmes.

"After I was apprised of the situation in the tavern and found the remains of your assistants, I set them loose on the island. These hunters do not fail. Hyde is no longer a worry."

Relief mixed with loathing washed like a wave over Robert. "Was he so easy for you to destroy?"

"Again with your naiveté! Do you think I would be such a fool as to let such a monster have his unfettered way with the world? A man of my stature? No way to run a business, Walton. Now, if you will excuse me, my plane awaits. Do not bother with the mess. These men will see to it once I am gone, and you are safely back in the cottage."

Then, as easy as that, Simeon Ravenskald, whose only difference with Edward Hyde was that he could more amply pay to cover up his cruelties, was gone.

It was then that Robert, amidst the bloody remains of his failures, allowed himself to weep.

CHAPTER 30

The (wholly just) demise of Robert Peary Walton.

Before I begin this section of the narrative, I must take a moment to explain the use of parentheses in the title.

My publishers were not pleased that I made such a strong statement against Robert Peary Walton, whom they initially conceived of as the hero of this tale.

I must respectfully disagree.

Who then? Certainly not myself, your humble narrator, although, as you will soon enough see, I was forced to undertake the central role in the story's final act. They were quick to agree with my assessment of this as well, most strenuously in fact, after our loud and admittedly volatile exchange in their smoky Fleet Street offices.

An aging, jaded journalist should never be anyone's hero.

The Costa family, who carried on, managing to thrive and do abundant good with the money the captain left them, have my primary vote, for reasons you shall later read.

Other heroes of this tale must include all those who gave their lives in service, directly and indirectly, to the mad pursuits of the three Gothic doctors and RP Walton. Their misunderstandings and often naiveté about the darker aspects of their employers' work we must unconditionally forgive. I think here of Costa's crewmen, the engineer and chemist on the Orkney islands, and all those whom Edward Hyde tortured and destroyed.

And Victor Frankenstein's friend, the poet Henry Clerval, his brother William, and his brand new bride, Elizabeth, whom he caught up in a maelstrom that rent them limb from limb.

Even the Sayer of the Law and all of the hybrid creations that came from Moreau's lab we must look upon with pity.

And, quite most of all, Tom Paris, of whom I shall now speak.

*****

Please, suh... I am still inside of 'im. 'Elp me Robert! I see what 'e sees! I see what 'e does! They are my 'ands that grip the knife, the

cane, the cord. My fingers that press upon the throat, drainin' out a life! An' my face, distorted tho it be, is the last thing that they see!
ROBERT!

Waking from this nightmare, which he had dreamed in an endless loop for hours, Robert fumbled in the darkness for his water glass, filled with the remains of his latest dose of a tincture of opium. Draining it, he leaned back against the headboard, pushing strands of limp wet hair from his stinging, aching eyes.

Could Tom truly still be trapped within the Hyde-beast's body? Conscious of all that was happening? Robert did not think it possible. He had read enough of Freud and Jung to know that these were shadows of his guilt. He had not used Tom's heart. Had not transferred his brain into the hybrid body that Hyde and Moreau had made.

At least there was that.

Still, he feared that Tom's soul *could* see all he had described. That he had not traveled to a mythical realm of angels—because now Robert knew the truth of the guile of all dark demons to come to the genius in the guise of wings and light!

Running his finger along the inside rim of the glass to collect the dregs of the laudanum powder, Robert licked it clean and settled back for sleep. He had become desperate for some minutes here and there. Anything to give his body a chance to heal.

Letting the laudanum do its work, he thought of a song he knew as a child. A song about faire days in the countryside, where simple pleasures and an utter lack of care for a boy of barely twelve could be conjured, assured, and treasured.

The notes of the melody cradled his mind in their gentle undulations, so sweet the memories and their sounds. Then a pause before the words, which he had sung while climbing trees and catching fish, long before he heard the voice of Hyde, in the guise of his nameless angel.

Jam on fresh baked bread. His mother, so pale and lovely, his father for once relaxed.

The melody, just before the words…

"Rahhhhhhhh-berrrrrrrrrrt. Rah-berrrrrt Walllllll-tonnnn…"

Those were not the words! That was not the memory that he loved.

Opening his eyes, Robert gasped. There was the Hyde-thing, in opera cloak and top hat—Lon Chaney's evil disguise in *London After Midnight* come to life, just as Ravenskald said!—his steel grey irises betraying that it was not Tom Paris, whose eyes were so innocent, so green, who stood there gazing upon him.

As Hyde removed his hat and undid the clasp of his cloak, the dim light of the sunrise more fully illuminated the sutured and scarred visage, revealing patches of coarse hair along the jaws, beneath the nose, and hanging from the chin.

"You try to make yourself seem human by implanting hair in your face!" Robert yelled, fully appalled by the ruse.

"I am a work in progress," Hyde said, no trace of the uneducated, rough and tumble Cockney Tom and he, through some cruel trick of fate, had shared. The voice, however, remained both deep and hard.

No doubt a product of the boar's throat structure, not made for human words.

"What are you thinking, Robert?" Hyde sat upon the bed, as though he was an old bridge partner checking up on an injured friend. "I do miss the days when I could feel your every thought, puerile though they are. Ah... I know. My voice! I am to be a man of society now. No more playing the thug. Whores and sailors are fine for a fickle fix, but I now require a higher brand of humanity to satiate my needs. My desires. So, I must leave the Orkneys and be off to civilization. But I could not depart without a final goodbye."

Robert fought the effects of the laudanum. He needed to be coherent to say what he must.

"The hunters Ravenskald hired. He said they were the best..."

"No doubt they were. I was simply better. There, there, good son. Do not cry. I was kind to them. Made it quick. After all, I too am a hunter. I know the price one must sometimes pay in the stalking quest for prey. Ha!"

The prolonged laughter that lava'd up from the Hyde-beast's throat made Robert want to vomit.

"Damn you for seeing me cry. Damn you for all you have done. When Ravenskald is made aware—"

"Shhh now, Robert. He won't be. There won't be anyone to tell him. I had a letter sent, signed by the hunters, saying they were heading direct for Senegal, for buffalo and warthogs. To wire the bounty there. Of course, *I* will be there to receive it, eventually."

"I will not let you—"

"But your corpse will." Hyde lifted his hands—*Tom's* hands—each sporting rings on several fingers, and pinned Robert by the wrists. "I have been thinking for some time now how you would kill yourself. Then it came to me." In an instant, Hyde had both of

Robert's wrists in one of his, his free one producing a Colt Cloverleaf revolver from the back of his belt. "Recognize this? You read about it over and over."

"Just like Jekyll's."

"Just like Jekyll's. How fitting, yes? And, being a man who wrote his heart out in journals, you had no words left for a suicide note. There was nothing left to say. Truly, truly, Robert. We have come to the end of the words between us. Only the bullet remains."

And so it was that RP Walton died.

Placing the gun in the dead man's hand, after carefully wiping the butt, Hyde put on his top hat and cloak. As he exited out the window into the early Orkney dawn, he looked directly into a bright, powerful sun emerging over Eynhallow Sound, where a small boat and two hired sailors waited for him to depart.

Crossing a field with a schoolboy's ready-for-holiday strides, he said to himself, "Now the world shall see what Edward Hyde can do. And I think I will start in London."

CHAPTER 31

How I came to be involved.

My Dear Reader:

The murder of Robert Peary Walton by the monster Edward Hyde marks a clearly delineated end to the narrative I have thus far told, a final draft of which I completed on the occasion of my sixty-eighth birthday, 31 October 1930.

The story, as conceived of initially in my outlines, was the short rise and bloody fall of Walton, my ultimately weak-willed antagonist, intermixed with the tales of those he admired and upon whom he modelled himself.

But a series of events over the next five years have necessitated a longer narrative, for unforeseen events made me no longer just reporter but *participant* in the gruesome aftermath of the events that concluded with Walton's death.

You see, it was Walton's former fiancée, Katherine Beaumont, who came to me at the end of 1929, as the market crashes were taking full effect and chaos began to reign in England and the world. As she sat across from me over the course of an hour, such were her tone of worry and weeping words of concern that I could not turn her away, as much as I initially thought it prudent to do exactly that.

I know what you are thinking, Loyal Reader: This has become a trope in this tale—he who knows better than to sally forth but does, despite the dangers.

Of my complicity in this theme, I can only say in my defence that, should you have spent that hour with Katherine Beaumont, so beautiful and desperate as she was, you would have to possess a heart as black and soulless as Hyde's to have turned her coldly away.

I must admit, for that afternoon, I sorely regretted having lived a life of such solitude and discipline.

Miss Beaumont entered my rented rooms on Fleet Street on Tuesday, which was Christmas Eve, rather than waiting until Thursday to come to my *Evening Standard* office on Derry Street in Kensington. I had also been doing by then some intermittent correspondence work for the *Daily Telegraph* and the *Times* on matters of criminals and the occult.

I mention this only to indicate that my extensive connections in London and even internationally and access to the growing technology available to men such as myself made the investigations that I did subsequent to our Christmas Eve meeting possible.

A cousin of John Watson's deceased wife, Mary Marsten, Miss Beaumont—I cannot bring myself to call her Katherine, even now, many years later, when we have continued our odd companionship in Sunday parks and for Thursday morning tea—had contacted the doctor in his retirement. He had in turn sent her to me, knowing of my interest in the cases of Moreau and Jekyll and my success with locating a variety of missing persons over the years.

This was precisely the skills she sought. Tom Paris had not been faithful in his promise to write to Miss Beaumont whenever possible as they traveled from England to the South Pacific. In truth, not a single letter arrived. Given Tom's unquestionable character and integrity, she rightly became concerned.

When they had not returned for the holidays, she knew in her heart that something was dreadfully wrong.

How heartbreakingly accurate her female intuition would turn out to be.

Assuring her at the end of the hour that I would do all I could to enquire as to the whereabouts of the missing Walton and Paris, I wished her a Happy Christmas despite her unhappy circumstances. I then sat at my writing desk smoking pipe after pipe full of strong Turkish tobacco as I contemplated—so unconsciously Sherlock Holmes—all that she had told me of Walton's obsessions. It was from her that I originally learned of his finding Captain Walton's journal, which had set him on his quest and about the auction prior to his departure with Tom Paris that put the secrets of Henry Jekyll finally before him.

On 26 December, having spent a quiet Christmas with JM Barrie to celebrate his recent donation of the copyright of *Peter Pan*—his most lucrative creation—to Great Ormond Street Hospital, I entered the archive room at the *Evening Standard*, where I also kept my records from my years at the *Pall Mall Gazette*. Pouring over the files, I searched for clues as to the location of Moreau's island, where Miss Beaumont had known Walton and Paris to be heading.

I began with the notes from my interviews with Edward Prendick, who had settled on HG Wells as the man to tell his tale, rather than myself. And why would he not? You must not think I mention this out of malice. It is simply the facts of the case.

Prendick had been careful not to divulge the location of the island. He was unsure of what had become of its malformed, cruelly created population, limited as it was.

But all one needs is a single breadcrumb at a time with which to track a trail, no matter how obscurely laid, and I found one, after many hours, in a passing mention of Prendick's that the list of tramp steamers that passed anywhere near to this island was indeed rather narrow.

The following day, despite the Baltic Exchange and many shipping offices closing their doors for the holiday week, and on the pretense of doing a story on the shipping industry in the South Pacific, I contacted several companies enquiring about passage to the more obscure islands. There were plenty available for those wanting to go to Fiji, Tahiti, Samoa, or the Solomon or Cook Islands, they told me, but I protested. My piece was going to focus on out of the way places and the special requirements and challenges that go along with reaching them.

I will spare you the details of the tedium of my pursuits with the shipping industry and her fearless and able captains… Let me summate by saying that 1929 became 1930 as I followed the breadcrumbs hours upon hours of enquiries managed to yield.

Though, over and over, one specific name came up.

Simeon Ravenskald, shipping magnate and head of the family that has been inextricably linked with my own since the Golden Age of Piracy.

As much as I could give in to the urge to devote thousands of words to the history of this mostly contentious, often bloody, relationship, I will apply restraint and tell you only what you need to know—here and in subsequent narratives—about the Stanton–Ravenskald rivalry.

At present, it will suffice to say that I was not yet willing to contact Simeon Ravenskald on this or any other matter.

However, as is so often the case in our families' mutual history, he was the one who contacted me, but some months would yet pass as I continued in my pursuit of the truth of what had befallen Walton and Paris in the South Pacific before that fateful occurrence befell me.

When I was not pursuing clues gleaned from conversations with shipping offices and captains, I poured over the case files and newspaper articles having to do with Henry Jekyll and Abraham

Moreau. I read the fictionalized accounts of their actions and even spent a weekend with Holmes and Watson, occupied with various pursuits in their quiet latter years, coaxing from their minds all I could of what they knew about these cases.

As winter went to sleep and we entered the pleasant weeks of early spring, I found myself woefully short of information, making my twice-weekly visits with Miss Beaumont increasingly painful for us both.

And then, as I found myself beginning to despair, a series of ugly murders were brought to my attention from in and around London, mostly through my friend, Scotland Yard's Inspector Jonathan Newcomen. Strangulations, merciless beatings, mutilations, and dismemberments of all kinds—the victims of whom were the sort of fringe of humanity that no one missed, paid attention to, or mourned.

You must keep in mind that, given the embarrassment and panic caused by the supposedly unsolved Ripper murders four decades before, both Scotland Yard and the members of the venerable Fourth Estate, such as myself, were careful to suppress murders such as these as best we could. If we made any mention at all, it was a few brief paragraphs deep within the daily edition. Only the most salacious and low-class rags sensationalized these crimes, and their editors and reporters were just as happy to be paid off by the police and other interested parties to keep their typewriters still.

I studied these cases with interest, traveling down to the docks and fetid back alleys, to the flophouses and abandoned warehouses where these atrocities occurred, and what I was discovering disturbed my soul no end. Not since Saucy Jack himself were such unholy actions carried out with such unbridled savagery upon the human form.

This perpetrator—and all indications pointed toward a single actor—had a taste for human flesh and predilections that no writer, no matter how desperate for sales, should ever put into print.

There were never any witnesses. The Yard had named no suspects.

It all seemed so familiar, yet different enough to assure us that the Ripper had not returned.

Then, one Sunday evening in mid-July, Inspector Newcomen paid me an unexpected visit in Hyde Park as I walked with Miss Beaumont past a herd of sheep grazing on the grass to keep it trimmed.

"A moment of your time, Mister Stanton, if you don't mind," he said, dropping his voice to add, "And it is best if the lady does not hear."

Excusing myself and walking with Newcomen a prudent distance away, I asked him what was so urgent to detain us both from simple pleasures on a Sunday.

"It's the cane of Edward Hyde, Judah," he said. "It's gone missing from the Black Museum at Scotland Yard again."

"My God," I whispered, leaning on his capable arm for support.

"And there is more. We believe it has already been used, on a sailor leaving the Black Anchor after a couple of pints late in the evening just passed."

Cutting short my walk with Miss Beaumont on the pretext of having to meet an urgent deadline for the Monday morning edition, I stopped by my office at the *Evening Standard* to update my files with this latest case of murder. Thorough notes made, I headed to my Fleet Street rooms, intending to visit the doctor in charge of the sailor's remains first thing in the morning and requiring a restful night's sleep in order to be able to face what would no doubt be a most unsettling experience.

Unlocking my door, I saw before me, in the center of the room, a sealed envelope. Someone had no doubt slid it through the gap while I was out.

Pouring myself a whiskey, I removed my coat, loosened my tie and grasped the envelope. Sitting at my desk, I lit the wick on my lamp and carefully examined the bone-toned linen envelope, but there was not a mark upon it. Nor was it sealed. Lifting the flap, I pulled forth a single page, written in a careful hand.

Lighting my pipe, I leaned in close to the lamp and began to read the text.

CHAPTER 32

Wherein the contents of the letter [and others] are revealed.

A Glorious Summer Not Far frumm York, 1930

Jotter:

Greetings, Judah. Been awhile, ain't it?

A couple a' lifetimes. Nuthin' tho, ta 'portant men like us.

I have Chosen ya ta write ta for a single, simple reason:

You were the one who almost solved them.

There in '88.

I was watchin'. As all the bucks n birds were watchin' the false as fuck interpretation of me on an illegitimate stage, Cunt dracula's playhouse, I was watchin' YOU.

A worthy opponent to a cunnin' cunny of a dodger.

So now I am findin' myself in dire need a' same.

In a word or two, you'll do.

Let me ask you—Judah Philemon Stanton—right off the bat... Just to give you a little clue: Have you seen the Devil? Given the goat his due?

No ya say?

Then Pay a Penny & walk the hell inside.

And when you gaze upon him, squattin' near the filth, I will also come inside and ask ye:

O have you seen the devle with his mikerscope and scalpel?

Lookin' at a kidney with a slide cocked up?

You maybe can't at present, but you will 'fore this month's end.

Ha ha. Hint. Ha ha.

I was quiet for awhile, Judah.   I shall be no more.

What a racket I've begun.

A little bit a'style, a smorgasbord of fun

Back again I am & up to the old smash n slash 'em tricks. Do what ya will, good son—you will never nap again.

Take a moment, Judah... You might remember me if you try and think a little

Ha Ha. Hint. Ha ha.

The good old times have come for thee and me and us tahgetha, oh purveyor wit' the pen.

I've grown bored at present. Scribblin' 'way the days.

Sose I suppose, outta nuthin' else fer now, to make my way to Cornwall and try my little games—

Goodbye for the present, from the [newest, truest] dodger

Ha ha and ta ta

Two days later, as my mind reeled from the first, a second letter arrived, also without a postmark, as I sat at my desk, pouring over the madman's initial missive.

July the twenty-third, nineteen and thirty

Just a line—

Ya see—I am still knockin' about. Poor news 'bout them kids in Cornwall.

O have you seen the devle with his mikerscope and scalpel?
Lookin' at a kidney with a slide cocked up?

No? You shall see it soon enough. Piece a' it, anyways...

Twas a jolly nice lark. Heads cave clean wit' a cane made a' hick'ry

Weather sailor or child. One skull a little thicker is all.

Oh, what a dance I am leadin'!

Don't laugh tho: I think I have been very good up ta now. Praktasin subtle restraint.

Oh No more.

Now when I strike, you shall feel it in your bones.

I passed a policeman yestaday & he didnd take no notice of me.

I am very much amused by The coppers... They Think Themselves devilish clever. Donkeys, double-faced asses. They are the ones whot won't be blamed for nuthin.

They never caught me and never will.

You tho, Judah. Who came so close in '88, Tah savin' pretty Polly spreadin' by the Gate.

Poor old carved up Mary, en cunty, pungent Kate. Lizzie girl en Mary Ann.

Couldn't be a single man.

Couldn't be, just wouldn't be.

And it won't again.

P.S. You can't trace me by this writin' so it's no use ta try.

As I pondered and prayed against the evil actions of their scribe, I kept the pair of letters and their contents for the present to myself, as I puzzled out the clues—of which there were many—yet a third arrived, along with a package the contents of which you might well guess.

July 29... still '30, near as I can tell.

From a little lefta Hell.

I've no time for clever riddles.

Check the police reports. The donor of the kidney will be obvious to find, though I send you only part. Promised you I would.

Tother piece I fried and ate. It was vey nise

With much regret I send this all along to inform you that I must now change the game.

This composite body is no longer holding up. It cannot do the work I so often ask of it. The fingers no longer capable of the precision I require. This sewn-together face, part man, part boar, part jaguar, part ME. It has now become too obvious. No amount of makeup, no ingeniously made disguise can hide the truth away.

So I must find other ways, other helpers, other tastes.

I have just begun to eat.

You're invited to the Feast.

After Eden, Cain went East

That's when he BECAME the Beast.

God, how WE shall eat... and eat and feast and eat!

Yours in Spirit.

Ha ha. Hint. Ha ha.

Not quite Edward Hyde

CHAPTER 33

What the horrid letters meant.

I cannot hope to describe my mounting agitation as the letters arrived and I carefully, line by line, processed their meaning. Not that Edward Hyde had gone to any great lengths to mask himself—a wholly apt, yet inappropriate turn of phrase. I know that well enough. Yet I believed that there may be clues embedded in the hybrid text of the words of Hyde and the dozens of hands that penned the Ripper letters in '88—some from the primal source, many others not—and so I set about to find out what I could.

   With the arrival of the second letter, my initial suspicions regarding their composer were confirmed. I had known well enough that the onset of communication was tied to my visits with Miss Beaumont and the news from Inspector Newcomen that Hyde's damnable hickory cane had gone missing once again. Although he had done his devilish work in not saying his name outright at the start, a trio of passages in that initial letter were key to proving my theory. Here is the first:

boys n birds were watchin' the false as fuck interpretation of me on an illegitimate stage, Cunt dracula's playhouse

   For it was in the midst of the Ripper murders that Henry Irving's Lyceum Theatre had featured a stage production of the tale of Jekyll and Hyde. Indeed, Martha Tabram was found just three days after the production had opened. I can say on good authority that Bram Stoker's Dracula was indeed a personification of Irving, as Hyde had intimated with his foul and fetid omission of the letter "o" in Count. Furthermore, Bram had been, for years, the ill-tempered actor–producer's suffering and servile assistant. Bram had most likely been inspired by Dr. Polidori's use of the blood-sucking Ruthven as his stand-in for Byron in *The Vampyre* (Polidori having been inspired by Caroline Lamb's *Glenarvon*, where Lord Ruthven, clearly Byron, first appeared). One need only look at Abraham/Bram to sense my statement's truth, although, as I said, despite my never being close with the aloof, enigmatic Stoker, a credible source informed me that this was indeed the case.

As to Hyde's poor opinion of Richard Mansfield's portrayal of him, this is the mark of the egomaniacal mind. Mansfield's performance was so convincing that one theatregoer accused him to the police of being *Jack the Ripper*, saying no man could be that convincing without himself being a homicidal maniac.

The second key in the initial letter was:

Then Pay a Penny & walk the hell inside.

Knowing this was familiar, but not exact to something I had read before, I spent several hours scanning the more than two hundred purported Ripper letters, postcards, and other communications held in the Public Records Office on Chancery Lane, City of London. At last I came upon a postcard dated 10 October 1888. "Pay a penny and walk inside" was the original.

Hyde was adding flair.

Not that those who penned the Ripper letters lacked it. In addition to the communications archived at the Public Records Office, there were letters received by WT Stead (my editor at the *Pall Mall Gazette*) and myself. Many of these have still not been made public, although I shall do so in a future narrative. Other letters and postcards were keep in their personal files by Inspector Frederick Abberline of the London Metropolitan Police and Commissioner of the Metro Police, Charles Warren.

I am making some effort to secure them.

The third key to the scribe's identity was:

O have you seen the devle with his mikerscope and scalpel?
Lookin' at a kidney with a slide cocked up?

Taken direct from the Dr. Openshaw Letter, dated 29 October 1888, this adapted line from a Cornwall folktale penned seventeen years earlier has been the subject of debate and investigation for the last four decades.

The original is thus:

Here's to the devil, with his wooden pick and shovel. Digging tin by the bushel, With his tail cock'd up

The Ripper(s)'s corruption of the original was of course a reference to the piece of kidney and "From Hell" letter addressed to George Lusk, head of the Mile End Vigilance Committee two weeks earlier.

Used by Edward Hyde, it was also a remark upon the work of Henry Jekyll, Robert Peary Walton, and the rest.

Before I continue to the second and third letters, and knowing there is considerably more to share in a subsequent volume, I wish to mention that WT Stead thought the Ripper was Robert Donston Stephenson, aka Roslyn D'Onston. An occult practitioner with whom I had been well acquainted, Stephenson (the similarity in name to the author of the altered account of the sordid tale of Jekyll and Hyde is quite remarkable), penned an article, "The Real Origin of 'She' by One Who Knew Her," which appeared in the *Pall Mall Gazette* on 3 January 1889. He talked of the popular book by H Rider Haggard, as well as the West African coastal religion known as Obeeyah or Obeah.

I am well versed on the latter subject, as it was Obeah that led to the disfigurement of the slave trader named Devon Ross who sailed in the early 1700s with my ancestor, Joseph. I mentioned this in my opening. I will only add here the irony that Ross—who was responsible for the death of Joseph's father and the undoing of his family—like Hyde and Leroux's Phantom of the Opera, wore a mask to hide his hideous visage.

The forces of our Universe laugh as they intertwine us.

As to D'Onston, or any one particular Ripper suspect, there are too many letters, often sent in too close a timeframe from two different, distant locations, for a single hand to have penned them. The variety of hands, syntaxes, spellings, and so on are more than one man could manage. Oh, it is clear that Hyde has done it in his trio of notes, but it is far too clumsy and obvious. He is showing off. Phonetic spellings such as "Praktasin" are clearly too contrived.

And I know full well he meant it to be so, hence, in the second letter:

P.S. You can't trace me by this writing so it's no use ta try.

The tricks of language the Ripper(s) employed ensured the police, the newsmen, and those walking the streets of London day and night were looking for the wrong type of suspect, so whole-cloth were the prejudices against the working classes and foreigners, which remain intact today.

Rather than go any further, line-by-line, through Hyde's second letter, I briefly wish to remark that the following are all bits and pieces, nearly verbatim, from the Ripper notes (and the infamous Goulston Street graffito):

Now when I strike, you shall feel it in your bones.

I passed a policeman yestaday & he didnd take no notice of me.

I am very much amused by The coppers... They Think Themselves devilish clever. Donkeys, double-faced asses. They are the ones whot won't be blamed for nuthin.

They never caught me and never will.

The references to the "hick'ry" cane and the sailor were obvious enough and it was a few moments' work to confirm the brutal deaths by blunt force trauma of two young lads in Cornwall.

After the third letter arrived with its grisly package, the most obvious in its homages, intents, and identities by far (the bastard finally signed his name), I knew just what it was myself and the police were facing, evident in these lines:

This composite body is no longer holding up. It cannot do the work I so often ask of it. The fingers no longer capable of the precision I require. This sewn-together face, part man, part boar, part jaguar, part ME. It's now become too obvious. No amount of makeup, no ingeniously made disguise can hide the truth away.

So I must find other ways, other helpers, other tastes.

I have just begun to eat.

Out of respect for the family, I will withhold the name, although the victim to whom the missing kidney belonged was discovered in the dressing room of a certain music hall hours after the letter and package arrived.

Hyde had not only turned himself to cannibalism—he was now recruiting.

And I, perhaps better than anyone, know the long lines of willing evil-doers waiting for a leader like Edward Hyde.

As though this were not foul enough a fact, a visit to my rooms on Fleet Street by a most unexpected guest sent my mind to reeling with what "So I must find other ways, other helpers, other tastes" truly, chillingly meant.

CHAPTER 34

Circumstances force me to make the enemy of my enemy my friend.

We were not far into August when my unexpected visitor arrived at my door just after the sun began to rise on a Saturday. I had barely completed my daily morning ablutions when I heard a business-like voice and a pair of insistent knocks.

"Stanton—you awake? I must speak to you immediately on a matter of the utmost urgency."

Putting a flame beneath my morning pot of coffee before tucking my always-loaded Colt police revolver into the back of my trousers, I unlocked the trio of security mechanisms I had recently installed on my door. Opening it just enough to see into the hallway, I commanded the figure before me to identify himself.

The reply sent a shiver down my neck and spine.

"Simeon Ravenskald. Let me in."

Placing my right hand on the butt of the revolver behind my back, I opened the door with my left and ushered him inside.

Looking with a cold, appraising eye around my modest rooms, the current head of the most despicable family my own has ever known said with a disarming smile, "You have not done as poorly for yourself in this dastardly business of reporting as I would have thought, Stanton. Good for you."

Offering him coffee, which he accepted, I motioned for him to sit by my writing desk. "You disapprove of my profession?" I asked, preparing his coffee with his requested amounts of milk and sugar.

"It has its uses. You're an associate of Sherlock Holmes... What was it he said about the press?"

"Essentially what you just did... It is a most valuable institution if you only know how to use it."

Sipping his coffee and nodding, Ravenskald said, "And I do. Take William Randolph Hearst. His going to war with Pulitzer was exactly what I wanted, as was his making so much of the incident with the USS *Maine*. The Spanish-American War was essential to our progress. It's a shame he has taken lately to the errant myths of Jeffersonianism. Although Jefferson himself was an ally of ours to the absolute end of his days."

Having heard and read similar statements—the boasting and bragging of master chess players using a board the size of the world—from members of this shadowy familial power behind the banking and political systems of the majority of nations, I did not bother to react.

"I am sure you have not come all this way to talk to me about the plusses and minuses of the fourth estate?"

Putting aside his coffee, which I appreciated his not complaining about, Ravenskald looked me in the eyes, motioning for me to sit on my bed, not far from his chair.

"I know your background, Judah Stanton. I have followed your work for the newspapers and your interest in the occult. I applaud you on the discoveries you have made. Should I have wished it, they would have been made public, although you must see, wise as you are, that the masses are ill equipped to handle that level of truth. This is why my family has been the gatekeeper of occult knowledge for more than a thousand years."

Having nothing to lose by being open, I shook my head. "You have been the gatekeepers because you found it good for business. And your brand of the occult is not mine, although it no doubt pays much better."

Belching forth a derisive laugh, Ravenskald slapped his knee as further evidence of my idiocy.

"How naïve you Stantons are. I had honestly hoped for more from you, Judah. You have a bravery about you. I know you have seen things, faced things head on, from which lesser men have run. Our fortune became sufficient by the end of the 1600s. Not long before our two families first clashed in the time of the Caribbean pirates. This is not about money. You must never think that. This is about knowledge. Who has it... what they do with it. The ancient Mystery Schools of Egypt and Greece existed for a reason. And it is my wholehearted pursuit of knowledge that has brought me to these modest rooms today."

I had to admit to myself that Ravenskald's honesty was unexpected. I pressed him to continue.

"Our interests of course overlap, as have the affairs of our two families for several hundred centuries. Perhaps even longer. As you may know, the Ravenskald history and that of Orkney are intimately tied together. We have funded the work of the University of Edinburgh's Professor V. Gordon Childe at Skara Brae on the Mainland since 1927, a dig on which your brother has been employed."

I turned my head on some pretext or another to keep him from seeing my surprise. Turning back, I said, "Very few people know that."

Ravenskald laughed. "I make it my business to know what people tied to my projects are doing. Most especially Stantons. For instance—and do not for a moment consider this coincidence—your brother was part of an expedition funded by us in 1911 in the Andes."

"Hiram Bingham's discovery of Machu Picchu."

Again the bully laughed. "Discovery is far too strong a word. All secrets have their time to be revealed."

"Is my brother aware of who actually signed his cheques?"

"Irrelevant. But you should know, since we are being honest, that my family also funded the digs he was on with Sir Charles Leonard Woolley when he excavated the extravagant death pits of Ur. The Sumerians are more important than anyone knows, Judah. You should be proud of your brother. His work with TE Lawrence and Woolley on the Hittite City of Carchemish was without question of the very highest quality."

"British Naval Intelligence certainly thought so," I said, stunned by Ravenskald's revelations.

"They did indeed. But you need not be concerned that your brother is wound up inextricably in our web. The projects of most interest to your brother are not at present a focus of our own. One area only is meaningful for us now. And that is the funding and support of the scientific genius pushing the boundaries of what man can accomplish to surpass the work of God."

I could not help but grunt at the way his eyes brightened at the thought.

"There are lambs and there are lions. You and yours, for all your righteousness and morality, are lambs. It is the job, the truest destiny and purpose of the lion, to foster the genius in his work. To guide and to fund him. To provide him with material and human support. My ancestors did it with Victor Frankenstein and Abraham Moreau and I myself with Robert Peary Walton."

He had come to it at last.

"Is Walton alive? As you no doubt are aware, his former fiancée has asked for my assistance in finding him and his associate, Thomas Paris."

Ravenskald nodded. "As I just said, it is my business to know what those included amongst my employees are doing. Walton's no longer amongst them."

"And his assistant?"

Rising from his chair to lock the trio of mechanisms on my door, Ravenskald lowered his voice and told me all he knew of what had transpired with Walton and Paris since they had left London following the Uttersons' estate sale at Salisbury and Sons in March of '29.

When Ravenskald had come to the end of his tale the morning was gone and I found myself willing my eyes not to weep. "My God. How utterly horrific. I do not know how I shall ever find a way to tell Miss Beaumont the truth."

Raising his voice in the manner of a father correcting his son, Ravenskald said, "You shant. You must tell her that they were lost at sea on the way to do what no doubt would have been groundbreaking work in the South Pacific. Anything else would be needless torture. She came to you for closure, not details."

Finding myself in agreement, I asked, "Why are you here, Mister Ravenskald? Certainly a telegram would have sufficed were it only to tell me what has become of Walton and Paris..."

"Sometime in the next few days you are going to receive a delivery of journals and other papers and objects that will further serve to illuminate the details of this narrative, but for now I must impress upon you that Edward Hyde is without a doubt the most dangerous foe either of us has faced. He managed to not only elude but also murder two of my most skilled and seasoned hunters. Men with impeccable pedigree. Hyde has undertaken the most foul acts and heinous indiscretions. Ergo, he must be destroyed, and I believe that you can help."

As I poured and dressed a second cup of coffee for my guest, Ravenskald related to me his impressions of Hyde. He then turned his attention—and my head—by speaking of the device he called the Ezekiel Wheel and a black mirror with all manner of supernatural powers, the exact details of which he chose not to share at that time.

"Both items were stolen from my home in Switzerland. For any mere mortal to penetrate the walls of that fortress would be impossible. And yet Hyde was able to get in and out without detection."

Placing the coffee on the desk beside him as he rose again from his chair to stretch his muscled frame, I asked, although it was merely perfunctory, "Are you sure that it was Hyde?"

"Who else?" he asked, leaving the coffee for the moment untouched. "As I just told you, our ancestral home is impregnable. I keep in my employ a unit of Special Forces commanders who test its defences monthly. There are items in that castle that are priceless. Men would kill their mothers just to be able to touch them for a moment, to say they saw them and verify they exist. Only Hyde could have the ability to circumvent such multilayered security."

"And why does he want these objects? I am sure they would fetch a pretty penny on the black market..." Seeing a shadow pass over Ravenskald's vision, I added, "Which you no doubt already have in process..."

Slamming his fist into the surface of the desk so the coffee cup rattled on its saucer, Ravenskald hissed, "You again infer that this is a matter of money. It is not. Those objects—and others like them—could be used for no less than to upset the cosmic order. But that is not the aim of Edward Hyde. No, Judah. He has no doubt outgrown the body that he and Walton cobbled together for him. He is desperate for other means of survival and the mirror and wheel could, in time, provide them.

Asking him to shift to his left, I opened a drawer in my desk, pulling out the three letters Hyde had sent me and directing his attention to the following lines:

This composite body is no longer holding up. It cannot do the work I so often ask of it. The fingers no longer capable of the precision I require. This sewn-together face, part man, part boar, part jaguar, part ME. It's now become too obvious. No amount of makeup, no ingeniously made disguise can hide the truth away.

So I must find other ways, other helpers, other tastes.

I have just begun to eat.

"It appears your assessment is correct and fears well founded," I whispered, as he first read the lines I pointed out before reading each of the letters twice through while I sat in silence on the edge of my bed.

Closing his eyes and leaning back while keeping possession of the letters, Ravenskald said, "'Yours in spirit.' That is how he closes. I do not take this metaphorically. It was in the period between the dates on the second and third letters that he broke into my home. We will have a job to catch him, Stanton. But we must. And soon."

I will spare you the details of the conclusion of our conversation and parting of the ways, except to say that Ravenskald again mentioned that a parcel would be arriving for me within days and that I was to contact him after I had thoroughly digested its contents.

Locking the door behind me as he disappeared down the hall, I lay upon my bed and began to ponder all that he had told me, before turning my attention to the matter of Ravenskald's request—and my own compulsion—to assist him in Hyde's capture and destruction.

As you can well imagine, my age—sixty-eight years old—gave me the greatest pause, although rigorous and even dangerous adventuring after nearly seven decades upon Earth was not without its precedent, a fact of which I quickly reminded myself. There was Allan Quartermain, who gave his life at precisely my age while in the wilds of Africa in 1899, as his biographer, H Rider Haggard, reported it. Sherlock Holmes was somewhere in his sixties when he at last gave up his career. My friend John Watson, though wounded in the Boer War, could have remained active on cases well past that age. And perhaps most appropriate to the task now before me, Abraham Van Helsing (a *nom de guerre*) was in his seventies when he confronted the undead blood-drinker fictionalized by Stoker and re-styled as Dracula.

I say fictionalized because vampyres—the plague-carrying *nosferatu*, in the etymology of the Greeks and Slavs—are not a creation of bitter writers' minds. They are, most assuredly, real.

Perhaps one day I will share the story of how I know.

CHAPTER 35

I study the contents of the package, after attending to some urgent and heartbreaking matters.

O ut of the great respect I maintain to this day for Katherine Beaumont, I will refrain from setting down the particulars of our conversation later that day, as we sat together over a grim pot of tea in a drawing room in her father's home in Belgravia.

Knowing in my soul that Ravenskald was correct, I relayed to the poor girl that both of the men for whom she had been so concerned had been lost in a violent storm in the South Pacific without ever reaching the island. This lie of course covered many sins, the most crucial of which being that, having been lost in the vast waters of the ocean, there was no hope of recovering their corpses. Nor would it be possible to recover their belongings or for her to ever know what it was they had done on Moreau's mysterious island. In addition, it explained their lack of communication.

This terrible deed behind me, I sought to fill my time until the package of journals and objects arrived. Hyde's three letters in hand, I considered taking a tedious train trip to consult with Watson and Holmes, although I pushed the thought immediately from my mind. Best to leave them in the peace they had more than earned and not subject them to working with or keeping the company of one such as Simeon Ravenskald. Both these esteemed gentlemen knew well enough the dark deeds and machinations of this despicable family of influencers and manipulators. After all, the Ravenskalds had funded the operations of the "Napoleon of Crime" himself, Professor James Moriarty. Although, as a side note, I must point out that Holmes borrowed this overly generous phrase from a Scotland Yard inspector referring to one of Moriarty's associates, Adam Worth.

I spent the rest of Saturday and much of Sunday visiting the sites where the Rippers had murdered their seven victims. I know what you are thinking, Gentle Reader—there were only five. All I can do is ask you to trust me at present so as not to slow the current narrative down.

It was my hope that Hyde had left me clues in these places, but I found myself more than passing disappointed.

He was managing the game with the utmost cunning and cruelty, making his mysteries known to me only as it suited his will.

Checking into the offices of the *Evening Standard* first thing Monday morning, I followed up on a few easy leads and fact-checks pertaining to a number of articles I was working up on a variety of subjects before heading home in the mid-afternoon to await the arrival of the package.

Hearing horse and wagon beneath my window as the clock struck four, I looked out the window to find the postman lifting a good-sized parcel from the back of the wagon and glancing up to confirm the number of my building. Not willing to wait a moment more than necessary to have the package in my hands, I left my room and descended the steps, meeting him in the building's cramped foyer.

Scribbling my name on a crumpled receipt and accepting the bill of lading, I took the package and, glancing past the retreating postman into the street and then behind the stairs until I was sure that no one was watching, I made my way back up to my rooms. Locking the door without letting the parcel leave my arms, I placed it on the bed, slicing through the layers of twine holding together its plain brown packaging with a penknife from my pocket.

As I mentioned in my opening, the parcel contained a bloodstained, well-weathered haversack. Unbuckling its pair of leather straps, I found at the top two journals. I can tell you now that these were the ones penned by Robert Peary Walton prior to and during his time on Moreau's island and on Rousay. Beneath them were a Colt Cloverleaf revolver, schematics of several complex scientific instruments, a map marked in pencil of Walton's journey from the South Pacific to Rousay (with several stops along the way correlating with Captain Costa's journal—although I would not be able to confirm this for several days), and the journals of the three infamous doctors—Frankenstein, Jekyll, and Moreau.

Imagine my thoughts, the jolt of lightning that my deep, cultivated curiosity sent up my spine, as I ran my hands over these items; as I flipped through the pages of the journals that served as the foundation for not only Walton's misguided experiments, but the most frightful and well-selling Gothic literature of the last more than one hundred years! Though my fingers trembled, I lifted the Cloverleaf revolver, its walnut grips faded and cold to the touch.

Such dark visions of violence embraced me as I held it to my chest! Later, as I read a neatly typed letter from Simeon Ravenskald cataloging the contents and offering explanations and guidance on how I should proceed with them, I learned that this was the very same pistol that Hyde had used to murder Robert Peary Walton—although he had gone to some pains to make it seem a suicide. The pistol, I also knew, was the exact model used by Henry Jekyll to end his own life and, so he thought, that of Edward Hyde.

It was as fitting as it was macabre.

Feigning a fever due to overwork, I remained in my rooms the next several days, reading the five journals and doing my best to make sense of the schematics. It was clear that the stolen mirror and so-called Ezekiel Wheel could be used together to generate immense amounts of power—perhaps sufficient amounts to open doors to other dimensions.

Rubbing my tired eyes as Monday became Tuesday, I asked myself a single, simple question: If the devices shown in the schematics and mentioned in the second of Walton's journals could be used to *transfer Hyde's essence into a body*, could they also be *used to take it back out?*

My answer was a resounding, disturbing yes.

This was clearly Hyde's next move.

Pouring a generous dose of bourbon into a chipped and coffee-stained mug, I moved on to my next vexing query.

Where would it be safe for him to do so? The Orkney islands were out of the question. Ravenskald no doubt had them monitored—especially Rousay. Besides, his letter had mentioned that his people had moved the last of the machinery to an undisclosed and well-guarded location.

As well guarded as your ancestral fortress? I asked the air.

I almost expected an answer.

After a shave and bath late in the day on Wednesday, I checked into my office before having dinner with Miss Beaumont near her home. The poor child looked as though she had managed to sleep nearly not at all since our dreadful meeting the Saturday prior. Assuring her that I was not yet willing to let the case go cold, I talked in vagaries about various leads that I was pursuing, even as I silently resolved to make good on one of them the following day.

I must take the train to Lisbon, a journey of just over two full days, in order to speak with Gonçalo Costa's widow. Simeon Ravenskald confided to me that her husband had sent her a record of the fateful voyage from Moreau's island to Orkney, including the details of the hired boy's change of heart. This he did to no doubt further impress upon me Hyde's despicable, deadly viciousness. Perhaps the captain had also verbally shared with his wife some pertinent remembrances of the initial journey to the South Pacific island and the later journey to Rousay.

CHAPTER 36

What I learned in Lisbon from the Widow Costa.

Although I had made it clear to the Widow Costa that no special arrangements were required to meet me at the train—I would be happy to secure my own transportation to her home—I found waiting for me Costa's two daughters, Renata and Beatriz, who led me to an impressively appointed carriage.

During the five-mile journey to their newly acquired home, the articulate and friendly pair pointed out various sites, including their former neighborhood, in which a carriage such as this would have been unthinkable.

As we approached the house, which was reached by a gravel road lined with manicured trees and an abundance of flowers and shrubs, I noticed a look of embarrassment on the faces of the girls as I remarked on the stables, gazebo, and other structures on the perimeter of the property.

Their situation had been greatly improved due to the death of their father.

Being surrounded by such beauty and comfort while bearing the guilt of why one had it must truly be a terrible burden to bear.

As we reached the entrance to the lavish two-story home, with its wrought iron balconies and precision stonework, I half expected to see liveried staff emerge to take my bag and escort me to my room.

To my relief, at the front door appeared a beautiful woman in her forties, dressed and veiled in black, and two boys.

This was Mariana, and her sons, Agostinho and Aleixo.

"Senhor Stanton," Mariana said, bowing her head. "Welcome to our home." Giving the boy to her right a gentle nudge forward, she whispered, "Aleixo. Take Senhor Stanton's bag and take it upstairs to the room we have prepared."

Thanking the boy as he and his brother headed indoors, I then thanked Renata and Beatriz, who were following their brothers inside.

"You have a beautiful family," I said to the Widow Costa when we were alone.

As the carriage driver headed the horses for the stables, my hostess motioned that we would be going in the opposite direction, off to the side instead of entering the house.

"I thought it best that we talk privately, in the garden, about the matters for which you have journeyed to Lisbon," she said, leading me into a small but carefully cultivated area filled with all manner of flowers, shrubs, and hedges, amongst which were statues of angels, abstract sculptures, bird baths, and a central fountain that brought the design of the garden together in a glistening focal point.

Indicating that I should sit on a curved stone bench, the legs of which were sculpted ocean waves, the widow produced from beneath her shawl the journal Ravenskald had told me that she possessed in the letter that had accompanied the package from the Orkney islands.

Not knowing how to begin—although she had shown me she had the journal, the widow made no move to hand it to me—I said, "I am not sure what you were told, but my intention in coming here is to honor your husband by bringing his murderer—and all those who assisted this demon—to justice."

Clasping the journal to her chest, the widow sat beside me, careful to keep an open space between us. "I know that you are not *polícia* but *jornalista*. My husband did not approve of those who read or wrote too much. He would not approve of the education I am arranging for our sons in Geneva with the blood money that these brutal men have provided to us in exchange for Gonçalo's suffering and our own."

She looked at the house and its surroundings with nothing short of disdain.

"The man who made this possible is the one who sent me," I replied, choosing my words with care. In truth, I wished nothing more than to have her give me the journal and permission to sequester myself in my room to read it. "Simeon Ravenskald most ardently wishes to see this justice done. If he had any inkling of—"

"You are surprisingly naïve," the widow replied in an ungentle voice. "As was he. Money and power are nothing in the face of such a *demônio* as my husband describes in these pages. Baron Riviera thought to expand his holdings by agreeing to Ravenskald's demands. To first make my Renata sick and then to further punish her, as well as Beatriz, because Gonçalo dared to defy them. The money they give us, because it is replaced in their coffers in the blink of an eye, is a poor replacement. This property, Senhor Stanton, drowns in a sea of blood."

I wished to place my hand upon hers, which was lightly gripping the edge of the bench, in order to comfort her, but I knew I could not. "Why not sell the house and property and make a new start? Surely you would fetch a generous price for all of this splendor."

Her reply surprised me. "It is not mine to sell. The house, the carriage, the few staff these lords have supplied... none of this is ours. I am to be watched, Senhor Stanton, for the rest of my life. After all, even to the end, Gonçalo defied them, by paying the village boy to send me this journal. I told you that Agostinho and Aleixo are to attend school in Switzerland. What I did not reveal, though I choose to now, is that the decision was not mine. How could it be? Further insurance of my compliance for the Ravenskalds. Further anguish for me. Were events not as dire as your presence here at these men's command suggests, I would not be holding his journal now. They would have taken it for good and made me suffer for not sending it to them as soon as I received it without that *desgraçado* having to ask."

Finding my nerves suddenly set on edge, I requested the widow's permission to light my pipe, which she granted. Blowing a thick cloud of smoke into the late afternoon air, I ran my fingers through my hair, willing myself to settle down. How the Widow Costa was managing to keep from having a nervous episode I could not imagine.

But her children were fortunate to have a mother of such impressive fortitude and strength of heart.

"Please believe I wish to help," I said after a few moments of uncomfortable silence. "I am not in Ravenskald's employ. I have never spoken to Baron Riviera, nor do I wish to. You must understand... my family and the Ravenskalds have had an unpleasant relationship for many centuries. As you yourself have said, were not the situation dire, I would not even know your husband's journal exists."

"Tell me what you need."

Taking another long drag on my pipe, I leaned forward while still respecting the space between us. "I would, of course, need to read the journal. I will not take it with me. But I need to spend some time alone with it, to process all it says. To compare it to what I know of the circumstances and see if I can make sense of what transpired."

"Then you shall have it. And, if you have any pity for me at all, you will take it with you when you leave. As you know, Ravenskald took it from me for a time, and now I feel it is soiled."

Nodding my agreement and my thanks, I continued. "What can you tell me about your husband's thoughts on taking this commission to bring Walton to the island?"

It was at this point that I learned of Captain Costa's visits to the local parish priest and to the *curandeira* that I already shared. Having had considerable experience with seers, shamans, and others of that ilk, I found the *curandeira*'s supposed lack of insight to be another ploy.

Filing those facts away, I turned my attention to other matters. "It is my understanding that your husband had dinner with you while the *Boa Sorte* was docked in Lisbon." This had also been included in Ravenskald's letter. "I need you to tell me, in all the detail you can manage, what transpired between you. What did he tell you? I most especially need to know what he may have said in confidence that he did not dare to share in the journal."

Closing her eyes and laying the journal in her lap, the Widow Costa told me all she remembered of that horrible July night.

"I made Gonçalo's favorite dinner—*bacalhou* and *enchidos*—and made sure to have plenty of his favorite liquor, *ginjinha*, on the table. I had fed the two boys and Beatriz earlier in the evening and they were playing in their rooms. I tell you the truth, Senhor Stanton—we talked of nothings in front of the children and I had no sooner poured Gonçalo another glass of *ginjinha* and set about clearing the table than our door was broken open and the *soldados de infantaria* entered and dragged him away, despite my cries of protest. That was the last time I saw him. I attempted to board the *Boa Sorte* the following day, but the harbormaster's *rufiões* prevented me. I knew in my heart that he saw me, and this journal confirms it. Here, Senhor Stanton. There is nothing more I can tell you. Now you must read."

Taking the journal from her trembling hands, I headed for the house.

CHAPTER 37

I pay two surprise visits before leaving Lisbon.

As I have already shared with you the relevant contents of Gonçalo Costa's journal earlier in this narrative, I need not reiterate them here. It might be wise, before continuing, for you to re-read them, if you have the stomach to do so. They served me as equal parts revelation and confirmation of all I had discovered, been told, and surmised prior to reading them. This was clearly a man being frightened out of his wits. A man whose faith, family, and fortunes were crumbling before him despite a strong will and unwavering determination.

The news that the Ravenskalds had terrorized his family in the early 1700s, same as mine, made my commitment to seeing justice done for him and his family all the stronger.

It also gave me pause.

What Universal designs work upon our lives?

May these journal entries serve as a lesson for us all.

Of Captain Costa's theories, I can tell you only this. I too believe that his daughter Renata's fever was not an act of nature but a means of ensuring that he would do Simeon Ravenskald's will. As you have read, his widow also felt it to be true. I know only too well that Tom Paris was not from Orkney. And, most of all, I believe that the *curandeira*, Senhora Martinez, lied about what she saw.

More on her in a moment.

Costa's journal, the handwriting in which became more haphazard and harder to read with each dated entry, served to confirm that all that Walton had written and Ravenskald had told me was true. Their experiments had met with success. Walton had ultimately faltered, finally awakened from the nightmare in the guise of a dream to find his Nameless Angel, now named, had woven a web around him, but it had been too late. I almost felt sympathy for him, thinking of what he had aided Hyde in doing—against his will—to poor Tom Paris.

To Costa and his crewmen.

It was all too clear from Costa's entries that Edward Hyde was not one with whom to be trifled. He had outwitted them all.

Would he do the same to me?

Turning my mind to more practical thoughts, I began to plan next moves. The family who tried to make the best of their tragedies with stop and start laughter in the drawing room below me had no more need of my intrusion. I would leave as early the next morning as the carriage would be available to carry me away.

Although it was not the train station for which I would be headed.

I was determined to get the truth from the deceitful *curandeira* about all that she had seen and why she had chosen to lie.

*****

After a simple breakfast of coffee and buttered bread in a café in the city, I checked the four .41 caliber rounds I had procured through my contacts in London, which I had inserted into the Colt Cloverleaf before my departure. Satisfied that the pistol would perform if called upon to do so, I tucked it into my jacket pocket. I am hard pressed even now to explain why I chose this cursed weapon over my own tried and true police revolver, which I had left in London. The choice, however, proved to be inspired.

Having rented a bicycle from a local shop—and leaving my overnight bag with the owner as collateral and convenience—I made my way first to the Port of Balboa, where I knew the *Boa Sorte* to be docked. There I found her new owner, Costa's former navigator, who was as cool a customer as one could be as I asked him questions about the voyages on which Walton was a passenger.

Ravenskald had no doubt paid him well—many of the *Boa Sorte*'s pieces of equipment, piping, and the like looked to be new and a painting crew was hard at work above and below the decks. Perhaps he was also frightened enough by what he knew had happened to his predecessor and three of his former fellow crewmen not to tell me anything of value. Anything he was sure I did not already know.

Certain bits of this narrative, such as the argument during the storm near Moreau's island, are the result of this interview, brief as it was. Anything that could be useful to my pursuit of Hyde, however, I left the ship without.

Getting back on the rented bicycle, I headed for Senhora Martinez's cottage, grateful that the weather was on my side. Although my mind was heavy, the scenery outside of Lisbon was breathtaking and the ride for a time was pleasant.

After an hour, however, I found myself peddling harder in anger as I thought of the Widow Costa and her quartet of offspring, deprived evermore of enjoying these surroundings with the brutally murdered Gonçalo.

Arriving at the cottage, I patted the hidden Cloverleaf for reassurance and approached its oaken door.

Before I could knock, it began to open, creaking loudly on its heavy hinges. In the dim light just beyond, I could see an old woman's form. Although her grey and silver hair was as wild and tangled as one would expect, she met none of the other stereotypes for one of her profession. She was nearly as tall as I, with a straight back and unblemished face. Once upon a time, I imagine men had called her beautiful, and the ensuing years had only barely begun to alter that assessment. Her eyes shone brightly in the dim light of the cottage.

"Senhora Martinez?" I asked, fully knowing the answer but unsure how else to begin.

"What is it you want, senhor? I am deeply engaged at the moment. A rush job for a client. They are always in a rush. No one *plans*, eh? Perhaps you will return tomorrow, in the early morning?"

Her accent was thick but pleasant to the ears, like the Widow Costa's.

Do not let this sorceress charm you, I commanded myself. *Think always of the widow and her children.*

Shaking my head, I said with authority, "Tomorrow morning will not do. I have a train to catch this evening. I will make it worth your while."

Smiling wide enough to reveal that she still had all her teeth, the *curandeira* motioned me inside. As I took in the details of the room that I later incorporated into my text on Costa's useless visit, Senhora Martinez took a length of canvas from a shelf, throwing it over whatever it was she had been working on when I had arrived.

"As I say, always in a rush. Tell me what you want and I will tell you what it costs."

Moving to the door and engaging the lock, I pulled the Cloverleaf from my jacket pocket and turned around to face her.

To my utter surprise she let out a horrified cry and retreated into a corner, her hands raised to her face.

"Infernal instrument! Keep it away from me!"

Pressing the advantage, I drew closer to her, pistol outstretched and aimed at her heart. "You will answer all of my questions, witch, or I will kill you where you stand."

"Yes, yes!" she answered, pressing her body into the cold stone walls behind her. "Only put that devil's-device away!"

Keeping my distance but not lowering the Cloverleaf, I indicated that she should sit upon a stool in the middle of the space, well out of arm's reach from any of the potentially lethal instruments of her trade arrayed around the room.

"I want to know why you lied to Gonçalo Costa though he paid you for your services and desperately needed your help."

When she did not immediately offer an answer, I pulled back the hammer on the Cloverleaf, which prompted a thorough response.

"Ai, he paid me... but others paid me better! Paid me for the suffering I have all my life endured. Shunned, sequestered... forced to live in the woods. Threatened by husbands when wives succumb to childbirth. Slapped and cursed at when the tea leaves tell a story the client does not care to hear. God has given me these gifts—to all the first-born women in my family for generations back in time— and I am not rewarded, but *cursed*. So comes these men... sacks full of money. Interest in my gifts... I have seen you in my nightmares, Judah Philemon Stanton! You know who runs these men. You know the depths of his power! That of his family! Hundreds of years! You know the winged beasts and demons to whom they have sold their souls. I cannot speak their names... I pray you will not either!"

Taking in what she told me—some of which I knew, some of which I would later corroborate through other sources—I used the barrel of the Cloverleaf to indicate she should continue.

"If I would have told him what I saw—this evil creature Hyde, the ghastly operations, the murder of Walton's friend! He never would have gone. And I would not have lived! You ask me what I saw? I saw his destiny! His fate! Each man has his path, Judah Philemon Stanton—even you. I see yours clear as day! Shall I tell *you* what I see, as payment for Costa's life?"

Closing the space between us in an instant, I placed the barrel of the pistol just above her eyes, pressing it into her flesh. "Do not tell me a word about myself! You gave Walton a poison, which he used to kill three of Costa's crew... That is enough in itself to see you hanged. What else did you give him? *What else*?"

As much as I wished to get away from the shrieks erupting from the full-toothed mouth of the *curandeira*, I remained where I was, pressing the barrel into her forehead even deeper, until it started to bleed.

Wiping the blood from her eyes, she hissed, "Nothing of note! Some rare herbs and tinctures for their experiments... for the *transference*! I am sure you know full well, as do I, how that devilry all turned out! I have seen it—every detail of it—in my dreams! The things they did to Costa! To his crewmen! How Hyde rewards a girl with savagery who dares to take his coin. Such horrid things I've seen!"

Seeing the fear in her eyes, how she folded up her body like a recently beaten child, I moved a few steps back, though my arm still held the Cloverleaf level with her head. "How is it that you can see these things? It is not the mere fact of their coming to your cottage... I know of these things, sorceress, so do not lie to me."

"It is because of Hyde! He made himself known to me in the time that Walton was here. It was he who did the talking, he who made the requests, he who made my life a fractured living hell after promising to make me a *tlahuelpuchi* or *bruxa*, capable of shedding my skin as can he!"

I found myself repulsed. "To feed on the blood of infants? To transform into a rat or a raven? How can you wish such things?"

The *curandeira* shook her head and laughed at me dismissively. "So narrow minded, inclining to believe the Roman church's lies. Hyde showed me *power*. True power."

"How did he manage to do this?"

Pointing a long, crooked finger at the table behind her, the *curandeira* said, "By means of that scrying mirror there."

Knowing all I did of Hyde's use of mirrors as a doorway to our world, I did not bother to even glance at it, much less bother to move to the table.

Uncocking the pistol, I wiped cold beads of sweat from my forehead and backed toward the door, never for an instant taking my eyes from those of the now sobbing *curandeira.*

"You are paying the price for your mistakes," I said, unlocking the door. "He will not stop your torment. Not for an instant. And if you are connected, then he knows I have come and he knows what you have told me. The price will grow steeper indeed."

As I turned to leave, the *curandeira*, her sobs suddenly stopped, rose of a sudden from her stool. Whipping around while re-cocking the Cloverleaf, I watched in wonder and terror as her eyes bulged from their sockets and her tongue flailed in her mouth as her body straightened and her feet rose slowly from the floor, as though she were being lifted and choked by an unseen attacker.

I knew in an instant, it was Hyde.

As if to confirm it, as the *curandeira*'s lifeless body fell like a sack to the floor, I heard the bastard's wicked laugh echo through the cottage.

CHAPTER 38

A four-year chase begins.

T he sound of Hyde's mocking laughter would be a needle poking my eardrum time and time again in the handful of years to come, its chilling effect surpassed only by the occasional whispered taunt or cleverly concealed clue that he shared when I lost the trail or he otherwise grew temporarily tired of our game.

In the pages that follow, I will endeavor to be succinct, to encapsulate as best as I am able, the key events that led to the final resolution of my personal conflict with Edward Hyde. They span the years 1930 through early January 1935 and cover numerous countries and locations. There are names and events that any reasonably educated reader will recognize and remember.

At times in my pursuit, it felt as though I were Victor Frankenstein and Hyde were the Creature, always a taunting step ahead of me. There were also long periods of silence that allowed me to recover from the efforts and perils of such prolonged pursuit and to keep my positions at the *Evening Standard* and elsewhere so I could pay my bills.

Inspector Jonathan Newcomen aided me greatly in London and, dare I say, Simeon Ravenskald and his extensive contacts helped in large measure when my travels took me for prolonged periods to America.

I also owe a debt of gratitude (and more) to my brother Connor, an archaeology professor in New Jersey in the United States, whose role in this drama I soon shall introduce.

This difficult piece of the narrative, what would be the fourth and fifth acts were we in a Shakespearean drama, began on the most bitter of notes. I arrived back in London after my interviews in Lisbon to the news that a maid had found Daphne Utterson, niece to Henry Jekyll's lawyer, murdered in her bedroom in the apartment she still kept in the city after her family's relocation to East Sussex, most likely bludgeoned to death with Hyde's infernal hickory cane.

The fiend had been in London!

The time of the victim's death, as indicated on the coroner's hurriedly scribbled report, made it not twelve hours after I had witnessed Hyde take the life of the *curandeira*.

Given that it was Daphne who was the instrument by which Walton received the journal of Henry Jekyll before departing for the South Pacific, I could not at the time fathom why Hyde would end her life.

When I learned the truth, I remember that, for some long moments, I was wholly incapable of breath.

I shall leave that revelation for a more appropriate time.

As I sat at my desk, Inspector Newcomen beside me, carefully studying the autopsy photos, two nagging dilemmas pecked with their terrible beaks at the base of my skull:

The first—how to track the fiend as disembodied essence—was nothing I could answer, so I turned to the second, more practical and perhaps more urgent of the two:

How would I be able to keep Katherine Beaumont safe? The fiend would no doubt come for her. Hyde's interest in her was clear. It was only a matter of time before he would enact yet another insult on one of the four doctors through violence to their families and friends.

Determined to act with haste, I contacted Simeon Ravenskald, updating him on my visit to Lisbon, the brutal murder of Daphne Utterson, and my concerns regarding Miss Beaumont.

True to form, he professed to know of both the murder and the details of my visit to Lisbon, which combined to make me more than a little uncomfortable.

He then sent to me the following telegram:

AUGUST 1930, CASTLE RUSHEN, ISLE OF MAN

JUDAH:

FOLLOWING THE EVENTS THAT HAVE TRANSPIRED AS OF LATE, I HAVE MOVED MY COMMAND CENTER FROM OUR ANCESTRAL HOME IN SWITZERLAND TO OUR STRONGHOLD IN TIMES OF WAR.

AND BELIEVE ME, SIR—THIS IS NOW A TIME OF WAR.

AN UPDATE: SINCE OUR LAST CONVERSATION, I HAVE DIRECTED A TEAM OF SPECIALISTS TO SET ABLAZE—TO BIBLICALLY RAZE—ALL OF THE BUILDINGS ON MOREAU'S FORMER ISLAND.

SHOULD HYDE TRAVEL THERE TO USE ITS FACILITIES, HE SHALL FIND IT ALL BUT BONE AND ASH.

MY TEAM IS FURTHER DIRECTED TO SOW ITS ACRES WITH SALT.

AS YOU ARE AWARE, THE ORKNEY LABORATORY HAS BEEN STRIPPED OF ALL USEABLE INSTRUMENTS AND MACHINERY. HYDE SHALL ALSO FIND IT USELESS. I HAVE ARRANGED FOR CONTINUAL SURVEILLANCE SHOULD HE BE SO FOOLISH AS TO TRY.

DO I THINK HE WILL? I DO NOT. BUT ALL EFFORT MUST BE MADE TO THWART HIS ABILITY TO INHABIT ANOTHER BODY.

OR BODIES.

KNOWING YOU AS I THINK I DO, YOU HAVE ALREADY SKIMMED THIS TELEGRAM FOR MISS BEAUMONT'S NAME, AS I AM WELL AWARE THAT HER SAFETY IS FOREMOST IN YOUR MIND. I WILL SEND SOMEONE FOR HER WITH ALL HASTE. MAKE HER READY, JUDAH. IT IS YOU SHE TRUSTS. IT IS YOU TO WHOM SHE WILL LISTEN.

WE HAVE ADDED CONSIDERABLY TO THE CASTLE'S SECURITY GIVEN THE BREACH IN SWITZERLAND, BOTH BY CONVENTIONAL MEANS AND WITH THE AID OF WARDING. AN ADVANCED COPY OF OUR MUTUAL FRIEND DF'S "PSYCHIC SELF DEFENSE" HAS PROVEN TO BE USEFUL.

I TRUST, BEING AS INTELLIGENT AS YOU ARE, THAT I NEED NOT SPEND THE INK TO EXPLAIN TO YOU WHY THIS IS OUR HOME IN TIMES OF WAR.

WE WILL MEET AGAIN SOON TO FORMULATE A PLAN TO DEAL WITH OUR DEVIL. IT IS BEST THAT I REMAIN HERE TO GREET YOUR KATHERINE UPON HER ARRIVAL.

UNTIL THEN I REMAIN—

YOUR OBEDIENT COLLABORATOR—

SIMEON RAVENSKALD

Despite Ravenskald's somewhat reassuring words, I knew that I was taking a risk in sending Katherine to Castle Rushen. It would not be beyond my old family enemy to use her as nothing less than bait to bring Hyde within range of his formidable private army— although the question of the means by which even the most elite military killers in the world could fight a disembodied demon was still well beyond my faculties to answer.

And Ravenskald, as always, was correct... I am well familiar with the design and history of Castle Rushen, as well as the occult work of our friend, DF... which stands for Dion Fortune. She and I worked together on several intriguing cases over the years, going back to her theories that deceased Eastern European soldiers had attached themselves to young British fighters during World War I. I was also of some minor assistance in clearing her rooms of a nasty energy when she inadvertently conjured a *tulpa* of Fenrir, the ferocious wolf of Norse mythology.

Hyde himself being a form of *tulpa*, I knew that Ravenskald's mention of Dion's book was deliberate and meant to draw my attention.

As to Castle Rushen. For those readers familiar, I promise to be succinct. In order to understand the Ravenskalds, one must understand the places they call home.

Especially in times of war.

Castle Rushen, built by the Kings of Mann—longtime Ravenskald allies—in the late twelfth century, consisted at first of nothing more than a utilitarian keep. In the ensuing hundreds of years—long past the time of its last king, Magnús Óláfsson, who died within its walls in 1265—the castle was converted into a proper medieval fortification with the addition of towers, walls, and gatehouses.

To this very day, in order to enter the keep, one must find a way to cross a drawbridge, fortified gatehouse, and an area between two portcullises where potential invaders will meet an onslaught of attacks from unseen assailants arrayed around and above them.

There are other features best left unmentioned.

Evidence of the castle's long history as a fortress for the powerful includes a clock tower built at the behest and expense of Queen Elizabeth in 1597, when the English controlled the island.

When I say the English, it is according to the pages of history.

It was well before that time that the Ravenskalds had made it their own, just another means of coercion and bargaining as they built their leviathan-like empire.

After the time of the Norse-Gaelic rulers, the castle was controlled from everyone from Dungal MacDouall and Robert the Bruce in 1313 to Edward Longshanks soon thereafter.

From the early fifteenth century, the Stanley family, under the title of either king or lord of Mann, maintained it.

The Stanleys, as you no doubt will have guessed, are longtime Ravenskald allies, crucial players in their carefully engineered instigation of the English Civil War, when Lord Stanley and his kin at the time were assigned the role of Royalists while others were employed to balance the scales on the side of Oliver Cromwell.

You must remember—the key to the Ravenskald juggernaut is accumulation of wealth and consolidation of power no matter the outcome of the events they engineer.

Were it not so sinister, one would call it brilliant.

Following the Restoration, the castle was converted to an administrative center. It was during these years—when my pirate ancestor Joseph inaugurated the course of conflict between the Ravenskalds and Stantons—that the Ravenskalds, led by their patriarch Athelstan, assisted by his twin sons, Absalom and Adonijah (note the Anglo-Saxon and biblical names, a family practice on both sides of our conflict), benefited beyond comprehension by what history has come to call the Golden Age of Piracy. It was in Castle Rushen that Adonijah met with the traitor to the crown and Stuart supporter George Seton in September 1717. Seton, due to hang, had been freed from the Tower of London thirteen months earlier by unwitting allies of the Ravenskalds—working as they all were for the exiled Old Pretender—while Athelstan and his sons were also working with agents in the employ of George the First.

I trust you see how this works.

In the 1800s, the castle became a prison and asylum for the insane.

All the more to make it their stronghold. Impenetrable and horrific in its dangers.

Potent in its hauntings.

A ready means to punish those who dare defy them.

*****

A few days after I received Ravenskald's telegram, I met with Katherine Beaumont in the drawing room of her home, convincing her to trust me in the matter of going to the Isle of Man, to which, after some resistance, she agreed. As I was taking my leave, I received a phone call from Inspector Newcomen, who reported yet another death with which to contend—a death, most thankfully, not related directly to Edward Hyde. That masterful portrayer of monsters, Lon Chaney, who had consulted with the young inspector about him and his uncle for his role as Burke in *London after Midnight* and with whom I had spent a handful of pleasant evenings over the years, had succumbed to cancer, preventing him from portraying that most quintessential of all pseudo-mythic monsters, Count Dracula.

I cannot but feel that Stoker would have much preferred Chaney's interpretation to that of Bela Lugosi.

Then again, it is probably wisest to leave the theatre criticism to my colleagues in that field.

Lest you think this mention of Dracula random, best you now read on.

Chapter 39

Enter the vampires.

Amongst the papers of Joseph Stanton—of which there are regrettably few—there are passing mentions of a number of benevolent ancient organizations charged with keeping the balance of Light and Dark in the face of other ancient organizations whispered to have given their souls—and blood—in exchange for power and wealth.

Although these organizations—lodges, orders, councils, and the like—date back at least to the times of the Sumerians, Babylonians, and Egyptians, most of what we know about them—even in the occult circles in which I travel—is based on whispers and fragments of documents and diaries.

One of these organizations, which I here shall call *SQ*, oversaw an order of knights who swore eternal allegiance to a saint of which there is no mention in the hagiographies. This secret saint I shall refer to here as *G*—a purposeful overlap with one of the focal points of the Freemasons.

The SQ and the knights devoted to G still do exist, so I must be discrete.

Joseph refers to a companion with whom he had a rather tempestuous relationship during his days *Out on the Account*. A Scottish Highlander, he is said to have sailed with the notorious Blackbeard and other key captains during the Golden Age of Piracy. Charged with serving as scribe under the nom de guerre of "Quill," this pirate kept careful diaries—stolen by Crown Agents in 1724, recovered, and then eventually lost to the sand and the sea decades later—of not only the public events of his time but the private. His dealings with both the SQ and the knights devoted to G are said to be extensive and tied to a number of biblical objects of which I now know the Ezekiel Wheel to be only one.

There are eleven others, some of which I have seen.

Within these ancient organizations were specially trained warrior-monks from many countries and cultures tasked with hunting and eliminating monsters.

One such monster is the vampire.

Laugh not, my skeptical reader. As I have mentioned, Bram Stoker's story may have been metaphorical, though not mythological. Vampires do exist—in Eastern Europe, in China, on the West African Coast, and on the islands of the Caribbean.

A close friend and colleague, the Protestant minister turned (in truth, recruited by the SQ) Catholic priest, Montague Summers, has undertaken two thorough studies of the vampire: *The Vampire: His Kith and Kin* (1928) and *The Vampire in Europe* (1929).

My ancestor Joseph fought a number of these demons, which nearly took his life.

I will admit it now, although I was less than honest in my opening:

It is, to this day, part of my family's work.

It is this detailed knowledge of vampires—to which I am privy through an impeccable network of sources—that allowed me to act without hesitation when, in February 1931, after having no contact from or evidence of Edward Hyde for many months, I was informed through my contacts in the SQ about Peter Kürten, whom the German press had dubbed "The Vampire of Düsseldorf" and the "Düsseldorf Monster."

Kürten was accused of committing a series of chilling murders and sexual assaults in that city during the whole of 1929—nine murders in August alone—that provided his moniker. Here is what I found of interest. In the years before these bloodthirsty acts, Kürten had amassed an impressive police record for relatively petty crimes, such as arson. He had attempted murder prior to his spree and was usually unsuccessful. He was unorganized and inefficient.

I should mention, in the interest of thorough disclosure that, after his arrest in 1930, he confessed to the 1913 murders of a nine-year-old girl in Mülheim am Rhein and a seventeen-year-old girl in Düsseldorf.

So what do we make of his mutilations, blood drinking, decapitations, and other ultra-deviant acts during 1929?

It is my contention that he was a bit of a rehearsal, a warmup, for Edward Hyde.

As the fiend had played the Nameless Angel for Robert Peary Walton by whispering in his ear, Hyde was at present escalating to possession.

A killer with prior experience was absolutely essential.

The crime reports from Düsseldorf, which I have thoroughly examined, match in myriad ways the crimes committed by Hyde at Rousay in Orkney and elsewhere. His mode of dress provides a clue.

He was playing the *wampyr* as actors were playing him.

To further my confidence in my theory, near to the time of Kürten's execution in early July 1931, I received a visit from a friend of my brother Connor, the journalist turned successful playwright John Balderston, who had attended Columbia University in New York while my brother was lecturing there. After working as a journalist in Philadelphia for a handful of years, Balderston moved to London as chief correspondent for the *New York World*. This was 1915 and I was happy to fulfill my brother's request to befriend him. In truth, we had a great deal in common, in both vocation and avocation.

In 1927, Balderston, already a reasonably successful playwright, was hired to update Hamilton Deane's *Dracula* for a new production on Broadway to star the Hungarian Bela Lugosi. Florence Stoker, Bram's strong-willed widow, disliked the producer but was amicable to Balderston, whose previous plays she admired.

If you saw this excellent (so I hear) production, either in New York, Los Angeles, or with the touring company, you will notice the absence of two key characters—the Texan Quincey P. Morris and the Honourable Arthur Holmwood. Deane, to accommodate an actress in his company, had rewritten Morris as a female.

So goes the official explanation.

In truth, this change of gender for Deane and their elimination altogether by Balderston was by personal request from Morris, made to the playwright through me.

How I know Quincey, and the fact that he was still alive to make the request after his encounter with Dracula, is a tale for another time. Although I shall whet the reader's appetite here by teasing that we met during my time on a case with Holmes and Watson. I will also share some further details a little later when I relate a conversation with my brother.

What brought Balderston to my office in summer '31 was his latest commission—an adaptation of Frankenstein, set to open the following year.

He asked for access to Frankenstein's journal.

I readily complied.

For a price, which he would pay in information.

Balderston, being a journalist, was not content to trade on the trope of the horror genre, following the novels note for note. He was of a peculiar, exacting mind, and he wished for firsthand accounts. His knowledge of the rites of ancient Egypt and the curious relationship of Francis Bacon and William Shakespeare (which plays a not insignificant part in the story of my pirate ancestor) made him a valuable ally in the circles in which I run.

"What do you know of the rise in vampiric acts tied to murderers and sexual deviants?" I asked him one evening in my modest rooms in Fleet Street, as I held the pieces of Frankenstein's journal tantalizingly in my hands.

"A sign of these uncertain times, perhaps," Balderston said, lighting a cigar and leaning back in his chair to enjoy the first inhale. "The markets, the uncertainty in Germany, the rise of the cinema..."

"Of course," I answered, lighting a cigar of my own. "I owe you congratulations. Browning's film adaptation, based of course on your play, is a smash."

Waving his hand dismissively in a swirling cloud of smoke, Balderston smiled. "I would have done it differently, of course. And I doubt very much that the speech they gave to Edward Van Sloan's Van Helsing cautioning the audience that vampires are real will survive in the film in the future. The executives at Universal are already concerned about the effect it will have on religious groups. But back to the rash of vampirism. The world is getting bigger, Judah. And the powers that be don't like it. A few control the many. The masses are being systematically drained to feed the elitist few. But the masses interpret this literally and a few have followed suit. It shall only get worse. Now... I am due to have a draft for the producers within the week, so... may I?"

He was referring of course to the journal, which I promptly handed over.

We spoke for as long as the cigars remained about his thoughts on Kürten and other matters, the details of which I have promised not to disclose.

As I lay on my bed that evening, I thought of Simeon Ravenskald.

If the sort of *symbolic* vampires, feeding not on the blood but on the *energetic essence* of others, as with the earliest popular vampire tales, that Balderston was alluding to also existed, then that bastard was their king.

Such are not the thoughts conducive to a sound and peaceful sleep, a luxury I would forego for several years to come.

*****

Ask any investigator, be it journalist or police—there is nothing more frustrating, more mentally debilitating and emasculating, than the trail going cold due to inaction by the suspect.

This was the case from July of '31 to May of '32. Although Newcomen, Ravenskald, our networks, and myself remained active in our inquiries and vigilance, it was impossible to investigate each case of murder or sexual assault that came across our desks. This is a cruel and heartless world, especially in this decade, when people are poor and afraid and countries with breathtakingly destructive weapons of war are at each other's throats, shaking their metaphorical fists in tandem with their literal ones.

All we could do was wait for Hyde to come to us, or to be so obvious in his work that it served to be a signature.

In May of '32, he did both.

On the third, in my office at the *Evening Standard*, I received the following letter:

Mayday, mayday, MAY DAY!

Greetings, my good son.
Been awhile, ain't it?
I was quiet for awhile... I shant be no more.
Back again I am... up to smash n slash 'em tricks.
With a bit a flair for laughter.
Try what ya try, my son—I know full well yer troubles... you will never nap again.
Ya must not have a doubt, I am knockin' back about
And I have just begun ta drink.
You're invited ta the Brink.
After Nod, cold Cain went North
Which is where he was Reborn.
Wilted Lilly, corruptive pistil
My stamen it ain't thistled
There are ways into a whore—
Danker, darker doors
God, how I did slurp... and lick and thrust and hurt!
Yours in Spirit—(not for long!)
Ha ha ha.
And now I'm gone...

The next morning a report came over the wire that brought the crux of the letter to light.

In Stockholm, Sweden (After Nod, cold Cain went North), in the so-called Atlas neighborhood, a streetwalker named Lilly Lindeström was discovered in her apartment, her head smashed in and not a drop of blood in her body.

Wilted Lilly, corruptive pistil
My stamen it ain't thistled
There are ways into a whore—
Danker, darker doors
God, how I did slurp... and lick and thrust and hurt!

While I am choosing to refrain from specifics, the preceding lines of Hyde's taunting missive match without a doubt the modes and methods of the assault and what came after.

I choose to tell you this—near the body was a ladle.

God, how I did slurp...

More of his games of vampirism!

The police had interviewed Miss Lindeström's (extensive) client list.

Not a single arrest was made.

As with the women who fell to Jack the Ripper, justice is not done. Most of her neighbors and clients will all too soon forget.

Hyde's barely revised homages to that evil entity's letters aside, there was one more line that gave me pause:

Yours in Spirit—(not for long!)

In little more than a month, I would learn just what that meant.

CHAPTER 40

To America… and my brother.

As the Lockheed Vega 5b began its landing at New Metropolitan Airport in the American state of New Jersey, I reflected on the breathtaking views—and more than a few heart-stopping moments—since I had left London as the red aeroplane's sole passenger a few days earlier.

My pilot, a man of few words in the employ of Simeon Ravenskald, was, I suppose, one of the best available, although, having never before traveled by air, I had no one with whom to compare him.

After all, it had been but weeks since Amelia Earhart had made her solo transatlantic flight in this very model of plane.

Half a day later, we landed in Newfoundland, a beautiful land from what little I saw of it. After sandwiches and coffee, the excitement of the novel events of the day overwhelmed me and I took myself to bed.

As the Vega came to a chattering stop on the airstrip in the growing city of Newark, I stretched my legs as best I could and looked out the window to see my brother, Connor, awaiting me, smiling like a schoolboy at our long-delayed reunion.

Thirteen years my junior—my parents had quietly referred to him now and again as "The Surprise"—Connor was an archaeologist, as I have mentioned, as well as holding the position of professor at Pinelands State University, a prestigious institution whose education, although not its pomp, was on par with that of the Ivies.

"How was your turn as a bird?" my brother asked, his British accent all but vanished due to his years in America and abroad.

"I much prefer the train," I said, embracing him.

"Spoken like a true son of Britannia." Extricating himself from my long, entwining arms, Connor picked up my suitcases. "No hotel, by the way. You will be staying with us. Emma insists on it. And Uriah will be coming in by train from Manhattan special tomorrow to see you. He is quite proud of the work he is doing at the *Times*."

Too tired to argue, I nodded. I would not admit it—also like a true son of Britannia—but the idea of home-cooked meals and a bed upon which not a thousand men had laid their weary backs appealed to me no end.

That, and the fact that Ravenskald's men would have had a much easier time watching over me at the hotel he had secured— near to Lakehurst Naval Air Station—than at my brother's home.

Making our way to the parking area, I was surprised to see my brother approach a two-tone black and medium blue automobile and proceed to place my bags in the spacious back seat.

"This is yours?" I asked, duly impressed.

"It is, elder brother," he answered, indicating for me to take the front passenger seat. "A Wolseley Hornet. Two years old, actually."

As we headed for his home, I could not help but remark, as older brothers will, "I did not know there was such excellent money in professorships and archeological digs…"

"Save it, my good son," Connor answered. "Your *inference* is no inference at all. Yes… I have been part of digs funded by our supposed enemy."

"Supposed?"

"Please, Judah." Connor's voice had taken on such a tone as to make me think that *he* was the elder sibling. "Life is complicated enough. From Washington to Baltimore to New York City, there is a vast web of espionage and sabotage being spun by agents from Germany, Japan, and Russia. The election of our family friend Franklin Delano to the presidency has opened up a new world of possibilities for both alliances and enemies. Moscow in particular is pushing hard for diplomatic recognition, which means an embassy in Washington. We must not limit the Stanton family mission to only offering balance against a single force of evil. The Ravenskalds are only one of several internationally connected families maneuvering to undermine our democracy. And, let us not forget that you are not here on family holiday. You are here as part of an alliance with Simeon Ravenskald, with whose purposes we are unquestionably at present aligned. The ransacking of the laboratory at the university is causing considerable concern. Some colleagues in the biology and chemistry departments were doing advanced experimentations in a number of classified areas."

My eyes grew wide at this last. "Which means the U.S. military."

"Yes, and other interests as well. Do not say the name—I hear it forming on your tongue like water turning to ice. There are things of which you have not been made privy, brother. You know of course, that my longtime favored mentor is Professor Vellum-Verlag."

"I do indeed," I answered, having honestly forgotten.

Which was thoroughly inexcusable.

Edgar Vellum-Verlag—rare book and object collector and dealer—oversaw his generations-old family business, also in New Jersey, while keeping an impressive schedule of travel around the world in search of same. Rumor had it that E.V.'s Antiquarian Books and Optical Oddities had long been a meeting place for all manner of power brokers and international criminals.

Connor had made himself cozy with a veritable viper's den of dangerous men.

And he with a wife and (albeit grown) child.

Due to the demands of his schooling and early struggles as he sought to establish himself, he and Emma had waited until they had passed their fortieth year to have Uriah.

Bringing me out of my concerns and reveries, Connor continued. "Edgar is not the scoundrel people profess him to be. He holds no seat on the SQ and, as far as I know, he has never participated in any of the counterbalance rituals of our enemies. Enough of him for now. The lab is what is important. Parts and pieces of various apparatus were taken, as well as a plethora of schematics and some tissue and other samples. I am sure Mister Ravenskald will share the details if he chooses."

Nodding, I allowed myself to believe with all my heart a fact I had been preventing myself from embracing.

It was the work of Edward Hyde.

"There is something you aren't telling me, Connor. Don't make me hear it from…"

"Very well," Connor answered. "There was something else in the underground lab. Something called the Jeshua Cask. I am certain you have—"

"Bloody well right I know of it!" I said, grasping the doorframe as Connor took a turn at a higher than advisable speed. "Purported to contain the dried blood of Christ."

If he had enjoyed my fright, he did not show it. "Not purported, Judah. Fact. Since you know about the cask, you also know it is but one of a dozen legendary objects of Biblical or equally ancient origin."

"I do indeed. I have heard rumors of some… a bowl, a blade… Most are said to be lost to time."

"Some are. Others are not. To possess them is the equivalent of possessing the Spear of Destiny. And you know how that's been contested."

"I do," I said, finding myself uncharacteristically losing my patience. "As has this conversation, to a degree. Tell me what you know, Connor. Tell me what it means. Why I was put on a private plane at great expense and brought here."

Letting go a breath as he made the decision to comply, Connor said, "There were two objects taken by Hyde from the Ravenskald stronghold in Switzerland…"

Suddenly I understood.

The mirror and Ezekiel Wheel.

"Which are also part of the twelve…" I whispered.

We drove the additional miles in a heavy, contemplative silence.

*****

After a hearty chicken dinner—fried American style—followed by a generous slice of peach cobbler with ice cream, Connor and I left Emma to her knitting and made our way to a small shack behind their cottage home, overlooking the Manasquan Inlet, for good cigars and brandy.

And a serious discussion about what it was we faced.

"I have to admit," I said around the tip of the cigar, "your considerable risks have certainly come with rewards."

Connor nodded, pulling several books from the crammed shelves around us. "I am not a bit ashamed. The work I do is important, and I do it well. Now, before we get into the lore… What word of you from Quincey Morris? He could be of service with some of this."

"Forced retirement in Texas. His extensive adventures have taken their toll beyond the natural progression of age. His letters since we parted company in '94 have grown scarcer every year. He paid a heavy price to capture his final prey. And then there was the matter of the count…"

"Unfortunate," Connor answered, flipping through one of the books in search of something specific. "His experiences with various creatures in Korea, the South Seas, and South America are unique. And that beastly bit in Sumatra…"

"Of which we are never to publicly speak," I reminded him. "Quincey is certainly one for bats… and rats…"

"Indeed. Have a look at this." He passed me the book, which smelled of dust and age. In the center of a page of tiny text was a charcoal drawing of a man-bat.

"The camazotz," I answered, flipping past the page to others filled with various lore of vampires and other supernatural creatures. "Mayan, correct? Said to be able to cut a man's head from his shoulders with its knife-like nose."

Pouring us both another brandy, Connor replied, "I am glad there is no scoffing in your tone, dear brother. These things are all too real, despite the desires of the elite to fund books, plays, and films guaranteed to make them appear a fantasy. There is just released another one—*The Dream of David Gray*."

"C.T. Dreyer's film," I said. "That's not its name in Denmark, you know. There they call it *Vampyr*. I have yet to see it."

Connor raised a brow. "Why would you, having seen these monsters and many others like them for real?" Opening another of the books, he turned it around to face me. "With this one, I have firsthand experience, at least in the sense of archaeological proof."

Placing my finger over the frightening claws and fangs of the camazotz before closing the book I held in my lap, I answered, "You certainly have my attention."

Looking at the book my brother held, I saw before me a series of photos of petroglyphs of what appeared to be mummified men dancing in a circle as a golden beam of brilliant light engulfed them.

"These are the Aztec priests of the flayed god Xipe Totec. In honor of him, they would skin their captives alive and feast upon their flesh. Afterwards, they wore the skin in a secret ritual we know virtually nothing about."

"Vulgar," I answered, unable to turn away.

"This," he said, handing me yet another book, "is the *obayifo*. From the West African coast. Our ancestor Joseph was there. It is a vampire–witch hybrid. Old women making pacts with some demon or another. Sucking the blood of preferably children through invisible means, although they are often witnessed as balls of light. The Haitian version, brought there by African slaves, where it mixed with the French *loup-garou*, is the similarly named *loogaroo*. In the Philippines they are called *aswang*, or *danag*, or *mandurugo*. There are, of course, versions amongst the Dutch and English, as well as the Romanians. The Hasidei Ashkenaz called them *estries*, similar to the Italian *strega* or Greek *lamia*. The theme is one of cannibals feasting on blood and corpses. Like vampires, one can kill them by impalement on a sharpened stake. If, that is, they materialize long enough to capture them. In the darkest lore of the *obayifo*, they remove the skins of their victims, and hang them on the Jumbie tree."

"My God!" I exclaimed, rising from my chair, book still in hand. "Joseph Stanton wrote in letters of the Jumbie!"

Closing his book hard for emphasis, Connor said, "Exactly right! And your Edward Hyde now has several of the items Joseph and the other pirates of his time were so desperate to get their hands upon. He is no doubt using the methods and rituals of the Aztec priests of Xipe Totec and the *obayifo* to quench his thirst for blood until he can construct a suitable body."

I nodded in dumb agreement. "There was a *curandeira*, in Lisbon... he promised to make her, as she called it, a *tlahuelpuchi* or *bruxa*. More maddening names of this seemingly universal entity. And this bit about hanging flesh upon the Jumbie tree... skin grafting is an integral part of what these damned doctors... Moreau and the rest... were up to. It cannot be coincidence."

Draining his brandy glass in a single go, Connor whispered, "Nor is his ransacking a laboratory so close to your brother's home."

CHAPTER 41

Mayhem and murder, '32 and '33.

I arrived home to London a few days after my unsettling, eye-opening meeting with my brother in an anxious, irritable mood. Although I had visited the ransacked laboratory, I was able to offer nothing in the way of analysis or additional clues. Adding to the stress, my nephew Uriah had made it clear to me that he had no intention of abandoning his chosen life as a journalist, no matter the strength of my case advising against it, so our rare and precious afternoon together wound up utterly wasted. As a result, I found myself unable to mind my manners or suffer the fools that paraded daily into and out of my office my first week back, looking for publicity for their businesses or angling to stir up a row of one sort or another using the instruments of the Fourth Estate.

My editor, four days in, suggested that I take a few days off, his tone circumventing any possibility on my part of refusal.

The months passed this way, with my inability to focus and build good will with almost anyone, through the summer and into the fall, with no word of Hyde nor any clues as to where he had set up his required facilities.

It was not until early autumn 1932 that the trail again grew warm.

It was Hyde again who made it so.

His target was New Orleans, the mysterious city called The Crescent, so rife with the lore of voodoo, séance, and the secrets of the Cajuns and Creoles in its cemeteries and swamps.

To my *Evening Standard* office he sent a dirty, crumpled envelope containing an article from September 1932 in the *New Orleans Times Picayune*, detailing the arrest and hanging of two brothers, John and Wayne Carter, admitted vampires who fed from the wrists of their victims each evening. Who knows for how long their crimes, committed in the French Quarter in their second-floor apartment at Royal and St. Ann Streets, would have gone on unnoticed—the police found a pair of corpses and four tied and gagged victims when they entered—if an eleven-year-old girl had not escaped and told the police.

Scrawled in red (His blood? Someone else's?) upon the paper were the words:

A precious pair, a demon's prayer. Made them drink, made them swear...

How many more go unaware??

I've plenty more ta spare.

Then there was nothing, not a word or bragged-on deed, until spring of '33.

It is a damned difficult reality that life is not like a novel. There are, as you have witnessed, gaps in the narrative where virtually nothing happens. My much more talented friends of the pen preach the arts of *heightening* and *compressing*. But this particular narrative—although dressed in the trappings and tropes of the adventure novel and Gothic horrors so popular with the public—is so firmly held by the facts that birthed it that I am bound to summarize these gaps as succinctly as I can and concentrate on the relevant periods of action.

It is a truth that I have learned through many decades of study and experience that we can weigh the times in which we live in a moral, political sense by the monsters that they breed.

Nowhere was this more prevalent in the timeframe of this story than in that rising Leviathan of an occult-obsessed military state, Germany herself.

If you have even a more than passing interest in secret societies and their rites, you have no doubt heard of Thule and Vril. The Hermetic Order of the Golden Dawn and the Ordo Templi Orientis. Names like Blavatsky and Crowley.

There are others, devoted to demonic ideas and demons made manifest through complex rituals and the manipulation of electricity, against whom my family has fought for more than two hundred years.

Societies that would make most horrendous use of a disembodied, cannibalistic, vampiric lunatic such as Edward Hyde.

It was nearly a decade earlier, in 1923, that Fritz Kloppe founded the Organisation Wehrwolf, formed in response to the French occupation of the Ruhr. This group of ruthless fighters lived up to its name in their bloodlust and degradations.

From as early as 1911, the German political machine also drew its inspiration from the thinly veiled nationalist and then Nazi propaganda masquerading as monster stories, written by Hanns Heinz Ewers, a tool of Goebbels and Rohm. In November 1932, his novel, *Rider in the German Night*, was published after he had met with Hitler for forty-five minutes at the future Fuhrer's headquarters the prior year, where Adolph requested a hero's tale worthy of inspiring the growing Nazi party.

Stories have power, Innocent Reader. You must never forget this.

A colleague reported that well over sixteen thousand storm troopers, SS, and Hitler Youth were in attendance at the gravesite of the hero upon which the book was based.

I mention Ewers not only to illustrate the power of the Word—for he who controls it controls the World—but because of one of his acquaintances, Erik Jan Hanussen, who figures directly into our story.

Masquerading as a Danish aristocrat, although he was in fact a Moravian Jew, the subject of our focus was born Hermann (Herschel Chaim) Steinschneider.

Just how many of these Nazi warmongers are also playing a false-faced role and game of name change to hide their Jewish ancestry anyone can guess.

But I have it on good authority—from Ravenskald himself—that Adolf Hitler, whose paternal grandmother was a servant in his ancestors' castle, has at least an eighth of a dose of Jewish blood.

Make of that secret what you will.

As to Erik Jan Hanussen—he made of himself a star performer at La Scala in Berlin and elsewhere with his hypnosis and mind reading, hobnobbing with the elite and playing the political provocateur in the process.

It was Hanussen who brought Ewers to Hitler in 1931. But being a mere connector of powerful people was not Hanussen's aim and, in November 1932, Hanussen began teaching Hitler crowd control techniques, including the use of strategic caesura and rigorously rehearsed gesture.

Hanussen published a journal, to which I subscribed through a pseudonym and false address, titled *Palace of the Occult*. He also took to making predictions as a demonstration of his powers of clairvoyance, including that of the Reichstag fire, a false flag operation—do not let the prevalent opinion fool you, I know damned well who set it—that gave the newly named Chancellor Hitler his current chokehold on the government.

On 25 March 1933, nearly two months to the day after Hitler's chancellorship, and a month after the fire, supposed *parties unknown* assassinated Hanussen, most likely for his poor decision to reveal the operation ahead of time to further his career.

The truth is, Gentle Reader, the killer was Edward Hyde.

The bastard told me so in a letter, full of his Ripperesque poetry and taunts, that has since been stolen from my rooms.

The truth that Edward Hyde was doing the dirty work of Hitler and the Nazis could ill afford to be published, and I do so now at my peril.

Of course, absent the letter, it is easier for you to dismiss it.

Speaking of, there were other events in 1933 that involved the devil Hyde, though I warn you, despite all that you have read thus far, the next run of text might break any hope of your continued, generous trust.

I have every reason to believe that Hyde engaged in the continued possession of a railroad gandy dancer, primarily in Cleveland, Ohio (whom I must keep nameless for lack of formal evidence), causing the tortured soul to commit horrific murders with an axe.

For some inexplicable reason, Hyde would return to Cleveland (in Ohio *and* Mississippi) time and time again in different bodies over the course of the next few years.

As you will see in the chapters that remain, my suspicions about his varied possessions continued to accumulate over time beyond what we knew of Walton and the others, proof upon proof, until there was no doubt.

Another of his actions, the motive for which is more than mere bloodlust, was the murder of Broadway dancer Joan Winters in the Garden of Gethsemane outside Jerusalem that October. Winters had been spending time with a local civil servant who was an operative for Edgar Vellum-Verlag.

Although the operative died of gunshots, Winters succumbed to trauma of the head.

I could not help but feel, as I read the coroner's report, that she was yet another stand-in for Katherine Beaumont.

At the time that they were killed, my sources tell me that the civil servant had been preparing to transport something known as the Tiber Vial—another of the twelve sacred objects—to Vellum-Verlag, who no doubt had a seller ready and waiting to buy it.

According to Connor, the Tiber Vial contains water from the river that gives it its name. On a tragic day in antiquity, for only a moment or two, at a particular spot on the banks of the Tiber, the water there turned red, having been blessed by the blood of the obscure, crucified saint I referred to earlier as G—whose order of warrior-monks have long been associated with both the Stantons and the Ravenskalds.

More blood-magick.

Now we knew Edward Hyde had four of the sacred objects in his possession.

And that he was working in middle-America.

So, after several months of fact-checking, interviews, and other essential preparations, I also made my return.

CHAPTER 42

Mayhem and murder in 1934 America.

O f the means of my return to America, I am sworn to say nothing. With time of the utmost essence, Simeon Ravenskald arranged for transportation the likes of which you would not believe if I told you.

I tremble with fear at the technological future of our world.

Fritz Lang's Moloch thrives.

Arriving in Texas in the spring of '34, I met with law enforcement agents near Elmendorf who had once been colleagues of Quincey Morris during his years in the Texas Rangers. Quincey, who was too ill to travel to meet me in person, had sent me a letter describing the suspicious activities of a criminal named Joe Ball, a former bootlegger and present owner of a nondescript, whitewashed inn in Elmendorf. A rough and tumble personality, Ball was the great-great grandson of John Hart Crenshaw, who had made his money and reputation in Illinois trading and breeding slaves in Gallatin County.

Back behind the inn, which he had named, with no doubt more than a little irony, the Sociable, he had dug a pond as a home for half a dozen alligators. Locals and travelers could pay a modest fee to watch him feed these carnivores living cats and dogs.

Given the drunken whispers from petty criminals looking to swing a deal and the notably high percentage of missing women in the area, including one of Ball's former girlfriends, the alligators were feasting on more than cats and dogs.

Ugly ancestry and exposure to violence in the Great War aside, Ball was popular, his family being one of the richest in town. So his turning to (as yet unproven) savagery in the form of feeding people to the 'gators, as the people of Texas call them, drew the attention of Quincey's allies on the police force.

That, and the fact that a truck full of body parts had been stopped leaving the Sociable one evening, for a headlight being out.

Why take body parts elsewhere if you are disposing of the bulk of those to whom they belonged in such an efficient, thorough fashion?

Ball was powerful enough in Elmendorf to have the matter go away, but the police are paying attention.

I am sure, in time, they will catch him.

As to the matter of why, the answers—and the link to Edward Hyde—lie in one of my later stops in America—Cleveland, in Mississippi, although from there I would return to its namesake in Ohio for the remainder of the year.

Convicted for grave robbing in Michigan in the late 1920s, Alonzo Robinson (aka James H. Coyner) had once again taken up his abhorrent predilections in Mississippi's Cleveland.

This time, I am sure, at the behest of Edward Hyde, whose supply of body parts from Texas Ball, on the side of caution, was no longer providing.

Coincidence, you claim.

Robinson was a cannibal. Need more? On 9 December 1934, he murdered a married couple *with an axe*.

Not enough? The link is in the commonality of Cleveland.

You may have heard of the so-called Torso Murders in Ohio. The 5 September 1934 Lady of the Lake incident is notable, although there have been over a dozen.

The cases, which are ongoing, are disturbing enough to have led J. Edgar Hoover, head of the Federal Bureau of Investigation, to assign famous agent Eliot Ness to work them.

Four years earlier, I had followed, enrapt, as had so many others, as Ness and his idealistic squad of Untouchables went after and ultimately took down Chicago mobster Al Capone.

Working with Ness for several weeks in Cleveland in 1934, I can say of him with confidence that his commitment was equaled only by his manners and professionalism.

If it were not for the unique abilities of the spectral Edward Hyde, inhabiting unsuspecting souls to do his dirty work of amassing a selection of heads and limbs for his diabolical work, I have no hesitation in saying that Eliot Ness would have captured him.

Lest you still think me spurious in tying all of these macabre murders and diabolical undertakings to Edward Hyde, I have saved the most unassailable evidence for last, which I will follow with a pair of letters I received from the demon himself during that fateful six months in America.

What do you know, my Dear Reader, of the serial killer, rapist, torturer, cannibal, and vampire Hamilton Howard "Albert" Fish, whose nicknames ranged from the Vampire of Brooklyn to the Werewolf of Wysteria to the Gray Man?

As my old boss WT Stead would attest, readers crave a memorable nickname.

I will not be so crude and salacious as to go into any detail about Fish's sick proclivities. The details are readily available in myriad print.

Here I offer only the barest and most essential of summations:

1. Fish began to hear phantom voices in 1917. He thought it was John the Apostle. It was not. Would such a spirit tell him to embed needles in his flesh? In his groin and abdomen? Would the Apostle instruct him to hit himself with a paddle studded with nails or insert a wad of wool into his body and set it alight? He would not.

Only Edward Hyde, testing his powers, feeding on the energy of pain, would serve up such instructions to an apostle of his own.

Fish did not disappoint.

2. On the contrary—he then indulged in cannibalism, feasting on the hacked up remains of victims he dispatched with cleaver, knife, and saw. As the years passed, working his way through the twenties, it was God, so he claimed, who told him what to do—to torture and mutilate children.

No, it was not God. It was Edward Hyde.

3. What ultimately undid Fish was an obscenely graphic letter he sent to the mother of one of his victims in November '34.

A *letter*. Because, by this time, Hyde was well and truly done with him.

Fish was arrested on 13 December.

Four days earlier, Hyde inhabited Alonzo Robinson many miles away, to indulge his bloodlust with an axe.

My time in New York following up on the Fish case was some of my most difficult, so unsettling were the crime scene photos to study and police and coroners' reports to read.

Fish's own narrative, from his time in Bellevue and post-arrest interviews, was nothing less than demonic.

One afternoon, needing a break from the macabre and compelled by a morbid sense of curiosity, I visited the cluster of art deco buildings that comprise the ongoing Rockefeller Center in midtown Manhattan, the first half dozen of which were completed the year before. As I stood before Paul Manship's eighteen-foot-tall bronze sculpture of Prometheus delivering fire to humanity I found myself making connections.

While it was John D. Rockefeller, Jr. who had spearheaded this monument to hubris, I knew well enough the involvement of the Ravenskalds in the enterprise. Simeon is known to be close with Junior's son, Nelson Aldrich, who was named for his maternal grandfather, a powerful senator who had been an architect of the Federal Reserve Act. He and his cronies—all representatives of the big banking families—chose Georgia's Jekyll Island as their meeting place. It is clear who their idols are (recall as well the subtitle of Mary Shelley's *Frankenstein*). I could not help but imagine the face of Simeon himself on the statue—the features are wholly Ravenskald—as he delivered the applications of Walton et al.'s work to any and all who could afford to pay what he was asking.

If it were not for the pleasant company of my nephew Uriah during that period, who graciously offered a daybed and an already well-worn copy of Thomas Wolfe's *Look Homeward, Angel* in his simple Manhattan apartment, I do not know that I would have survived it.

I promised you letters.

Read them if you dare.

Untied [sic (k)] States of America, 1934

Greetings from Hades.

Here I sit wit Moloch. Mammon says HELL-o.
Hear the kiddies cry?
Just before they fry?

Chomp chomp chomp chompchomp—
Scaly cold-hearts in a swamp
Better cleanin' than a mop.

I have got a chained up ball
And brother that ain't all...

I can get in with no key
Mystic ether, alchemy.

What a monster I must be.

Look ya lousy lout--I am knockin' still about
See the future, see the fire, see the corpsey cunts conspire
Risin' ever, ever hire
Til I kiss the razor wire...

Comes the Winter of my malcontent
On a mission, martyr-sent
My cocky cane, it bashed-n-bent

Do you think me Vial?

Always, E.

*****

Cleaverland, Ohio (etc.), Still '34. THE FALL.

My weary, bleary friend.

I have a list of items. Tools 'a the trade:
Knife. Saw. Needles (29). Cleaver. Axe. Another axe. Ropes. Spits.
Garlic, sage, and salt.
Tennnnnnnderizers alllllll....

Boy can these boys COOK!

Funny how they nod, thinking I am god.
(And Who's to say I'm not?)

Apostle, disciple, deceived...
It feels good to be INSIDE.

But nothing is fun if it lasts.

I have become a Collector.

What is missing is my stock—

Livers in the rivers
Torsos on the shore.
Kept a tibia from Texas
Perhaps a wee bit more...

Heads and limbs amissin'
Bodies found by fukks while fishin'
Judah, Say hello to G-man.
I shall touch him with my kissing.
Dirty nails... we've done some digging.

Bodies, after all, are a dozen for a dime.

The gandy, he was dandy
But the fish, a dish of CANDY!

You're invited to the Feast.
Bored of Cleaveland, I went East
That's when AL became the Beast.
God, how WE did eat... and eat and feast and eat!

Soon a vessel be complete.

The correlations are clear. Pause and make your notes.

As much as I would have liked to remain in New York, with the prospect of Christmas dinner with my brother, his wife, and Uriah, in mid-December I was summoned to Chicago.

Ravenskald's agents had at last located Edward's secret lab.

CHAPTER 43

Echoes of horrors past and plenty for the present.

In my decades as a newspaperman, I have taken note of the admiration certain master criminals and serial killers have for one another. In some cases, there is a "copycat effect," a term that came into vogue at the time of Jack the Ripper. In others—the most dangerous—there is a game of high stakes one-upmanship that is paid by innocent victims in pounds of flesh and quarts of blood.

There is a third manifestation of this phenomenon of the deviant's brain that leads admirers to walk in the footsteps of those that came before.

Knowing this existed, it was with minimal surprise that I received word that Ravenskald's network of spies, which included the fabled and morally ambiguous Pinkertons—with whom I have had extensive dealings—had tracked Hyde through a number of recent crimes to the so-called Murder Castle on Sixty-Third and Wallace in Chicago.

Left abandoned since November 1894, when its designer, owner, and chief denizen was arrested in Boston, the World's Fair Hotel, as it was formally called, consisted of one hundred rooms on three floors, plus a basement.

Named to take advantage of the large influx of visitors coming to town for the 1893 Chicago Columbia Exposition, the hotel was the perfect location to take advantage of the thousands of women laborers and prostitutes seeking employment.

Hundreds of women went missing at that time, from all over the world.

The owner of the Murder Castle was directly responsible for abducting and murdering God knows how many dozens of them.

When police made a search of the building after the scope of the owner's crimes began to come to light, they found a macabre maze of rooms, further complicated by trap doors, false stairs leading to bricked doorways, hallways to nowhere, and a Hollywood-like assortment of false partitions and hinged and iron-plated walls.

Those last to stifle screams.

In some of the rooms, there were hidden grates to pump in poison gas.

In order to keep such a horrid design a secret, he frequently changed architects, builders, and laborers.

How many wound up dead when they discovered a bit too much?

As to the suite of rooms kept by the monster himself. The investigators found a trap door in the bathroom, which led via staircase to a windowless room containing a chute to the basement.

Ah, the basement. Now we come to the meat of the matter (pardon my indelicacy).

A true monster's lair, in the vein of the labs of Frankenstein, Moreau, and Walton.

Although the aim in this subterranean den of secrets was not Life but Death.

There the policemen found a large stove for burning corpses; several operating tables—one still covered with blood; a torture device the details of which were not released, although rumor has it the owner bought it from the descendants of a powerful English slave trader and politician from the first half of the 1700s; and shelves full of surgical instruments, tools of torture, and various acids suitable for dissolving muscle and flesh.

There were also an array of bones, both animal and human, some from at least one child as young as six.

I am sure you can see why a disembodied devil such as Edward Hyde would admire the demi-human who created such a perfect killing-box and monument to all things abhorrent and evil.

And that man's name, which I have until this moment withheld?

Herman Webster Mudgett, although in Chicago he was known as Henry Howard Holmes.

Holmes... An homage? A taunt at the world's foremost detective?

Sherlock did consult on certain elements of the case. Elements involving Mudgett's probable time in London during the Ripper murders.

I will share that story in a follow-up volume to this one.

Here I shall only reveal that, in 1891, less than a mile from the Astor House in New York where Mudgett/Holmes was residing, there was discovered a prostitute so similarly mutilated to the Ripper victims that my good friend and future collaborator, Jonathan Newcomen, as a newly minted inspector at Scotland Yard, was sent to America to investigate.

He was convinced that Mudgett had been involved in the Ripper's dirty deeds.

I concur.

So what do we know of Herman Webster Mudgett?

More than perhaps we should. After his arrest, he sold his story to William Randolph Hearst for $7500. My feelings on how this egomaniacal gamester used his newspaper for nefarious means, such as stoking the fires of the Spanish-American War at the behest of the Ravenskalds and other powerful banking families I have already intimated, although I could go further—they writhe in a deep abyss.

Mudgett/Holmes's story is full to the brim with exaggerations and outright lies.

He claimed to have killed nearly thirty people. Problem was, some of those he named were later found alive.

The numbers of his victims are no doubt so much higher.

He could have given their families and friends some peace by dealing in truths, but, like Poe's unreliable narrators, his mind was so far gone in the blood-glut of his deeds that it was as twisted and deadly a maze as the Murder Castle he built.

What I now wish to share I base on reliable information gleaned from an array of investigators and my own interviews over the years.

Like many serial killers, Mudgett showed signs of violence and a dark turn of mind by the time he was a teen. Some of his cousins went missing. It is probable he killed them. We know he tortured and mutilated animals before going on to medical schools, including the University of Michigan, for whom he robbed graves for cadavers, although his clients for organs and skeletons did not stop there. This was 1882. He was also known to have altered cadavers in an anatomy lab to work an insurance scam.

It was in 1886 that he made his way to the Windy City, buying the lot for the Murder Castle a year later.

All in preparation for the influx of faceless masses that would come with Chicago's fair.

There is extensive evidence that Herman Webster Mudgett, similar to Albert Fish, was a victim of demonic influence. He said it himself: "I was born with the devil in me." And a few years after his arrest, he claimed that he was *turning into the devil, his face taking on a most demonic visage*.

On occasion, even the most unreliable manage the truth.

There were demons all around him—one of which is intimately related to the infamous Ripper case—and, as you soon shall see, one of his greatest admirers, who learned from him an array of cruelties he applied to Fish, Robinson, Ball, and others, was our own Edward Hyde.

Many of those who came into constellation with Mudgett/Holmes—on both sides of the law—found themselves the victims of early or horrible deaths.

His Murder Castle caretaker, Patrick Quinlan, who must have by necessity known almost as much as his master, prior to taking his own life, wrote the following note, stating simply:

"I could not sleep."

*****

Relying on the notion that Hyde's habits had not changed from his time in Orkney, and assuming that he had completed a suitable body within which to contain his essence, it was decided amongst the Pinkertons and police that would accompany me to the Murder Castle that we would approach the building in the middle of the night. While some of the two dozen men assigned to the task secured the perimeter, the rest stationed themselves strategically throughout the interior—coordinated by a veteran officer that had been one of those tasked with mapping the one hundred rooms and cataloging their often-macabre contents.

As for me, armed with both the Cloverleaf and my Colt police revolver, I would follow the lead officer up to Mudgett/Holmes's second floor bedroom suite, using the stairs into the windowless room and then the chute so that I could enter the basement.

It was our hope that I could recover the mirror, Ezekiel Wheel, Jeshua Cask, and Tiber Vial and exit into safety while the Pinkertons and police awaited and apprehended Hyde returning from one of his typical nights of debauchery.

Such a sound plan, but it was never meant to be.

All went swimmingly until the moment I exited the chute and entered the basement.

There, hunched over a dimly lit, crowded table full of books, flasks, and surgical tools, was a figure I could only guess was the cobbled-together vessel of the villain Edward Hyde.

It seemed to be sewing—though what, I could not tell.

"At last, at last you have come," he whispered, his voice reminding me of an Oxford don and not the working-class laborer his letters had (falsely) evoked. "Will you sit with me, Judah? I have much to tell."

Such sincerity. And my rampant curiosity, the core tool of my trade, was pulling me forward while my more rational half begged it to call for help.

"You can if you want to," Hyde whispered, "but old Herman Webster lined these walls with iron. Besides, when I was not at work on this body, I was making some adjustments to the pipes. There will be corpses to account for come the sunrise, laddie. You can bank on that for sure. Now, please... you have journeyed all this way—and in such magnificent, secret style! Be a gentleman and sit."

Taking stock of the room as I proceeded to the table, where a metal stool awaited me, I saw, come to life before me, the descriptions of the various laboratories I had read about in the journals. A complicated array of machinery, ready to writhe at the flip of a switch like half a dozen octopi with coils, wires, and tubes. Placed about, as if for fun-house effect, were corpses, and body parts, and all manner of detritus and gore.

God, how I wanted to run.

But I stood my ground, hesitating a moment before realizing what *was* not there amongst the machinery.

The Ezekiel Wheel and mirror.

"You did not think I would leave them out in the open now, did you?" Hyde asked, having no doubt read my gaze. "Why do you hesitate? You are armed, Judah. I am not. For the moment, you have the advantage. And I have the patience of Job. I really do. Something about this face... when I gaze upon it, I find myself at peace."

It was not just my gaze he could read. It was all of a sudden obvious. He was reading my mind. Which meant I had to watch what I thought. Not knowing how even to begin such a process, I decided it was best to do as he asked.

As I sat upon the stool, I wondered if the men arrayed on the three floors above me were beginning now to die.

"Does it matter?" Hyde asked, leaning closer to the table as he continued with his work.

As he did so, a lamp illuminated him. That is when I saw what he was sewing.

A hand. To his wrist.

His own.

"Damned inconvenient," he said, snapping the string with his yellow corncob teeth after pulling the sutures tight. "But hands are important. So you see there, packed in ice, I have a broad array."

I decided to take his word for it.

"Really, Judah. Such a prude. And after all you have seen. Have a look at this hand. Exquisite. From a Swiss-German master who created custom clocks. It does not exactly match this other one"—he raised the one that did the sewing so I could see—"but it is usually gloved."

"You wanted me to find you." So overwhelmed was I by what I had seen and heard, the words came out of my mouth unbidden.

"That has been the plan," he answered. "From the start. I want you to get it right. The details of it. When you tell my story. The Jesuit priest whose face I now wear—a teacher at Loyola with some dark tastes I was more than happy to join him in until I was ready to take his face—was infinitely patient. Who could guess a face could hold such an energy after death.

"Though it was not dead for long. Nothing lasts, Judah. And once I had done my work in the two Clevelands, New York, and elsewhere—laid out in my letters—I was anxious to go. I had been readying this laboratory—with the help of impressionable young laborers and my soldiers of the scalpel—for the past several years. Such a shame, a delicious construction such as this, laying empty and unused. Unattended. The locals call it cursed.

"I lovingly call it home."

His voice was trance inducing. And his skills with the scalpel and needle... the presentation was flawless. Far beyond the limitations of his predecessors.

The Jesuit's face... it could only be called handsome, its sutures strategically covered with great waves of thick raven hair.

"Transplanted from a poet. An homage to Frankenstein's Henry. Have I not become something of a wonder, Judah? A veritable sage.

"And these eyes. From one of the Cleveland torsos. As close as possible to Jekyll's. I truly miss that man...

"Now, to the story. I will be quick and efficient. Nothing more boring than a fiend who prattles on. Your work must be better than that, if we are to reach an appropriately sizable audience."

My God, I thought. *Our objectives are aligned.*

"Let us begin," Hyde said, using his newly attached hand to pull a pocket watch from his vest to take note of the time. "Belonged to the gandy dancer. Precise, precise, precise. Never loses a second, long as I keep it wound. And I do, Judah. I certainly, certainly do."

I was riveted by his charm. If he had offered me a brandy at that moment, I would have gladly toasted his talent.

"Point one. Up until the summer of 1930, I was a father. Yes, yes… it is true. A daughter born of rape, but no less beautiful, because God is vain and despises ugly things."

Up until the summer of 1930… I shuddered as I realized whom he meant.

"You were Daphne Utterson's father?"

"Bravo, Judah! Bravo! You truly are a scholar!"

"How…"

"Jekyll was courting her mother. No one was to know—Utterson had his doubts about his slowly slipping friend—but of course, *I did.* I knew everything. *Felt* everything. From the moment he created me in a flask. Ugh… I am imprecise… I must be like the pocket watch. From the moment he *birthed* me. And, since he was a terrible father, as was Frankenstein, as was Moreau, as was Robert Walton, I decided that I would be a better one.

"Her flailing and flouncing were delectable. Jekyll had been such a gentleman, so resistant to his *urges*—you know full well, having read the journals—and when I showed up for dinner in his stead—the mysterious and mischievous Edward Hyde—Utterson, in a huff, left for dinner with that damnable Danvers Carew. As for me, I dined on her instead.

"I tell you, laddie—she loved it."

"You murdered your own daughter."

"I gave her a chance to join me, Judah," Hyde replied, with no more emotion than if we were talking about asking a girl to a picnic. "She was unable to grasp the truth, much less the potential of an alliance. The girl no doubt had gifts. Deeply suppressed, wholly wasted. At least she did not suffer."

Careful now, Judah thought. *He may look like some wizened Jesuit angel, but he is the devil incarnate.*

"So why is it you lured me here, at the price of so many lives? I don't suppose it is to return the items that you stole."

Turning his face toward the light so it glowed an unholy red, Hyde showed for the first time in this place the signs of his true temper and malignant capabilities. "They are *all* stolen, time and time again, by one faction or another. Misused by all. The Ravenskalds and their associates most of all. Co-opted to gain power, and to squash the power of others. With me they belong, and with me they shall stay. I am wholly intent on gaining the other eight as well. Only I am worthy of their power."

Such an ego, Judah observed. *I shall make it his undoing.*

"So why then am I here?"

"Facts, Judah. As I said. Facts for the story. I know that you have questions. Perhaps my soliloquy will answer some or all. No matter what you wish… it is what *I* wish you to write that counts. Let us start small. 1885. My public pummeling of Sir Danvers Carew. He knew things he should not. Smartest of the bunch. The rest of that particular portion of my… I suppose you could call it life… is all in the journals and papers of the day. I have you to thank for some of that. So thanks.

"Now for the complicated. How did I survive Jekyll's suicide… Ah… I see that that one peaks your interest! There is an expansive ether that lies precisely in between what the religious call Heaven and Hell… which are so much more than the literature describes, and not so dichotomously separate as Good and Evil, Light and Dark, Cool and Hot. Those supposed biblical writers who have professed to hear the voices of angels and saints? Well, just ask Albert Fish how unreliable they can be.

"Anyhow, there I was, for the better part of two decades, in a place so utterly dark and black one might as well be blind. Not that time applies in an other-world such as that. Most of the souls there are sickeningly convinced they shall either soon be called to Heaven or have utterly given up.

"And then there was me. So angry at Jekyll's betrayal that I refused to be anything less than ever and always vigilant.

"My fortitude paid off.

"The first glimpse of anything but darkness was a golden ray of light emanating from the King's Chamber in the Great Pyramid of Giza. Looking in, I saw it was standing room only, filled as it was with all manner of winged beings, both demonic and angelic, vying for power in endless councils and debates. The most vocal and angry by far were the damnable djinn. Infuriatingly hard to manage. Impossible to work with. All the fault of Solomon, who enslaved both them and their leader Iblis to build his infamous temple—another house of secrets—by means of a magic ring. Ever since that time, they are wholly out for revenge. Horrific things they have done. You have honestly no idea. Makes my work look like a hobby. So there I was, looking into the light through a probable door of escape and not able to take advantage of it. Poor old Hyde… so atrophied and weak.

"There were other beings in the pyramid complex as well. Beneath the Sphinx, flying and crawling above and beneath the sands. Beings from distant star systems. Whole other galaxies.

Hitler's gang of mystics have been and are now especially interested in those.

"So I hope you are paying attention.

"As much as I wished to... needed to... I could not descend from the ether. Not just then. Not just there. Though I knew I could be patient.

"Hell... I had no choice.

"Then, in 1918, with the world so pained from war—with animated corpses and targeted possessions filling the alleys and forests, I caught another glimpse of light. In a section of the ether where no kind of light should be. A stronger, more insistent one, than the one I saw in Giza. So, despite the protestations of the wailing souls around me, I followed the trail, which took me to New York, where I spied a funny little fella, all big-headed and gloomy, answering a pyramid-hatted, amateur egoist's call.

"Big-head's name was Lam. I know you know that name."

I tried not to show how incredibly excited I was. "You entered Alistair Crowley's apartments during the Amalantrah Working..."

"Yes I did," Hyde answered, simply as you'd like. "In I went and out I came. There wasn't a reason to linger. As I said, Crowley's amateur hour. Best to be avoided. Mark my words. He plays to the highest bidder, like your Ravenskalds. So much less the master than Blavatsky or Samuel Liddell MacGregor Mathers, who, by the way, died in November 1918, not too long after Crowley opened the Amalantrah rift.

"He knew the purest days were done.

"Oh, and by the way... your ancestor... the pirate. He was closely associated with one of the MacGregors. *That's why* Mathers took the name. I bet you were not aware.

"But one day it could matter. There are journals. In code. You should make it your mission to find them.

"So, I crawled out on my ethereally scaly belly, completely unseen.

"Old muddle-minded Lam eyed me as I left, but he did not bother to say it.

"So then was I free. For a bit of time after, I kicked about, doing various and sundry, learning my powers, testing the limits. One of my earliest successes in possession—and I readily admit most of them were messes—morgues and madhouses filled with them—was Fritz Haarmann in Germany."

"The Vampire of Hanover," I whispered.

"Indeed, indeed he was. His bloodlust—that was something. Cannibalism—the closest thing to being in a body, having a body in me. Or, in me via the body I was in. See what an annoyance disembodiment can be?

"So I knew I needed a vessel. But how to get one? I obviously needed help.

"Then I found my shill in Walton. What a lovely, lucky find. Oh so ready to be whispered to. To have his dreams come true.

"Despite a certain... interference... we succeeded. Well... *I* did.

"That, along with my letters, brings us current, Judah. And now I take my leave. Your precious little Katherine has waited long enough."

Before I could reach for either of my guns, Hyde was on his feet, his hickory cane coming down in an arc.

And I was blacking out.

CHAPTER 44

An out of body experience with an unexpected ally.

I awoke in a local hospital nearly three weeks later, as a pleasant nurse informed me as I slowly came back to consciousness, with a knot of police and Pinkertons on guard outside the door.

"Hyde will not come here," I whispered, accepting her offer to take a sip of ice water up through a straw. "He has said his say for now."

Ignoring my remarks and instead adjusting my pillows, the nurse informed me that the injury to the side of my head was severe. My brain had swelled and a team of neurosurgeons had worked on me for hours.

For my protection, they had put me in a coma.

While I had slept a healing sleep, Christmas and New Years had passed.

I asked her for the date.

"January fourth, 1935."

Handing me a tiny cup with two large pills, she advised me to swallow them and try to get some sleep.

My head aching and eyes refusing to focus, I did as she suggested.

It was sometime after sundown when I next awoke. My head, which I realized was tightly wound with gauze, was throbbing. I was barely able to stifle a scream, so intense was the pain in the back of my skull and just behind my eyes.

Nursey-girl should have given you more than just a pair of those happy-tabs. Hyde nearly caved your skull.

Not seeing the speaker, I turned my head—at great effort— toward the door. *The guards must be off for coffee*, I thought. *They know the danger's passed.*

Turning back, I looked to the other side of the bed, where the visitor's chair was placed.

It was empty. Nor was there anyone at the foot of the bed, where my multi-page chart was hung.

I am not visible to you, Judah. Not at present. But you can trust that I am here.

My whispered response surprised me.

"Can you do something for the pain?"

I can take you away from here, psychically, for a time… somewhere pleasant, where the pain does not exist. Would you like that, Judah?

Perhaps it was the two tablets the nurse *had* given me, but I nodded without a single moment's thought.

Ah, ah, ah… too quick, Judah. Too quick by far. I have a counter-offer. I can diminish the pain so you can better function, and, in return for a teensy bit of suffering, I can show you something you need to see. Something that will help you kill that stitched-together bastard who nearly took you down.

Although it made me grit my teeth to keep from crying out, I nodded my head again, far more vigorously than before.

And then, after a series of rapid blinks of my eyes that I thought were signaling a seizure, I found myself out of my bed in the hospital and standing at the perimeter of a hotel room. Looking down, I saw myself still in the flower-patterned gown with the opening in back. Instinctively reaching behind to hold it closed, I heard my guide let out a laugh.

"No one can see you, nor hear us, Judah." His voice was like that of an angel, as was his visage and form, though I could barely make it out. His etheric hair was long, dark, and curled and his eyes were a glittering brown. He worn a poet's ruffled shirt, the tail pulled out over tailored chino pants.

My God, I suddenly realized. *We have met before.*

It was the "angel falling upward," as he often called himself.

Planner Forthright… his other *nom de guerre*.

Although I had questions in the dozens, my attention was pulled to the activity in the room. Several police officers and a photographer were collecting physical and photographic evidence of an obvious crime scene.

There was blood on the walls and the ceiling. And a puddle on the bed.

"Where are we?" I asked.

"Room 1046, in the Hotel President in Kansas City, Missouri. Notice it overlooks the courtyard. That is specifically what he requested. The victim checked in two days ago under the name of Roland T. Owen, although his actual name is Artemus Ogletree, which sounds a lot more interesting, don't you think?"

"Is he dead?"

"Not yet. Tomorrow sometime. I am not always informed of the details."

"And this was the doing of Hyde?"

"Yes indeed it was," my guide replied. Clapping me on the shoulder, which caused a sensation like the activation of embedded electric needles, he winked at me and motioned for me to sit on the bed, despite the puddle of blood.

Seeing my hesitation at the utter impropriety of it, he said, "They won't mind. Especially Roland/Artemus. I promise."

Acknowledging that, even in this less than solid state, I was dizzy and weak from the pain and my ordeal, I did as he suggested.

"Now," he said. "This man that Hyde worked over was part of a chain of highly specialized searchers and dealers—another of which was the doomed companion of Joan Winters in Jerusalem—who are committed to securing a certain set of items. Biblical. Magical. I know that you are aware of these, Judah, and that is why I am helping you. That and you're a Stanton."

I raised a psychic brow. "And that matters?"

"Of course it does. You *know* it does. How else could you and your ancestors have experienced so much. *Seen* so much. Then there are the Ravenskalds. You are the balance that the Universe requires. Some ancient cosmic law God and his lackeys devised. Never mind my explaining. There's never enough time... Instead, I am writing a book... Like you, Judah. We have so very much in common. You really have no idea..."

I watched in wonder as this angel-like being, though with a decidedly dark perimeter, pulsed and started to fracture, though he collected himself with a breath.

"It will take some time... eighteen months I hear... for the truth to come out—in a limited way, to a certain circle of men—that Artemus was in Egypt. Cairo, precisely. Securing an artifact—something called the Judas Coin, one guess to whom the thing belonged—for a contact that went by the name of 'Don.' There's Artemus's note to him, beside you on the table."

Unable to grasp the paper in my unnatural, ethereal state, I willed my still aching eyes to focus. In an uneasy hand he had written, "Don: I will be back in fifteen minutes. Wait."

"Don is Edward Hyde."

"You're a sharp one, Judah P. I tell you—I knew our brief, productive alliance in 1888 wasn't just a fluke. This was not their only communication. A maid who looked in on Mister Ogletree several times throughout his stay told the police not an hour before we arrived that she had heard him talking on the phone, telling this Don that he wasn't hungry... that he had had his breakfast already. She returned in the mid-afternoon with fresh towels and was told to go away by a voice that wasn't Ogletree's. Earlier today, some of the staff found him tied at the wrists and ankles, stabbed several times in the chest, with a skull-fracturing blow to the right side of the head that was severe enough to leave splatters of blood on the ceiling. Sound familiar?"

All too, I indicated with a nod.

"I have a friend of sorts. Edgar Vellum-Verlag. Ah... I see you know him. Artemus Ogletree was a runner in his employ. Had he stuck to the generous terms Edgar was quoting for the coin, he might have made a sidestep in his tap shoe dance with death. Listen to me, sounding like a pulp-paged gumshoe rag."

"So Hyde now has the coin."

"Yes. Which makes five of the items in all. And we cannot have that, Judah. What these items can do when combined, if one knows *how* to combine them... it is truly, truly cosmic in its consequences. I tried to avoid this. To reason with Walton... Free will is a stupid, stupid rule. Far from doing good, it allows all the worst to win. Now, we have to get you back. There are rules and risks, you know. Much longer out of body and the silver thread might snap, leaving you nothing more than an invisible vampire like the ones your brother studies. That, and I need you alive. You must continue to be the balance, until the next one's ready."

My eyes again began to blink, a dozen times in succession, until I found myself back in my hospital bed.

Gasping for air, I tried to sit up—the pain would not allow it. Then the nurse was beside me, saying, "Easy Mister Stanton. You must have had a nightmare. Your heart rate is through the roof. If you can settle down, there is someone here to see you. He says his name is Simeon."

CHAPTER 45

A second unexpected visit.

After several minutes of deep breathing and half of one of the two tablets the nurse offered in another tiny cup (I did not want my senses dulled with such a snake as Ravenskald in the room), I was able to bring my heart to an acceptable beats per minute for the nurse to feel comfortable opening the door.

Removing a beaver felt fedora that complemented his wool worsted three-piece suit and navy topcoat (odd the things we notice while under the influence of drugs), Ravenskald walked wordlessly to the chair on the far side of my bed.

Assured the nurse was well away up the hall, he said, with no more emotion than if he were reporting the latest price of onions, "Ten police and Pinkertons dead of gas exposure. Two others hospitalized. If they live, they will be vegetables."

"All so he could tell me his story. How are the newspapers handling it?"

"They aren't, thanks to a sizable contribution. And I have already sent some of my agents to the Hotel President in Kansas City. They will glean more from the witnesses and staff than local law enforcement and then make sure that no one discovers the truth. Or, if they do, it is too fantastical to believe."

"We operate at cross purposes, Simeon. You must realize that this uneasy partnership of ours cannot continue any longer. I will not be party to suppression of the truth."

Simeon let out a laugh. "Again with the naivety. Which I shall not hold against you, knowing all that you've endured. Papers print what men like me want them to. Nothing more. Your friend Holmes—another uneasy partnership of yours—got it wrong."

I inched myself further away from the edge of the bed near to where he sat.

"You did not come here to give me a body count for our failed operation at the World's Fair Hotel." I could not bring myself to call it by its more macabre, colloquial name. "I would think that you would have stayed at Rushen. Hyde is on his way. He told me as much."

Again the bastard laughed. "And did he also tell you of his stop-off in Missouri? When he comes, we shall be ready." Changing his tone and leaning in from the chair, he said, "Do you know how to keep a vampire at bay with a simple jar of seeds?"

Nodding, I answered, "Spread it on the floor. They will have to stop where they are and count the grains, be it millet, poppy, or rice. Probable nonsense, you know."

"I happen to know that it's not. Although that is not the point. Hyde now possesses five of the twelve sacred objects. His mission will not be complete until he possesses all twelve and uses them for their quite serious, quite irreversible purpose."

"'Truly, truly cosmic in its consequences,'" I whispered, knowing the words did not originate from my mind in that moment, but were placed directly on my tongue and teeth to speak.

"What did you just say?" Ravenskald asked, his green eyes going wide.

"You are not my only visitor today. Not that you will find a record of the first. A fallen angel—"

"Falling *upwards*," Ravenskald said, quite beside himself. "I should have realized he would find a loophole to join us in our game. Quite the entity, that one. Can we make of him an ally..." He was at that moment talking only to himself.

Before I could hazard an answer, Ravenskald collected himself and related to me what had happened in Orkney with the mirror.

I have already shared with you that dialogue, in its rightful chronological position in the narrative.

"This angel falling upward has no love for Hyde," I said, taking in what he had told me. "And he certainly does not want him to have the objects. What do you know of the other eight?"

Ravenskald stood, placing his fedora upon his head and buttoning his topcoat. "I am not at liberty to say. But there is a plan in place. A plan hinging on the fact that at least one of the objects he shall come for will function as the seeds that will stop him in his tracks."

CHAPTER 46

Home to London with a plan.

My return trip to London was again arranged by Simeon Ravenskald, made all the more secretive and exotic because of my still-concerning head injury and the perils it presented to conventional aircraft travel.

With my permission, I was given a series of sedatives for the duration of the journey by a medical staff of three that I surmised were in Ravenskald's private employ.

I awoke on 20 January on a newly installed mattress in my Fleet Street rooms. Getting up to use the loo, I saw that the larder and ice box were well stocked with a variety of foods and beverages a simple newspaperman like myself could never have hoped to afford.

He is trying to buy me, I thought, abandoning the idea of a bath as the room began to spin.

I'll be damned before I'm bought.

I spent the rest of the evening and the whole of the following day going over my private notes on all that had occurred since 1930, as well as the four doctors' journals.

It seemed to me, reading it all at a go, more of a madman's nightmare than at any time before.

The following morning, feeling for the first time on the mend, I was just sitting down to a cup of Colombian coffee and a pair of fancy Italian pastries (I certainly had no intention of wasting them) when some unseen hand slipped a note beneath my door. The contents, looking as though they were scribbled out in haste, welcomed me home, expressed regret for my injury, and requested that I meet Inspector Jonathan Newcomen at a certain address in the affluent London neighborhood of Belgravia as soon as I was able.

Eating the pastries in a few delicious bites, I washed my face and dressed myself in loose, comfortable clothing, allowing for the chance that an adventure was at hand. Placing the Cloverleaf and extra ammunition in the pocket of my coat, I made my way to the street, hailing a cab for the journey south along the Thames and west to my destination on Wilton Street.

Checking the paper against the number of the home, I saw that it was undergoing extensive renovations.

Paying the cabbie, I navigated the front steps with care, as they were stacked with loose bricks and encased in scaffolding. Knocking on the door, I was surprised to see it swinging slowly open, allowing me silent entry.

Closing the door behind me, and taking the precaution of throwing the bolt against anyone following me in, I found myself in the midst of piles of plaster and lathe, buckets of unused paint, and buckets and temporary tables made with sawhorses and sheets of plywood full of the tools of the carpenter's trade.

"Inspector Newcomen!" I yelled, to the rooms to the right and left of me and up the central staircase.

I heard nothing, so I called out again.

This time, from an upstairs room, I heard the faintest cry of suffering and pain.

Pulling the Cloverleaf from my pocket, I ascended the stairs, my heart beginning to race and my head becoming light. Gritting my teeth against it, I moved from room to room until, outside a door left half-ajar, I again heard the sounds of an injured, weakened male.

Catching my breath and looking toward the Heavens, though I do not know quite why, I pushed open the door with my foot, my arms extended and the Cloverleaf cocked and ready for business.

The scene that was before me made my blood run cold.

There, tied to a chair, was Inspector Newcomen, stripped naked and barely alive.

This last fact was a miracle... there were parts and pieces which God had given him when he was born, strewn about around him.

I tell you without shame, I barely made it to a half-filled bucket of plaster in the nearest corner of the room before I lost the pastries amid a burning stream of bile.

Collecting myself as best I could, I brought my face near to Newcomen's—a face that was missing an eyelid, an ear, and several of its teeth. One of his nostrils had been flayed open and there were deep gashes in both of his cheeks.

"My God, Newcomen...," I said, not knowing how to give him comfort, when all I wanted to do was run. "Did *he* do this? The fucking cunty bastard..."

Swallowing blood and bile in a painful attempt to speak, Newcomen at first choked, before managing to whisper, "Wanted... to show... his... handiwork... to an admirer..."

Shaking my head, I said, "I am no admirer, Jonathan, you must—"

"Not you," he spat out, along with a trickle of blood-tinged saliva. "Took photos. Scotland Yarder... big impressive prize... beat and... tortured and all. Second generation... all the more a... trophy."

"Son of a *bitch*," I said, frozen in place despite my willing myself to move, to help, to aid him in some way.

Although, as I glanced at the burns, cuts, and gouges on his chest and legs and groin, I knew there was no help to be had.

"Did have... a message for you, so... he said he hoped you'd... hurry." His eyes rolling back in his head and breathing becoming labored, I knew his time was nearly done.

"What is the message, Jonathan?"

"Katherine Beaumont's corpse will look so much worse than mine."

And with those words, Inspector Jonathan Newcomen, unsung hero of the Yard, breathed his final breath.

I sank to the floor in tears, all the horrors of the past half-decade washing over me like the sea.

CHAPTER 47

Like scattered seeds for a Vampire.

Ido not recall for how long it was that I lay like a child weeping at the feet of Jonathan Newcomen. As macabre as it sounds, surrounded as I was by gore, I must have at some point fallen asleep—my grief and the lingering effects of my head injury conspiring against my will—for it was well into the night before I gathered myself together, alerting a passing policeman on Wilton Street to the nightmare beyond the door.

The murder of a Scotland Yard inspector is paramount to an attack on no less than the sovereignty and safety of the Royal Family. Especially as vicious an attack as was this. The top men of the Yard, including Police Commissioner Hugh Trenchard, and a few of King George the Fifth's closest advisors, stood in the foyer of the house—whose owners would soon be contacted to apprise them of the goings on.

Whatever holiday enjoyment they might be having during the renovations would no doubt swiftly die.

An educated guess: Once the work was finished, the owners would place the house on the market through a trusted family agent, and they would never go there again.

It was nearly two in the morning before the policemen agreed to release me, satisfied that I had told them all that I could—which was very little beyond the fact that we had both received threats from a most unsavory character whose criminal enterprise we had been tracking and interfering with.

I was confident that Simeon Ravenskald would make the proper arrangements with Trenchard and the others. He did not disappoint. The commissioner announced within months of Newcomen's murder that the Yard had selected an architect to design a new building for them, paid for in full by the Ravenskald family.

Gratefully accepting a ride back to Fleet Street by a reporter from the *Evening Standard*, I wearily climbed the stairs to my rooms, my head throbbing and strength nearly once more spent. Just outside my door I took in the silhouette of a man, a trail of smoke and glowing red tip from his cigarette barely visible in the darkness, and I immediately knew who had sent him and why.

"What has happened?" I asked him, unlocking my door and inviting him inside.

As if the torture and murder of Inspector Newcomen were not enough.

Accepting my offer of a glass of water—there was no time for coffee he informed me—but not taking the expected step of identifying himself by name, Ravenskald's man told me the following, with nary an ounce of emotion:

"Approximately an hour ago, an attempt was made on Castle Rushen. An attack of some genius which the security team was barely successful in repelling."

"Miss Beaumont?" I asked, my blood going cold as I awaited the answer.

"Shaken but unharmed. Our losses were high, but the assassin did not succeed."

Assassin. Did this man not know the attacker's name, or was he too afraid to speak it?

The man instructed me to pack a bag as quickly as I could. I had a plane to catch.

I was expected at Castle Rushen, and that was all he would say.

Leaving from London City—the same airfield Hyde must have used—I arrived on the Isle of Man five hours later and was being dropped off by a silent chauffeur at the entrance to the castle just past the bridge and through the formidable-looking gatehouse half an hour after I landed.

"Where is Miss Beaumont, Ravenskald?" I asked of Simeon, too tired and in pain to bother to be polite, when he greeted me at the door. "I wish to see that she is safe. That the monster did not hurt her."

Pointing me to a door to his right instead of to the central stairway, Ravenskald said, "Calm yourself, Judah. Katherine is fine. I have locked her safely away and, after the stiff drink that I mixed her, she is probably sound asleep. You shall see her as long as you wish as soon as this is over. We have pressing business to which we must attend."

Leading me through a series of hallways and chambers, Ravenskald entered a small room, the walls of which were lined with floor-to-ceiling bookcases built from maple and oak and crammed to the point that the shelves were sagging in their centers.

Placing his hand underneath one of the straighter of the shelves, he moved it back and forth, after which I heard the grind of hidden machinery and, like a pivotal moment out of an old Gothic novel, two of the bookcases began to separate, revealing a secret passage.

"Your design?" I asked, admittedly impressed by the theatrics of it all.

"My grandfather's," he said, his voice softening with regret that the idea was not his own. "Though I have used it for decades. Ever since my initiation, after college graduation."

Pulling a flashlight from his pocket—I was disappointed there were no open-flame torches flickering in cast iron wall sconces—Ravenskald descended a set of curving stairs as I followed close behind him, until we were standing in what was clearly a ceremonial chamber. In its center was an oblong stone altar, long enough for a body of average height, above which were a series of complex carvings of symbols and sigils in the ceiling.

"There are things that I must tell you, Judah, because time is of the essence. Since our earliest days, the Ravenskalds have benefitted from an otherworldly energy. Other powerful families—under our guidance and control—have also been given a certain amount of access to this power, derived from a winged beast-god that answers to the call of Mammon—though we are not primitives... one could just as easily call it Kali, Moloch, or Tezcatlipoca. We have lodges all over the world... there was once one in London, beneath the home of Lord John Carteret, a powerful lord proprietor and governor of the Royal African Company. Your own forbear, Joseph Stanton, worked in his employ—or for those who did—early in his career."

"You are worshippers of Lucifer himself," I said, shocked to have confirmed as real what I had, for the sake of my faith, always conveniently considered myth. Gossip at best, propaganda at worst. "Fire and blood. Eaters of children! Moloch indeed! I have heard whispers of the so-called sixty families, over which you reign. You are no better than Edward Hyde..."

Foregoing his usual derisive laugh—it was clear he needed me to understand—Ravenskald answered, "Lucifer is in no way the same as these metaphors made manifest that our most dedicated loyalists worship. While there are light beings that will answer to the names of archangels, there are also a few genuine archangels. Lucifer is one. Though he is sitting on the sidelines, a mewling, puking defeatist. Planner Forthright is another." Glancing at an ornately filigreed pocket watch that must be a family heirloom, he exhaled a frustrated breath and shook his head. "This is no time for a theo-philosophical discussion, Judah. It is time to show you some of our millet, poppy, and rice."

Crossing the room—past a stone altar with channels carved into its weathered surface that I assumed directed blood— Ravenskald opened a cabinet covered in Egyptian hieroglyphs and Celtic runes and removed several items, which he laid side by side upon the altar. "These are the sacred objects called the Abraham Blade, Aaron Staff, and Baptist Bowl."

He then proceeded to explain each and its complicated history, using as few words as possible. Herein I shall provide only the briefest explanation, with consciousness of both the pacing of this final act of our narrative and the simple fact that some of the information I was given is too dangerous to reveal.

The first object, a bone-handled blade, was the very knife that Abraham intended to use to sacrifice Isaac. It was once in the care of Lord John Carteret. The second, the magical walking stick used by Moses and Aaron during the Exodus, had been in the Ravenskald family for hundreds of years, serving as the source of power for the Mammon Lodge in Dublin in the early 1700s under the leadership of Abonijah. The final object, the Baptist Bowl, was the skull of John the Baptist, leader of the Essenes, with the top cut out and lined with leather so that it was fit to hold liquids and other items. I will say of that holy-macabre thing that it was a central piece of evidence in the wrongful undoing of the Templars.

And the Ravenskalds were to blame, having planted it amongst them prior to the pope and French king's accusations of their blasphemy.

The skull had also contributed to mistaken information about a secret group toasting in a tower the death of Alexander Spotswood, lieutenant governor of Virginia, and the architect of Edward "Blackbeard" Thache's assassination by the Royal Navy in 1718.

The group was the SQ and the skull was the Baptist's, not Blackbeard's.

As I studied the objects in silence, my attention was drawn to a door being unbolted in a dark, obscured corner of the subterranean ritual room.

Through it walked Edgar Vellum-Verlag.

"I trust I am not late," the venerable antiques and oddities dealer said, as though he were Carroll's White Rabbit transformed into a man—complete with vest and umbrella.

"You are not," Ravenskald answered, not bothering with the formalities of an introduction. "Have you brought to me more seeds?"

Vellum-Verlag nodded, pulling from an inner pocket of his coat an item the size of a large harmonica wrapped in cheesecloth.

Taking it carefully in his hands, Ravenskald whispered with a reverence with which I had not believed him capable, "The Sheba Comb." Then, for my benefit, as he unwrapped it, he added, "Once possessed by a powerful queen of Spain. Secured at great expense of capital—monetary, political, and human."

"Isabella?" I asked.

"Iso*bel*," he replied. "Farnese."

Another link to Joseph's time.

Showing me the ancient honeycomb that lay within the cheesecloth, Ravenskald re-wrapped it and laid it beside the other items.

"Now gentlemen," Ravenskald said, as half a dozen robed and hooded figures entered the room, carrying candles and smoking censers full of an acrid, half-blinding resin. "I must activate these objects to send out our call. Hyde has attuned himself to them. He shall not be able to resist. With a third of the objects present, and he in possession of at least four of the others, the central energy that binds them will draw like the force of a magnet."

"Hold a moment," I said, suddenly confused and more than a bit put off by his plan. "Miss Beaumont is Hyde's central target. What shall keep him from dispatching her—despite your best efforts, which have not prevented theft from this very place and a nearly successful attack upon her person—and *then* coming for these objects?"

In answer, Ravenskald rang a bell on a side table and the door through which Vellum-Verlag had entered opened again, revealing two burly men in robes with Miss Beaumont, barefoot in a flimsy sleeveless nightgown, held between them.

"You bastard..." I said, vulgar in my language despite Miss Beaumont's presence. "It is not these objects, but *she* that shall be the scattered seeds!"

Motioning for the guards to place her on the table, to which she did not resist, Ravenskald smiled. "It is she *as well as* these. We cannot take a chance. He must be dealt with tonight. Here. On my terms. Yes, she is the bait. But no harm shall come to her. We shall protect her—here better than where she was. Now, we must begin. Stand beside Edgar and argue with me no more."

Smiling reassuringly at Miss Beaumont, who only looked back at me in a trance—she clearly had been drugged—I did as Ravenskald instructed.

Taking position behind the altar, and taking the Abraham Blade in his left hand, he began to intone the following: "*Wa hay-nah sa ma ka Edward Hyde. Mu-kah do hay-nah ka. Tach ma, tach mu, sa mu sa Edward Hyde. Co-mama sa. Co-mama sa Edward Hyde ...*"

The second time through, the eight hooded men joined in, their collective voices echoing and amplifying off the rocks that ringed the space, their acoustic features collecting and distributing the energies until I felt my body begin to tingle.

"*WA HAY-NAH SA MA KA EDWARD HYDE. MU-KAH DO HAY-NAH KA. TACH MA, TACH MU, SA MU SA EDWARD HYDE. CO-MAMA SA. CO-MAMA SA EDWARD HYDE ...*"

The volume was at a level far from what eight men's voices could produce. There was no doubt—and I had witnessed many fantastical things at séances and other rituals—that something occult was now occurring, that forces beyond our ken were being summoned in.

Then, just above us, the sounds of guns and dying men.

Then there was silence.

"It seems our guest has arrived," Vellum-Verlag whispered.

I heard movement past the levered bookshelves above and in a moment, there he stood—a demon with the face of an angel.

A cliché, yes, but also accurate.

"Greetings, boys," Hyde said, curls of smoke and the smell of cordite emerging from the barrels of a pair of Soviet AVS automatic rifles, which he dropped to the floor before approaching the altar, where he was met with a variety of knives and guns produced from beneath their robes by the eight hooded men.

Even Ravenskald produced a Luger to go with the Abraham Blade.

"Clever you are, Simeon. As all the Ravenskalds are. I have your family to thank, after all. As did Moreau and Frankenstein. And even Jekyll, by extension. But you must realize how this ends. There is no killing me. Body or not—the killing shall go on.

"And I am not alone. Not anymore. I have learned *so much*. And I have been having the most *exquisite* dreams, good sons—of bleeding crosses and bowls full of blood... of beating hearts and reeking livers, of cannibals and vampires singing out my songs. You cannot hope to staunch their ravenous thirst for blood. From caves and castles, from garages and gaols, from the bottoms of swamps and deep within the jungle. I too have my chants. I too have my calls. And they too, with the proper training, shall have their secret labs, their subterranean workshops, their backyard suburban sheds. They shall fill the fields with the flotsam and jetsam of failure. And then they shall fill the cities with the fruits of their success.

"Like old Matthew said, '*Ye shall know them by their fruits.*'

"Like Ball or Mudgett/Holmes, they shall be led by me to believe that disposing of the bodies with acid and gators and weighted sacks in lakes will keep them out of jail. Whom do they think coached Hanussen in the ways to coach our Adolph? Hanussen— such a prospect, 'til he believed the power was his. When the ego gets too large, the hour's arrived to die. Or to be turned over. Made to make mistakes, so the coppers come to call.

"There will be some great ones, the names of which you'll know. The Tacoma Axe-Murderer, the Acid Bath Murderer... The names shall lack any signs of imagination, though the acts themselves will not. Watch the papers, Judah. It may take some years, but it all shall come to pass. One of the most famous, equal in gruesomeness and grandeur, I shall choose because his name shall be homage to those two New Orleans brothers when I really made my start... Pogo and Patches, clowning in Chicago... Why, your eyes are asking... Because, as the master wizard Joyce encoded in *Ulysses*, from the mouth of his alter ego, God has sent a black panther vampire to prey upon the weak ones who worship him. And that God, you sodden cocks, is no one else but I. Until I have my sons.

"And I shall have me *many* sons. I have been practicing with the plumbing, here and there, in and out. It is down to the chemistry, gents. 'Cause the killing keeps me hard.

"I shall not be as the doctors, rejecting what I create. I shall love them as the Father never loved the masses. I shall raise them as ebony panthers, all too keen to prey—ushering in a new and evil era, stalking this pitiful plane, hand in glove with pulsing energy weapons and other deadly devices for mankind's great demise. *That's* what you want with these, Simeon. For war makes rich men kings!

"Watch how we will feast! Misery makes a rich and magnificent meal! And such a lovely buffet your greed and grasping have made—poverty and overpopulation, ravaging diseases created in a lab. The interstellar beings Thule and Vril let in are looking for their payments, like the ancient Gods of old.

"Payments made in gore, in the factories of war.

"*That's* Moloch! *That's* Mammon! Which the German expressionists *get*!

"They'll test even you, Simeon, and the dynasty you have built, in the decade that's to come."

"Are you finished?" Ravenskald asked, as if this extended monologue was nothing more than a child's drawn out tantrum.

Hyde, flushed with the power of his stream of vile vitriol, answered, "Nearly. I shall soon have eight of the twelve. And you, Edgar, showing up here, with the Comb, at such a crucial time. I know you know the locations of another pair of the objects—the two that are always together. I shall get their locations from you a cut and a tongue-lap at a time."

Although he had refrained since the moment I had arrived, Ravenskald now laughed, and full of mirth it was.

"If you manage to succeed in killing us all and getting off this now blockaded island," he said, "you shall not have the eight. You shall have these four. My agents are persistent and powerful, Edward. They are incredibly persuasive. As of an hour ago, *I* possess the eight."

If the priest whose face Hyde wore had ever doubted his faith in God, he must have displayed the look that Hyde was showing us now.

"Impossible!" Hyde yelled.

"Walton's grandmother's attic," Ravenskald countered. "That's where you hid them. Yes? You don't have to answer... I can see it in your—or whoever's—eyes."

It was true—Hyde looked ready to shake so hard his sutures would fail to hold. Ravenskald continued with his taunts.

"Quite an uninspired choice, Edward—ending where it began. Such fun you must have had, playing Walton like a puppet, luring him upstairs on a rainy day in a house near Kensington Gardens to find his ancestor's correspondence."

Letting loose a demonic howl, Hyde, grabbing the Aaron Staff off the table in lieu of his hickory cane, brought it down in a wide, death-dealing arc toward Ravenskald's head, yelling, "I shall possess them all, Ravenskald! I will! And as for your deaths—which will wholly be my pleasure to deliver—you are wrong again, for Katherine will not die! She shall be my Eve—what Frankenstein's creature was denied!"

"STOP!"

The staff, against the probabilities of physics, did, mere inches from Simeon's skull.

I recognized the voice.

An angel had arrived.

Along with a most unexpected companion, whose presence filled me with anger and dread.

Standing in the underground entranceway was not the Angel Falling Upward, but my nephew Uriah, all of twenty-one years old, holding the gilded mirror about which I had read and heard so much.

To cry out his name or even allow my shock and concern to register for a split second in front of Hyde was out of the question. I called upon my stiff-upper-lip British upbringing and awaited the unfolding of whatever was to come.

"You will not win, Edward Hyde!" came the voice of the complicated angel, projecting outward from deep within the mirror. With each word, as if he were walking a long, upwardly inclined hallway, Planner's voice grew louder. "LET GO OF THE STAFF AND MAKE NO FUTHER MOVE, YOU COBBLED TOGETHER HOMUNCULUS! I SWEAR TO OUR ABSENTEE FATHER-GOD I WILL KICK YOUR FUCKIN' FACE IN!"

The volume and vibration of the warning was so great, the straining of the polished obsidian in its oblong frame rebounded off the walls.

What if it did not hold?

Dropping the staff, Hyde, his face contorted into the visage of a gargoyle, charged at my nephew. Pulling my Cloverleaf from my pocket, I cocked it and took aim.

"Let it be, Judah!" Ravenskald yelled, simultaneously with my nephew's plea to do the same, delivered with different words and a remarkable sense of calm as he stood his ground, the mirror held before him, the polished obsidian surface facing Hyde.

"This has always been the plan. We must not get involved," Vellum-Verlag whispered, leaning into me. "Though you must keep the pistol cocked and at the ready, just in case..."

Rabid with rage, Hyde grasped the mirror, which Uriah did not relinquish. All pretext of civility lost, he reverted to his disposition in the time of Jekyll. "Back ta 'Ell wit' ya, angel! Ya rolled ya dice an' lost—you an' that worthless Lucifah! Ya hads ya time! This is *my* war... *my* epoch! I am willin' ta share... even the bird, once I had me fill a 'er... I won' even ask ya aid in dispatchin' this riff-raff. But I will be gettin' me items—ya canary singin' sonofa whore!"

Pressing his face against the obsidian, which again began to strain, Hyde fogged its surface with his ragged, fetid breath until the figure of the angel inside of it was totally obscured.

"What's ya an-sah, angel? I knows about ya, mate, shur 'nuff. A rebel amongst the rebels, ya be. Let's make an alliance!"

"An alluring little idea," Planner said, "although we must first get some things straight. To begin with, my mother was a nun and not a whore. Or, she will be... Regardless, there's clearly a difference... Equally as important, you will *not* ever again attempt to interpret Joyce. I spoke to Stephen Dedalus myself. Or I shall... no time to explain the particulars. It is bad form and a waste of time to speak of metaphors and myths you do not understand. Your interpretation—to say nothing of your ego—are off by an acre and embarrassingly out of size."

Looking wholly unaffected, Hyde replied, "Agreed."

Planner did not reply.

The room was as silent and still as the tomb it might become with further escalation.

Would the fallen angel turn? Was that not his nature?

The answer came in earnest as a clawed, muscled hand came flashing through the fogbank and the mirror, grasping Edward Hyde by his hair and yanking him inside.

Or his essence, as it were, leaving his sutured-together vessel falling like a grain sack to the ground.

"Quickly, Uriah! Bring the mirror here!"

The order came from Ravenskald, who still held in his left hand the ancient Abraham Blade. With his right, he undid the flap of the cheesecloth that held the Sheba Comb.

Grasping the honey-filled object, Ravenskald smeared it on the mirror in concentric circular motions, edge to center, uttering thrice the following mystical words: "*Sanco tupanché, tecco du mané, té-liggo, té-liggo supanché. Sanco du mené, geelo du ché ché. Sanco tupanché, tecco du mané, du mané, du mané. Clorra tume ché ché.*"

After the third utterance, a heart-stopping scream of frustration and defeat echoed within the mirror, followed by a string of obscenities from Planner urging Hyde to cease his embarrassing temper tantrum.

And then, again, a silence.

"I take it you succeeded?" Vellum-Verlag asked, taking a healthy pinch of snuff from a monogrammed silver case.

"He is now trapped, sent back into the ether, like a djinn within its lamp," Ravenskald explained, accepting the mirror from Uriah and placing it on the altar. "Perfectly done, my boy. You and your friend were marvelous." Then, to the hooded men, he said, "Take

Miss Beaumont to her rooms. See to it she has whatever she requests."

Mouthing to my unofficial ward that I would see her soon, I watched her walk away.

As Simeon and Edgar turned their attention to the mechanisms and properties of the gathered objects—apparently there was also an incantation to clear the mirror as well as to lock it—I took Uriah by the arm and moved him away from the crowd.

"How in the hell are you here?" I asked, all too aware of the answer.

"There is a war on, Uncle," he responded, his tone polite but firm.

To the end, he was his father's son.

"A war, yes," I answered, "and our oldest enemy was a fraction of a second from death. Why could you not wait?"

Uriah shook his head. "Centuries-old enmities must no longer fester. Father and I know of what he is capable, but we cannot win without him. All of this, going back years, was primarily Simeon's doing. The Ravenskalds have always been diplomats in their way—certainly unsurpassed strategists—and they shall not choose silver over survival with all that is to come. You must trust that without doubt, dear Uncle."

"How deeply are you in?"

"Further than you would like. I have helped my father and Mister Vellum-Verlag in my own unique ways on many an occasion. Since I was a child."

"Forgive me, Uriah... it is the journalist within me... But yet another question. Ravenskald spoke of 'your friend.' You know this Planner Forthright?"

Uriah dropped his voice. "Since I was a boy. A toddler. At least to hear his voice. Many Stantons have, Uncle, down through the years. I understand he helped you with the Ripper back in '88."

I nodded in affirmation. "What now for you, Nephew?"

"Now I must stand on my own. I will soon receive the capital—through a series of anonymous investors—to start my own paper, in New Jersey. The *Eastern Standard* I shall call it, in homage to the paper for which you work. I need your wisdom, Uncle. I need your advice and guidance. It must be a bastion against the likes of Hearst and others, who use their extensive holdings as a weapon."

"How soon will this happen?" I asked, intrigued and agitated in equal measure.

"It is rather hard to say… much depends on you. How much time you can give me as your pupil, as your eager protégé. I have already given notice to my editor in Manhattan. All my things are ready for transport to London. I only await your word."

Before I could answer, Ravenskald called out, "The other three objects, Uriah?"

"Safe, sir, and awaiting your retrieval."

Sir… How my heart clenched at this unearned honorific.

"Excellent. And the location of the others? Did Planner—?"

"All in the report. On the Gold Coast, as you thought. Only the pair, though. The last remains elusive."

Turning to Vellum-Verlag, Ravenskald said, sounding like a boy of twelve, "So it's off to Ghana, Edgar! And not a moment to lose!"

EPILOGUE: TWO YEARS LATER

In my business as a journalist, and more so as a novelist, we traffic in IOUs. WT Stead taught me that, with his brilliant invention of the investigative series.

I now shall pay them off.

What did I answer my nephew?

He returned to London with me, where he stayed, an apt and diligent pupil, working by my side for nearly a year before returning to New Jersey to found the *Evening Standard*.

As with every venture, it struggles at its birth, although its reputation—and circulation—grow. It is my sincerest hope that the *Evening Standard* shall be a bulwark against not only power mongers like Hearst, as Uriah pointed out, but those that would use them, such as Ravenskald and the Rockefellers.

As for my own career, I am retired now, except to offer advice when called upon, which is rarely as of late.

With this, I am content.

I still have stories left to tell.

What became of Katherine Beaumont?

After a prolonged recovery of many months under the care of a stable of doctors—specialists of body and mind—all paid for by Simeon Ravenskald, Miss Beaumont was once again able to have visitors, to walk in gardens and parks, more and more often with my nephew, whom she will join in marriage in the late summer of 1938.

What of the twelve ancient objects?

Of these, I now know nothing. My contact and alliance with Simeon Ravenskald ended that day at Rushen. I know not the names of the final three objects, nor if any were secured, as thought, in Ghana.

I do fear, however, that, as the Nazis continue to rise, the Ravenskalds are there, whispering to them and their enemies, using these powerful weapons to barter the future of Earth for their place as its shadowed kings.

What of Planner Forthright?

He visits me on occasion, for evening sessions mostly, full of philosophical poetry and prophet-like predictions. Almost all of the objects, after millennia, in the hands of so few is of utmost concern to him.

Ethereal being of light though this Planner professes to be, I think him rather mad.

What of Edward Hyde?

Of him or from him, most happily, I have heard not a single word.

Fleet Street, London
—November 1937

Finis

ABOUT THE AUTHOR

Joey Madia is a novelist, screenwriter, historical educator, playwright, actor, and director. He writes narratives and designs the puzzles for Escape Rooms, based on literature and historical events, often mixing mystery with the paranormal. He is founding editor of www.newmystics.com, a literary site created in 2002 that houses the work of over 120 writers and artists from around the world. His website is newmystics.com/joey. He also has profiles at Stage 32 (where he is a frequent blogger), Instagram, Facebook, Goodreads, Film Freeway, IMDb, and OnStellar. When he is not creating fictional stories, he is a paranormal investigator and cohost of *Into the Outer Realms*.

www.ingramcontent.com/pod-product-compliance
Lightning Source LLC
Chambersburg PA
CBHW030821020726
47499CB00006B/2013